THIS IS AMERICA

A Novel by
E. Nigma

To submit a manuscript for our review, email us at submissions@majorkeypublishing.com

SYNOPSIS

Civil unrest fills the city of Los Angeles with protesters flooding the streets making it uncomfortable for the LAPD. Watching minorities die from the corrupt police force has the neighborhoods wanting justice for their losses. The justice they're seeking is handed out by a group known as The Hand of God who is led by Damu, an ex-gang banger looking to even the score between the streets and police by targeting cops who the system let slide by.

Upset with the way his police force is handling the investigation into The Hand of God, Police Commissioner Billick decides on a different approach, by recruiting formally disgraced Cincinnati Police Officer Duke Mitchell to work his way undercover into the group's ranks in the hope of bringing down Damu and his followers from the inside.

While undercover, Duke starts to question his assignment as he starts to understand the motives of the group, and starts falling for Terricka, who is an attorney and activist that leads the charge looking for justice for the streets. Caught between doing his duty and his feelings for Terricka, Duke battles morality and must decide whether to back the blue or follow his heart. Taking place in today's social unrest society, see the story from both sides as you decide for yourself who the true villains and heroes are.

Prelude

It's a little after midnight in the city of Los Angeles with a full moon illuminating the block. The city is feeling a little unrest with the constant protests and riots randomly taking place earlier that day, and pretty much all month. About a month ago, Patrol Officer Stonebrook was involved in a police brutality case that went viral. The case left a twenty-two-year-old black male dead, which enraged the public. The video evidence was deemed inconclusive, which allowed Stonebrook to regain his posting. The public outcry was harsh with protests and riots abroad. The LAPD offered Stonebrook a desk job, just until things cooled down, but he declined. He is a street police, and he isn't about to back away from his job just because of a few hurt feelings on the part of protesters. In order to ease him back in, the department put him on the overnight shift, where things were slower. He's been with the force for fifteen years and felt disrespected being placed on an overnight shift. Compared to a desk job, however, it was better than nothing.

Stonebrook and rookie Patrol Officer Gentry exit their squad car and enter into an all-night diner. When they walk in, the area is pretty quiet, as expected around this time of night. The two officers take a seat at a nearby booth and make a quick order of coffee as they get comfortable. The years are weighing on Stonebrook, whose graying hair looks thin and brittle when he removes his hat and places it on the chair next to him. The negative press has been hard on him, but his smugness has him feeling little to no guilt. On the other hand, Gentry looks fresh and new, with thick red hair on top of his freckle filled face. He's been out of the academy for a little over a week and was thrilled to have a mentor as well-liked as Stonebrook showing him the ropes.

"What you gonna have, rookie?" Stonebrook asks with his grim voice.

"I don't know. I'm not really that hungry, to be honest," Gentry responds as he looks over the menu.

"Well, you better eat now cause we're gonna be in that car for the rest of the night if all goes well," Stonebrook points out.

Gentry scratches his head as the waitress comes back and takes Stonebrook's order. After a few moments, Gentry places his order as well as the waitress walks off quickly to fulfill their requests. Stonebrook takes a sip of his coffee and relaxes as a few thoughts run through the rookie's head.

"Sir, thanks for everything you taught me. You can't begin to understand how much this helps me," he responds, almost sucking up to the veteran officer. "I gotta ask you though, why patrolman? I mean, a man of your skillset could have went on to become detective, or maybe something else. I know it's personal, sir, but I gotta know why just patrol?"

Stonebrook chuckles before taking a sip of his coffee once more. He thinks for a moment before responding to the wide-eyed rookie.

"Look, kid, I've seen a lot of things in my time on the force," he replies. "I've seen stripes change a man. Once you start chasing the career, you lose something. I wasn't born to be a detective or any bullshit like that. I wasn't born to be commissioner like Billick either. I'm a front line police for the realest police squad on the force. The higher ups don't give a damn about keeping these streets clean. Not really, anyway. It's all a numbers game."

Gentry nods his head hanging on every word the veteran cop has to say.

"I guess that makes sense. Can't make a difference if you're sitting behind a desk all day," Gentry responds.

"Amen to that," Stonebrook says, impressed with the rookie's spunk. "Front line officers are the only ones who are out there putting ourselves on the line every damn day and night. Used to be you could take a perp down no matter what. Now everybody and their mother has a fuckin' camera to film everything you do. Who are they to judge how to do my job? I don't go to Burger King or McDonald's and tell them how to flip burgers, do I?"

Gentry chuckles as the waitress bring back their meals.

"Take that kid, that Malcolm Johnson," Stonebrook continues as he adds salt and pepper to his eggs. "Here's a guy with a criminal history longer than my grandmother's tits. I'm trying to place him under arrest for basically being an asshole. I was just talking to the kid, and he decides he wants to be the next

Zulu King and talk about his rights. What was supposed to be a simple traffic stop ended up having IA teeth marks all on my ass crack and me on the six o'clock news."

"Yeah, that was bullshit. I mean, based on the evidence, there was no way they could blame you for that," Gentry responds as Stonebrook nods his head before taking a bite of his food.

"Exactly my point," he responds with a mouth full of food. "I did what needed to be done to subdue the perp. They're trying to make his ass look like he was a saint. Get outta here with all of that. Now I got basketball and football players talking about I should be fired and charged. Maybe next time, I'll let the nigger get away so he can rob them or their family. I bet you they'll change their attitudes quick if the police don't respond. A bunch of millionaire babies."

Gentry's smile drops as he hadn't heard Stonebrook speak so freely up until this point. He takes a few bites of his meal before continuing with his conversation.

"I mean, I get that Malcolm Johnson was a perp and all, but you subdued him within the constraints of the law and training, right?" Gentry asks, looking for clarification. "I know how the media is treating it, making it look like Rodney King or some extreme bullshit like that, but we're still here to protect the people, right?"

Stonebrook chuckles with his partner's naivety.

"Kid, you've got a lot of learning to do," he responds to the rookie. "That black bastard, King, deserved the ass whoppin' he got. He resisted, and he got put down for it. If it was up to me, I would have shot him down in the streets like the animal he is."

Stonebrook can tell that his partner isn't feeling what he's saying.

"Oh, I get it. You're one of those," Stonebrook says with a smirk.

"I'm one of those?"

"Yeah. Those who won't do what it takes to clean up these streets," Stonebrook clarifies. "They're animals, Gentry. All of them. The niggers, the spics, they're all animals. Think about it. They kill each other daily over drugs, money, and whatever other illegal enterprises they can get their hands on. They all deserve to die because they're from a no good evil race."

Gentry chuckles nervously, thinking that the veteran is joking with him.

"Come on, sir. You can't believe that?" Gentry responds. "I'll admit, there are a lot of them out there who are as bad as you say, but not all blacks and Hispanics are bad. I mean, Obama was president. He's not an animal."

"No, he was an even bigger threat," Stonebrook points out while chewing on his food. "He's the one making these animals think they're like us. An animal is an animal no matter where you put them. Just because he was able to become president doesn't mean-"

Stonebrook's words are silenced as a bullet hits him in the middle of his forehead blowing out the back of his skull. A terrified Gentry is about to pull his weapon out when three black men all wearing masks surround him with their guns drawn.

"Don't even think about it, white boy," one of the masked gunmen says.

Gentry is shaking as he slowly raises his hands up.

"Please don't do this," he pleas as one of the masked gunmen reaches down and takes his weapon and radio.

He does the same from the body of Stonebrook, while Gentry continues to shake with fear.

"Please, I have a family. You don't have to do this."

"You know who had a family. Malcolm Johnson had a family," a voice behind Gentry says.

Brotha Damu walks over without a mask as he takes a look at the rookie cop. The diner has cleared out as Damu, wearing sunglasses at night, peers down to the fallen Stonebrook.

"It's funny how when the end is near everyone speaks about their family," Damu says, turning his attention to the young cop. "Malcolm Johnson pleaded for his family too as he was beat down by this racist pig that you see before you."

Although a thin older man, Damu was very intimidating as

he stares down Gentry through his glasses. Gentry is terrified by a man with hair straightened out, almost as if he were a pimp wearing dark clothing and holding a nine-millimeter gun. A shaking Gentry is breathing heavily as Damu points his gun towards his head.

"Let this be a lesson for you, Officer... Gentry," Damu says, reading the patrolman's badge. "We're not gonna sit around silently watching the blue kill our brothas anymore. Times are changing. We're not gonna fear the blue, but you will fear the black, you dig?"

Gentry slowly nods his head with his hands still raised.

"Make better decisions, Officer, than your partner did, or we'll come for you next," Damu says as he lowers the gun from Gentry's head. "When they ask, let them know that it was Brotha Damu and The Hand of God that did this. Let them know we're coming after all who kill our brothas and sistas. We didn't start this war, but we're damn sure gonna end it. Blood will be shed."

Damu motions the others out of the restaurant. The last masked gunman removes the clip and the bullet from the guns before handing back the officer his and Stonebrook's weapons. He rips the radios apart and tosses them to the side before hurrying outside of the diner as well. A relieved Gentry sighs as he can't believe he's still alive. After a sigh of relief, he looks at Stonebrook, terrified at what he sees. Stonebrook's eyes are still open, looking up at the ceiling almost as if he's looking for God. After a few moments, Gentry rises from the booth and quickly makes his way out of the diner, and into his squad car to call the murder of his partner in from his dashboard radio.

CHAPTER 1

Past Transgressions

The next day after the shooting at the late night diner, Police Commissioner Billick is sitting behind his desk in his office watching the news on a nearby TV. He frowns as the reporter discusses the shooting that killed Stonebrook early in the morning hours. Billick had hoped to eliminate this *Damu issue,* as he's called it in the past. Losing an officer in the line of duty is never a good thing, but when officers are targeted, it frustrates him even more. As he continues to watch the news broadcast, there is a knock at his door. Deputy Police Chief Irvin peeks his head in and is waved in by the commissioner.

"You see this, James," Billick says, pointing towards the TV. "It's not enough that we lost one in the line last night, but they have to report it like this? It's just the thing that'll inspire more of these thugs to take action against us."

"Yeah, I was watching it in my office. All that 'he was accused of this' garbage isn't going to help this investigation," Irvin says as he takes a seat across from the commissioner.

Billick cuts off the TV with his remote and grabs his head in frustration.

"Where are we with the investigation?" The white-haired Billick asks.

"Unfortunately, nowhere close to finding a suspect," Irvin responds. "There are no cameras in the diner, and all the men were wearing masks except-"

"Let me guess. Except Damu," Billick interrupts, finishing the statement. "Same description?"

"Yeah. Older black male, around six foot one, mid-fifties, no more than one hundred sixty-five pounds, long hair, wearing sunglasses," Irvin recites as if it was common knowledge. "He was accompanied by three other men, who all had masks covering their faces. All black. Only one of them spoke the entire time, but no tattoos or anything we can get from that."

"Well, I guess I should be happy it's the same mope doing this instead of copycats," Billick responds as he sighs. "This son of a bitch has killed six of my officers in the past seven months. Six, Deputy. Do you know how this looks, not only in the public's eyes but the department's as well?"

"Sir, not to justify any of this, but all the officers that have been killed thus far by this Damu have all been involved in police shootings and brutality cases," Irvin points out. "Maybe we need to announce a different approach when it comes to those cases. I'm not saying it will resolve the issue, but at least it'll take the heat off the department and may slow these protests."

Billick chuckles and looks at his deputy as if he's offended. Billick and Irvin would bump heads occasionally on any type of racial dispute, being that Billick is white, and his deputy is black.

"Deputy, let me explain something to you," Billick says, irritated. "Last night, we didn't lose one officer; we lost two. The rookie who was assigned to Stonebrook came in this morning and put in his papers. Apparently, the shooting took its toll on him. I say all this to say we can't let the media or the population dictate who and what we are. Most of those claims are frivolous and are cleared by departmental investigations. We're fighting a war out there, deputy. Instead of trying to figure out a way we can approach things differently in-house, how about you try and figure out a way to catch this son of a bitch who is killing our men."

Irvin sighs, not knowing what else he can do in the investigation of Damu and his followers.

"Sir, all due respect, what do you want us to do?" He replies. "I've got our major crime unit looking into Damu and his follower's whereabouts. I have the patrol division on high alert looking for any information we can get. I've checked with informants and the residents. Nobody knows anything, and if they do know anything, they aren't talking to us. He's a hero to them, battling in their name. They aren't going to give him up even if they could. I think changing our approach with these brutality cases would at least cool heads while we track down this son of a bitch."

Billick is silent as he ponders to himself. He didn't want to compromise anything, believing order needs to be kept on the streets. As he said, it is a war to him, and wars are won on the streets, not by compromise.

"Noted, Deputy," he responds, refusing to budge on his position. "Your top priority is Damu and his followers. I want a plan mapped out on my desk by the end of tomorrow. I want you to think outside of the box on this one, Irv. The mayor and the rest of city council are on my ass. We need to nip this cop killer in the bud before things get worse. Once Damu is brought to justice, then we can sit and discuss reform."

Irvin sighs before nodding his head with understanding. Billick dismisses his deputy before going back to the news reports he was watching before, still frowning at each word.

At a local corner store in a South Central neighborhood, the sun begins its descent, closing out another seventy-degree day. The neighborhood is filled with life in the run-down area, as local winos sip their brew hanging out in front of the store. Duke, who is one of the store's workers, walks out and runs the winos off the property. He sighs as he looks around the once prosperous neighborhood from his childhood filled with poverty and drugs. The shop, owned by his grandmother, is one of the few old neighborhood staples left. Most businesses have either relocated or have been bought out and replaced with chain businesses. After looking around the area once more, he enters the store and finishes sweeping up. It's not the line of work Duke was hoping for when he moved back home from Cincinnati, but after his grandfather passed away, he didn't want his grandmother, Evelyn, working the shop alone in this neighborhood. She is happy with him helping out, but she can tell the job isn't for him. Evelyn is finalizing the count on the register getting prepared for a deposit.

"Dookie, are you gonna have time to run this over to the bank after you get off?" She asks, causing her grandson to cringe.

He hated being called Dookie. He's a couple of years shy of thirty and hates when his grandmother called him by his childhood name.

"Yeah, grandma, I got it," he replies as he puts the broom behind the counter. "Yo, I'm gonna take me a break real fast, then I'll get that down to the bank."

"Alright. Don't take too long. I don't want you to have to go to the bank after dark," Evelyn warns.

Duke nods his head before heading outside of the shop. He takes a pack of cigarettes from his pocket and lights one up, enjoying his smoke break. He never understood why his grandmother worried so much about him. He was a cop in Cincinnati and is fully capable of taking care of himself. Would have still been a cop if things hadn't fallen apart as they did. His cop senses have him surveying the area looking for danger as he puffs on his cigarette. While he didn't notice any immediate threats, what he does notices is a beautiful female making her way down the street heading towards the shop. He's taken aback by her as he checks out her body in her skin tight jeans that almost look painted on. Her hair flows from below her black doo rag, with her eyes hidden behind her shades as Duke smiles when he notices her heading to the store entrance.

"Hey, how you doing?" he says, cutting her off. "Anything I can help you with?"

"Um, yeah, you can get out of my way," the female says, causing Duke to chuckle at her sassiness.

"Damn, I'm not tryin' holla at you or anything. I work here

13

and wanted to see if there is anything I can do to make your visit more pleasurable," a sly Duke says. "I mean, I could hook you up with a discount if you're looking for it."

The female lowers her glasses revealing her blue eyes, checking out Duke.

"Well, that's nice and all, but I'm sure I can get by without a discount for a pack of gum," she replies.

"Shit, you must don't know how much gum is nowadays," Duke replies, smirking. "I'm just sayin', a quarter saved is a quarter earned."

"Is that right?" The female replies.

"Yes, ma'am. I'm Duke, and you are?"

"Duke? You're Dookie? Evelyn's grandson?" The female inquires, causing Duke to sigh.

"Yeah, I'm Duke," he answers, emphasizing his name.

"Damn, I heard you was back in town. Heard them Cincinnati boys ran you outta there," the female replies, grinning.

"Wasn't anything like that," Duke quips. "Who are you again?"

"Terricka," she answers. "My dad and your dad used to run with them Pirus back in the day."

Duke looks at Terricka, trying to remember who she is, but is coming up short. She rolls her eyes in disbelief that he doesn't remember her.

"Centennial High? Does that jog your memory?" She says. "Ms. Richardson's history class?"

Duke ponders a few seconds more before snapping his fingers.

"Oh yeah, you was that skinny girl with glasses who sat in the front," he replies with a smirk. "Smart girl with all the answers."

He checks her out once more, impressed with how far she's come.

"Well, guess I can't call you skinny no more," he jokes, referring to her mature body.

"And I guess I can't call you the childish, playful, dumb ass nigga from the back of the class anymore," Terricka fires back. "Although looking at where you're at now, I can see you ended up right where I thought you would."

Duke chuckles off Terricka's insults.

"Okay. Still a lil' uppity. I see you," he replies. "Keep in mind, you're shopping at my people's business in the hood, so you can't throw stones, baby girl. Anyway, go ahead and get your gum."

Terricka glances at Duke before walking into the store. Duke continues to smoke his cigarette in peace, shaking his head after his interaction with his old classmate. From what he can remember, she was an honor roll student who had all the answers. She wasn't too appealing back in the day with her huge glasses and ponytail hairstyle, but she has certainly grown up to his liking.

He chuckles to himself, reminiscing on his high school days when he notices a police car pulling up on the side of the road, not too far from the store. Two white officers quickly exit the vehicle with their guns drawn out, pointing towards a person of interest on the corner. Some bystanders in the area scatter not wanting to be involved in the apprehension, while others took out their phones to record the incident. The targeted man quickly raises his hands and offers no resistance as the officers approach him. Duke finishes up his cigarette while watching the interaction, and is stunned when one of the officers kicks the targeted black male towards the ground before putting his knee into his back. Being a former officer himself, Duke knows this is not procedure as the victim showed no resistance. He flicks his cigarette butt to the side and starts to make his way over towards the incident just as Terricka exits the store.

"Hey, what the fuck are you doing?" Duke asks, catching the officer's attention. "He wasn't resisting or anything!"

"Sir, I need you to back away," one of the officers says watching his partner put the cuffs on the suspect.

"I'm just standing here, unarmed," Duke says with his arms up. "I'm saying, this shit is uncalled for! Ol' boy was just standing there with his hands up when your partner over there kicked him in the fuckin' back for no reason!"

"I said stay your ass back!" The standing officer says, now aiming his gun at Duke.

Duke chuckles, still standing with his hands up.

"Oh, you gonna shoot me now," he says, grinning. "In case you don't see it, there's like five folks out here recording, plus I'm sure a couple of traffic cams. Do what you gotta do, but know they gonna charge your dumb ass!"

Terricka looks on from a distance impressed with Duke challenging the police before deciding to walk over herself.

"Excuse me, Officer, but is all this necessary?" She calmly asks. "This man is doing nothing but talking, and you have a gun aimed right at him!"

"Ma'am, I need you and him to back away!" The office exclaims.

"Back away or what?" Duke challenges before looking down at the perp struggling to breathe after the officer moves his leg onto his neck. "Yo, my man, he can't breathe! What the fuck are you doing?"

As Duke tries to get the kneeling officer's attention, the other officer has had enough and quickly holsters his weapon before tackling Duke to the ground. A confused Duke grunts as he's held down on the ground.

"What are you doing?!" Terricka exclaims.

"Back the fuck up!" The officer yells back, angering Terricka.

Duke looks up and notices his old classmate's mood.

"Yo, it's cool, it's cool," he tells her. "Let me grandma know what's going down, please."

Terricka nods her head and watches as the officers lift both Duke and the perp from the ground, putting them in the back of their cruiser when they notice bystanders gathering in the area. She quickly makes her way back into the shop to let Evelyn know what's going on as the police cruiser pulls off. Duke shakes his head, sighing, questioning why did he choose to get involved with something that doesn't have anything to do with him.

Hours later, Duke finds himself sitting in an interrogation

room with his wrist handcuffed to the table at the local police station. He spent the first two hours in a holding cell and had finally been moved to the lone cold room. He isn't fazed by the room's intimidation as he's been in them plenty of times during his time as an officer, albeit on the other side. He knew their tactics and knew they were trying to make him sweat. Add on to the fact that he hadn't committed any crime to begin with. He is taking his time in the room with stride waiting for a chance to call a lawyer. Just outside the room, Deputy Irvin makes his way over to one of the officers keeping watch on Duke.

"Hello, Deputy, sir," the officer says as he hands Irvin a file.

Irvin looks through several items that pique his interest as he reads over the file. He checks Duke's photo file and some of his undercover photo files as well. He has a rough exterior and a hardened look that could fit well in any environment. He isn't clean-shaven and sports a beard that's popular currently, but his eyes and his glare are what impresses Irvin as he goes through the photos in the file.

"You sure that's him?" He asks the officer.

"Yes, sir. We double checked," the officer answers.

"What's the charge?" Irvin inquires.

"Failure to obey, loitering, and obstruction of justice by interfering with an arrest," the officer informs.

"So, in other words, bullshit," Irvin says as he hands the file back to the officer. "Has he asked for a lawyer yet?"

"We haven't been in to talk with him yet. Figured this wouldn't be too much work," the officer answers.

Irvin nods his head before walking into the interrogation room. Duke checks him out, and can immediately tell that Irvin's no regular cop as he watches the deputy take a seat across from him.

"My name is Deputy Commissioner James Irvin," he says, sizing Duke up. "I understand you're sort of a brother in arms from Cincinnati."

"Wow. It's not every day that a Deputy Commissioner visits a perp on some bullshit charge," Duke quips, smirking. "Look, all

I need for you to do is to contact my lawyer, that's it. You L.A. boys are wild out here."

"Same could be said about you, Mr. Mitchell," Irvin responds, referring to his past. "Eight years with the Cincinnati PD. I read your file. Impeccable work, that is up until the end. So, what happened? If you don't mind me asking."

The smirk from Duke's face drops, changing his mood.

"It's in the file I'm sure you saw," he responds. "What does this have to do with why I'm here?"

"Well, call me curious," Irvin says as he gets comfortable. "I know what's in the file. I've also been on this job long enough to know what's in the file isn't what really went on. Since we're sitting here, might as well talk about something."

Duke shakes his head, hating to have to discuss his past. He is unsure why the Deputy Commissioner would care, but decides to humor him.

"It was all bullshit," Duke answers. "I was running with this narcotics squad for about six months. We were our own unit in charge of building cases against high-end dealers. Nothing too fancy. It called for some undercover work, and it was a legit job taking assholes off the street."

"I've heard. It was one of the best units in your department, always getting results," Irvin says.

"Yeah, we were on it. When I first got there, we were takin' targets down like it wasn't nothing. That was until Shaper was promoted to lieutenant and took over the team," Duke explains. "He's the type of person who likes to run his own hit squad. Shoot first, and ask questions after you've laced your pockets a bit if you get what I'm saying."

Irvin nods his head as Duke continues.

"I told him I wasn't with it. I didn't sign on to basically rob drug dealers. It started to be more about the money than the actual work, so I requested a transfer," Duke says, pausing as his past still haunts him. "One night, as I'm leaving the post, I get into my car and am stopped by IA and other folks requesting a search of my car. Low and behold, there was a key of coke hidden in my trunk. I was charged with possession with the intent to distribute."

"Let me guess, it was your hit squad to set you up?" Irvin asks.

Duke doesn't respond, which all but confirms Irvin's suspicion.

"So why didn't you roll on your squad?" He inquires. "I mean, surely that could have saved you from everything that happened after that?"

"I'm no snitch," Duke replies, snapping back. "Besides, they didn't have shit on me. They couldn't find any evidence it was mine, nor could they prove it was planted. Eventually, they dropped the charges."

"But your career as a police officer was over," Irvin concludes.

Duke chuckles, thinking about all that he had gone through.

"Cost me my badge, and essentially blackballed me from every police post going forward," he says. "Did that feed your curiosity?"

Irvin smiles, nodding his head.

"It most certainly has, and I think I can help you out," he says, confusing Duke. "How would you like a chance to wear the badge again?"

"Wear the badge? With who? LAPD?" Duke inquires before bursting into laughter. "After what I seen out there today? Why would I want to do that?"

"Because unlike these poorly trained patrolmen we have on the frontline, you've actually done some criminal investigation work," Irvin points out. "Besides, it wouldn't be as a patrol personnel. I'm looking for someone who can handle a little undercover work. Someone who won't fold under pressure. Someone who knows the streets."

"I don't know the streets," Duke replies. "I've been in Cincinnati for the past ten years. Haven't been home long enough to know what's going down."

"But you know the culture, and it's in that aspect you can be valuable to us," Irvin responds. "I'm giving you a second chance. You may have been blackballed everywhere else, but we can give you what you want, and that's to be a cop again. Or, you can sit here and wait for your lawyer. Your choice."

Duke doesn't trust Irvin, but if there is the slightest chance that he could resurrect his law enforcement career, he didn't want to hesitate or turn down the offer. After a few moments, he slightly nods his head, much to Irvin's delight.

"Just hang tight," Irvin says while rising. "Let me make a few calls."

"How about doing something about this?" Duke responds, motioning towards his hand that is still cuffed to the table.

"I'll get someone to take care of it," Irvin says before making his way out of the room.

He pulls out his cell phone and dials Billick, with a cryptic smile on his face.

"Hello, sir... yes... I think I have a solution to our problem," he says with a sinister grin on his face.

He goes into describing his plan with his superior trying to convince him that this is the best way to take the war to the cop killers that roams the streets.

CHAPTER 2

The Detail

In an undisclosed safe house in the city, Detective Sargent Thomas Reid, who is head of the special unit known as the Terror Squad, sits across from a suspect eating an apple nonchalantly, looking towards his battered victim, who is surrounded by two of his unit crew, Dalton and Slater. The Terror Squad is known in the department and on the streets as being an aggressive special unit tasked with neutralizing some of the most dangerous criminal organizations in the city. Reid crafted this team in his own image, mainly white officers, with the exception of one, who were not afraid to get their hands dirty in the name of the job. The streets fear his buzz cut, frowning face when they see his car patrolling the area. His suspect, Jamal, is equally fearful shaking, wondering what the detective is going to do to him next.

"Come on, Jamal. Great name by the way. But we both know you know something about this Damu guy. Why not make this easy on yourself, so we can get out of here?" Reid pleads with the suspect. "All we want is him. You're nothing in the grand scheme of things. Just give the man up, and we'll send you on your way."

"Pl... please! I don't know anything about him. I've never met him in my life," Jamal responds. "If I knew, I'd tell you. Please... I have a wife and kids."

Reid shakes his head in disappointment before nodding to Dalton, who responds by slamming Jamal's head onto the table in front of him.

"You see, that's not what I heard," Reid says as he leans back in his chair, his gray eyes gazing at his victim. "I heard that you and a few others offered sanction to a few guys we were looking for that was directly associated with that crazy son of a bitch. I believe they called it an underground railroad for those involved in police shootings. You knew we were closing in on them, and decided to hide them at your house, or your store until they had a safe passage out of our great city. Aiding and abetting is a serious crime here in L.A., but I'm offering you the deal of a lifetime. You walk, and all I ask is for information regarding Damu. I think that's fair. Dalton, does that seem fair?"

"Extremely fair," the blonde hair blue eyed Dalton responds right on cue.

"What about you, Slater? You think I'm being fair?" The charismatic Reid says, turning his attention towards his other subordinate.

"I think you're being too fair, sir," the built like a tank, rugged, slicked-back, dark-haired Slater responds, smirking.

Reid chuckles before turning his attention back towards Jamal.

"Don't mind Slater," he calmly says. "He's a little more stern than I am. Has a little problem with anger management, unfortunately. I'm working with him on that. Either way, both of my men seem to think I'm being fair with you, so the question is if I'm being fair with you, why can't you be fair with me?"

Jamal doesn't respond causing his captor to sigh, before nodding his head at his officers once more. This time it's Slater who slams Jamal's head into the table, but unlike Dalton, he repeatedly slams Jamal's head until Reid waves him off.

"You see? There's that anger management I was talking about," a cryptic Reid says to Jamal. "I have all the time in the world here. So what's it going to be?"

A bloodied Jamal can barely speak when Reid's cell phone starts to ring, catching his attention.

"Excuse me for a moment," Reid says as he checks the caller

ID.

He gets up and walks to the corner of the room for a little privacy before answering the line.

"Yes, sir," he answers as the caller gives him a few instructions. "Understood. I'll be there in about thirty minutes.... Thank you, sir."

He hangs up the line and looks at Jamal once more before turning his attention towards Dalton.

"I gotta meeting at HQ. Our friend here looks a little dirty. Why don't you two get him cleaned up, and keep cleaning him until we get answers?" he commands to a smiling Dalton.

"Yes, sir," Dalton says before he and Slater drag Jamal to a nearby sink.

Slater quickly runs the water to fill up the old style sink anticipating the torture he's about to inflict on a defiant Jamal. After the sink is filled, he and Dalton begin to waterboard their captive. A slight grin enters Reid's face as he makes his way out of the safe house.

Thirty minutes later, at Billick's office, the commissioner is sitting behind his desk going over a few things, with Reid sitting across from him when Irvin leads Duke into the office. Reid stands up as a smiling Billick offers the two a seat across from him.

"Gentlemen, welcome," he says as both Irvin and Duke take a seat. "Can I offer you anything to drink?"

"No, I'm good," Duke says, trying to read those around him.

"So you're the guy who is going to make all things right for us," Billick says, smirking. "I've been reading your file, and outside of the last incident, your record was impeccable."

Duke nods his head, choosing to remain silent, hoping he can find out Billick's true intentions.

"So, did Irv fill you in on the job?" Billick inquires.

"He just said something about an undercover op, but no details beyond that," Duke answers.

Billick nods his head before getting comfortable in his chair.

"Well, I have a problem, Duke. Several of my officers have been targeted and killed by a gang who calls themselves 'The Hand of God,'" the commissioner explains. "They are part of this whole defund the police movement. The officers they have targeted have been officers who have been involved in brutality and shooting cases that were deemed unfounded by an investigative team. They are led by someone who calls himself Damu."

"With the way your officers handle folks, I can see why there's a movement," Duke quips. "I watched them kick down and put their knee on someone's neck who wasn't even resisting. Hell, I wasn't resisting, and they damn near took me out. I know protocols between here and Cincinnati may be slightly different, but Commissioner, I gotta say, what I saw was ruthless aggression, point blank."

Billick ponders for a moment before responding to Duke's concerns.

"I know we're not perfect. Some of my officers do tend to get a little aggressive at times, but I assure you it's all about the safety of my officers. If we're too lax, I end up having to contact next of kin. Have you ever had to make one of those calls?" Billick asks.

Duke shakes his head knowing how it must be difficult to handle such a burden.

"I wouldn't wish it on my worst enemy," Billick says before looking towards Irvin. "However, I think we can have this looked into, Irv. Investigate and see if we're at fault here. See if reprimands or suspensions are warranted."

"I'll look into it," Irvin says as the attention is back on Duke, who isn't fully satisfied with the matter, but moves the discussion on.

"So, Damu. As in blood gang Damu?" Duke questions.

"We're not one hundred percent sure if he's affiliated with any of the local Blood Gangs or not, although we did do a thorough investigation into some of their leadership," Billick answers, causing Reid to smirk knowing the *thorough investigation* the commissioner referred to was putting it mildly. "We've been running an investigation into the group for the past six or seven months, and have gotten nowhere. Reid, were you able to get anywhere with the known associate you brought in?"

"My squad is currently interrogating the suspect as we speak, but he hasn't given us anything to work with thus far," Reid reports in reference to Jamal. "Honestly, he's either the most loyal man on the planet, or he doesn't know anything."

Billick nods his head, turning his attention back to Duke.

"Detective Reid and his unit are the best there is on the streets, and as you can see, we're still not getting results," he says, causing Reid to shoot him a brief look.

"Alright, I get it. You have cop killers on your hand that you want me to flesh out, but all due respect, this sounds really thin," Duke says, trying to understand the point of the meeting. "I mean, you don't have any leads, or know who's even associated with this group outside of the one suspect who isn't giving you anything. If you don't know who's in the group, what good is that gonna do me? I can't go undercover if I don't know who to work.

Not only that, I'm an ex-cop, which with my past is easily searchable on the internet. That's why you don't do undercover ops in your own backyard. If these guys are as organized as you say they are, even a half-ass search will get me made."

"It's true. You're not going to be able to slide right in their ranks with an assumed identity," Billick admits. "From what little intelligence we have, it seems they like to recruit useful assets who have been so called victimized by the police in the past. You getting arrested already earned you points on the street; you just haven't realized it yet. We'll need a little more of a show however to make sure they really see you, assuming you take the assignment of course."

Duke takes a deep breath as he considers Billick's proposal. He has heard about the diner shooting where Officer Stonebrook was killed a few nights ago and knew there was some truth to a lot of what Billick is saying. He still didn't trust anyone in the office, especially Reid, who gave him a soldier vibe as he stood at attention awaiting a response.

"And if they never come calling? What then?" Duke inquires.

"Well, it will just be another waste of the tax payer's money," Billick answers, chuckling. "For now, if you accept, you'll be paid a sergeant's wage, let's say for the next six months. I hear you're working at a convenience store, is that right?"

Duke nods his head.

"I say you keep the job for appearances," Billick responds. "You're just one of the community. Who's going to question that?"

"Who will be my contact?" Duke asks.

"Well, for now, the only people I want to know about this operation are those in this room. Maybe one more," Billick answers before looking towards Reid. "You have one of your detail that you can trust to be the go-between and back up our friend here if need be?"

"Martinez can blend in with the best of them," Reid answers. "They would be perfect."

"So there we have it. Us three and Martinez will be the only ones who know about this operation," Billick says, turning his attention back towards Duke. "We're thinking that this organization has a mole in the department somewhere. I want to keep this as quiet as we can. So, am I speaking to the newest member of the Los Angeles Police Department?"

Duke thinks for a moment, still processing everything that's been told to him. His interaction with the police that arrested him has left a sour taste in his mouth regarding the LAPD and their officers, but all he's ever wanted to be since he was a child was a police officer. The incident in Cincinnati took that dream away from him, but he's being offered another chance to be what he's always wanted. Even though he didn't totally trust the detail he's being offered, he decides to take Billick up on his offer, slowly nodding his head with acceptance.

"I'm in," he replies to an ecstatic Billick.

"Great. Simply great," Billick responds. "Now, let's get you out of here. I'll leave you in the hands of Reid and the deputy now for the next stages. Make sure you keep them and me informed on anything you come across."

Duke nods his head, as both he and the commissioner rise from their seats and shake hands. Reid is about to walk out when Billick holds him back watching Irvin and Duke walk out of the office. After the door is closed, he turns to his most trusted detective, asking his opinion.

"So, what do you think of him?" Billick asks.

"I don't know. Too early to tell," Reid responds. "He might be a do-gooder, not really built to do what's necessary. If he's able to get in, I say we use him for information, and that's it. Let me and my unit do the dirty work."

Billick ponders for a moment before nodding his head.

"For now, keep him out of the loop," Billick responds. "I don't want any more of my force in the crossfire here. I'm dangling a worm for all to see. Make sure they see it."

"Yes, sir," Reid says before making his way out of the office as well.

Billick takes a seat behind his desk once again, satisfied that a plan has been put into place to take out the threat to his officers.

A few days later, Duke is back working his grandmother's convenience store working the register, and keeping an eye on a couple of customers that are in the store. He has continued to go on with his day to day life for the last few days without much going on, paying close attention to those around the neighborhood as of recent. He didn't know where to begin to make contact with this underground group but has plans in place to hopefully give him more exposure to the streets. He's also been doing his research as well, reading articles, and going over investigation files to see if there is anything the LAPD is missing during their analysis. One of the things he has noticed is that the non-fatal police victims were all attacked by their alleged atrocity being beaten, choked, or even shot just as their victims were and because their victims survived, the officers were also allowed to live. The worst of the bunch, however, was the cops who were involved in fatal altercations that found themselves dead, just as their victims were taken out being by choking or shot, with the exception of Stonebrook, which caught Duke's attention. The entire situation is disturbing in Duke's eyes, but until contact is made, he's not in the position to do anything about it.

While he continues to monitor the store, he's surprised when he notices Terricka walking into the store.

"Hey, you," he says as he comes from behind the register to greet her.

"Hey. I heard you got out," she replies. "You okay?"

"Yeah, it's all good," Duke answers. "I was bailed out, but they eventually dropped all the charges."

"How'd you pull that off?" a curious Terricka asks.

"Wasn't an issue really. They were bullshit charges to begin with," Duke points out. "Once they saw I was an ex-cop, they let me off with a warning. Whatever that means anyway."

"I guess blue lives do matter," Terricka says as she reaches for a pack of gum. "Y'all take care of y'all's own, I see."

"Trust me, they aren't mine," Duke answers before making his way behind the register once more to ring her up. "They broke like half a dozen protocols with that arrest. I filed a complaint as soon as they released me. That's the type of shit that gets fools killed, you know."

"Yeah, I do," Terricka says smirking as she pays for her gum. "Well, I was gonna offer you my services, but you seem to be straight."

"And what services might that be?" Duke says with a smile.

Terricka goes into her purse, pulls out her business card, and hands it to the stunned Duke.

"Wait a minute, you're a lawyer?" He asks.

"Yeah. Why you actin' all shocked?" She asks with a hint of attitude.

"I don't know. I mean, I guess it makes sense cause you always was a Ms. Know-it-all back in school," Duke jokes. "Why the hell are you always in the hood then? I mean I would think a lawyer would be in Beverly Hills or something."

"Not all of us forget where we came from, Mr. Cincinnati," Terricka quips. "While you were up north playing cops and robbers, shit got bad out here. Cops really started to wild out on us. I became a lawyer to help my people out here. After my brother was shot by a cop, I knew what I wanted to do with my life."

"Whoa, wait a minute. Reggie's dead?" A concerned Duke asks.

"Yeah. Happened around the time I graduated," Terricka responds somberly. "I ain't saying the boy was clean, cause I know my brother, but he wasn't armed when they shot him. Said they feared for their life, and he reached for something. There were a hundred and one ways they could have taken him down, but they chose to shoot first. It was at that moment that I knew what I had to do."

Duke is silent, shocked to hear about Terricka's brother. He was a few years older than him and got involved with the wrong crowd, eventually joining a gang.

"Wow, I didn't hear nothing about it. Sorry for your loss," expresses Duke.

"You didn't know about it because these cops have been getting away with it for years," Terricka points out. "There's a big movement going on now, and it's the perfect time to make sure our voices are heard. That means more to me than anything. Our people need help. What kind of a person would I be to turn my back on them?"

Terricka is passionate about her cause, which catches the former cop's eye. Duke tries to hand her card back to her, but she waves him off.

"Keep it," she says. "You never know when you might need it."

"Maybe I'll call you up and set up a dinner date," a flirting Duke responds.

"If you call that number, I bill at one fifty an hour," Terricka fires back with a smirk. "So if you're planning to take me out, that's a two hour minimum. Think you got three hundred to spare?"

Duke chuckles while looking her over once more.

"I may have to ask grandma for a loan cause I'm a little short," he replies.

"Well, call me when you can afford me," Terricka says before she starts making her way towards the exit.

"What happened to helpin' out the people in the neighborhood?" Duke asks.

"Next time you're locked up, give me a call. I got you," Terricka replies before walking out of the store.

Duke chuckles before putting her card in his pocket, knowing one day he will have his shot with the beauty.

Several blocks away, cruising down the street in their cruiser patrolling the area is veteran Officer James Williams and his partner David Murphy. Williams is an officer looking towards his retirement date after twenty-three years on the force. He looks at his partner, who is still in his early thirties, reminiscing on what life was like when he was Murphy's age, with much of his career still in front of him. With all the protests and anti-police agenda out in the world, Williams is happy it's almost his time. Too much violence and politics have made being a police officer difficult. Murphy, by contrast, welcomed the chaos in the world feeling that the police were on the side of good other than a few bad apples, and was ready to show the world that not all cops are bad men.

"So, still no regrets leaving your Malibu post for the shit detail?" Williams asks his partner. "Cause I gotta tell you, Malibu sounds pretty good right about now. I know it's been a couple of years, but you don't look back at the time and think 'what the fuck was I thinking'?"

"Come on, Will. You should know better than that?" Murphy responds, smirking. "Just cause you wanna cut and run doesn't mean the rest of us do. How are we gonna fix things out here if we don't challenge ourselves? Malibu was dead. Sure, it had its high profile cases every now and then, but this is where we need the most help. Not some preppy entitled white boys. This here, this is where the action is."

"Yeah, but you're white," Williams states pointing out the obvious. "I'm also white. We're not part of the natives if you get my drift. What makes you think you can do anything out here? These mopes don't trust us, and never will. We're just setting ourselves up for failure. I can see the writing, kid. It's not looking good for the department."

"That's why we need to be out here," Murphy says, continuing to navigate down the city streets. "Think about it, the residents still haven't recovered from that Rodney King thing from back in the day. It's just gotten worse. I wouldn't trust us either with all that's been going on."

"I get that, but where does it say that we have to be the ones to fix things?" Williams inquires. "The public is tired, and I get that. We're in a war right now. One where the public is demanding to defund us. Like that'll do any good. How do they expect us to do our jobs with limited funding? I swear, everyone hates us until they need us."

Murphy chuckles, in disbelief with his veteran partner's words.

"War? War is for soldiers. I thought our job was to protect and serve. When did war become a thing for the police?" He asks.

"When those animals started firing back," Williams quips. "You heard what they did to Stonebrook about a week ago, right? It became a war when cops started dying in the line of duty."

"Hey, I don't wish that on anybody, don't get me wrong but Stonebrook was a racist prick. You and I both know that," Murphy responds. "He didn't deserve to die, but when you conduct yourself like that it's bound to catch up to you."

Williams shakes his head, in disbelief with his partner's words as he reminisces about when he joined the force years ago. His old young, full of hope self has been replaced with an old crinkly skin, balding, battered down version of the man he once was. He and Williams had history, and the shooting was too close to home in his eyes.

"The man was no saint, I'll give you that, but me and him came up together. It was different back then. The war part of it came with the war on drugs. It was when these thugs started shooting us down with automatic weapons. You can't fight a war like that with a revolver. We needed to step up. Nowadays, it's more about the political stance more than anything. Doesn't help that every rap song is talking about killing us either. They start young with that shit and wonder why the next generation is scared of us," Williams explains to his partner.

Murphy doesn't respond as he and Williams always agree to disagree in these moments. He did agree with his partner on one aspect, and that the tension is rising between the police and the public. Stonebrook's murder was the latest attack on the department, and both he and Williams know there will be repercussions to follow on the streets. As the two officers continue to make their way down the street, they notice a couple arguing in the parking lot of a fast food establishment making a scene. Murphy looks at Williams, who shrugs.

"Why not," Williams says with a smirk. "Maybe we're lucky and this is an easy one. Get a quick stat out of it."

Murphy smiles as he quickly makes a U-turn and pulls into the parking lot where the couple is making a scene going back and forth. The two officers quickly analyze the situation as they look at the male, who is at least two-hundred-fifty pounds built solid. Williams, who is aging and not in the best of shape, and Murphy, who, while nicely toned, doesn't have anything on the male are both concerned in case this interaction gets out of hand. The female is a petite female but is the one making the most noise getting into the male's face pushing him around. The officers sigh as they exit the vehicle and approach the arguing couple.

"Hello, folks. What seems to be the problem here?" Murphy says, taking lead.

"Officer, this nigga stole my fuckin' car!" The female exclaims. "Y'all need to arrest his ass right now!"

"Hold up! It ain't even like that," the male says, backing away slightly. "It's my car. My name is on the bitch and everything. How can I steal my own car?"

"Nigga, I'm the one paying for the shit! Your ass don't do a fuckin' thing!" The female blasts back as Murphy tries to interject.

"Wait, let's just take it easy right now," he says, trying to calm the situation. "We can settle this real quick without all the drama, okay. I can run the car in the system, figure out ownership, and go from there."

"Fuck that," the female responds, becoming aggressive. "I don't care what that fuckin' system says. His name might be on it, but he don't pay it! I do! This nigga ain't did shit for the car, and now all of sudden wants to come around like it's his!"

The male sighs, shaking his head.

"Officer, it's not like that at all," he calmly responds. "I didn't roll through and just snatch her car like that. She got a bunch of unpaid tickets that get sent to me every other week. I then asked her to pay the shit multiple times, and she ain't doing it! Them niggas talkin' about they gonna suspend my license and shit over this! If she not gonna take care of the tickets, why the fuck should I let her keep the car?"

"Them shits ain't legit!" The female exclaims as she and her partner start going back and forth once again.

Murphy shakes his head, confused about how such a basic situation is causing so much drama. Williams, who's had his hand on his gun throughout the interaction, slowly approaches his partner.

"Look, let me just run their names, see what's what and get out of here," Williams says.

Murphy nods his head, approaching the couple once more.

"Alright! Alright! Settle down!" He yells, trying to calm the situation. "Look, my partner here is gonna run your names to see who owns what so we can move on."

"Hell nah! Y'all don't need to run shit on me!" The female

responds aggressively. "Don't y'all niggas shoot fools like him? Just do what y'all normally do to niggas like him!"

"Ma'am, I'm gonna need you to calm down, and show me some ID," Murphy replies.

"Fuck that, and fuck you!" The female says, getting into the officer's face. "I know my muthafuckin' rights, and I ain't gotta show you shit!"

Murphy remains calm, as the male hands his license over to Williams, who takes a look at his partner.

"You good?" He asks.

"I'm good," Murphy responds as Williams heads back to the squad car to look up the male's info into the computer.

The female backs away slightly but still is looking at Murphy eye to eye. He remains calm making sure to keep an eye on the male as well, looking for sudden movement from either of the couple. After a few moments, Williams returns and hands the male back his license.

"He's clean. The car is in his name," Williams responds. "However, there are about a thousand dollars' worth of tickets attached to the vehicle, with the vast majority being attached to a Nicole Tucker. Are you Nicole Tucker, ma'am?"

"Fuck you, old man! I don't know any Nicole Tucker," the female fires back.

Williams frowns as he's heard enough from the explicit laced female. She folds her arms as if she's daring the officer to do something, looking on with an attitude in her eyes.

"Ma'am, I'm going to need to see some ID," Williams insists.

"Fuck you, let me see your ID!" The female responds.

"Ma'am, there may be a possible warrant out for your arrest. So in order to determine you're not Nicole Tucker, I'll ask to see your ID once again," Williams responds trying to remain cool.

"I know my rights! I don't gotta show you nothing!" The female responds.

Williams has had enough as he takes out his cuffs and approaches the female.

"Ma'am, you have to right to remain silent. Anything you say can be used against you in the court of law," he says, reading her Miranda rights.

He tries to grab her arm to cuff her, but she quickly jerks her arm away from the officer, making Murphy nervous as he pulls out his gun.

"Get on the ground!" Murphy yells while pointing his weapon at her.

"Oh, what the fuck you gonna do? Shoot me? Look at all these folks out here! You gonna shoot me in front of them?" The female says, bringing attention to all the bystanders who have gathered around the area with their phones out recording the altercation.

"I'm not gonna ask you again! Get on the ground!" Murphy yells once more.

Williams shakes his head at his partner, thinking he's going too far with his weapon pulled out on the petite female.

"Ma'am, it doesn't need to go like this," he says, trying to bargain with the female. "Please follow the officer's instructions so we can avoid any issues."

The female looks towards Murphy and can tell he means business with a serious look in his eyes. She rolls her eyes as she slowly kneels on the ground with her hands in the air, not wanting to lose her life."

"This is some bullshit!" She says as Williams walks over and cuffs her.

As soon as she's secure, Murphy lowers his weapon, placing it back into his holster before looking towards the male.

"We're going to have to impound your vehicle," he explains to the male. "You can pick it up at the police impound lot on West MLK."

"But officer, the tickets are on her. What that gotta do-"

The male's words are silenced as Murphy shoots him a look, making him nervous.

"My bad, West MLK you said, right?" The male asks.

Murphy nods his head before going to his radio to order a vehicle pick up. Williams raises the female towards their cruiser and places her into the back seat. He looks back at his partner disappointed at the way he handled the situation.

After booking their suspect at the local lock-up, Williams makes his way out of the precinct and approaches Murphy, who is sitting on a bench just outside of the building.

"Well, I hope you're happy," Williams says, confusing his partner.

"Happy? What are you talking about?"

"We got the wrong perp," Williams explains. "Nicole is her seventeen-year-old daughter. We have Sharniece in custody right now."

"Well... I mean, if she would have just shown her ID, none of this shit would have happened," an unbothered Murphy replies.

"True, but did you have to pull your gun on the woman?" Williams fires back as he takes a seat next to his partner. "That was totally unnecessary. What's worse is you have about ten people with footage of the whole incident."

"Weren't you the one talking about how things have changed, and we need to make sure we take care of ourselves," Murphy points out. "I didn't do anything against protocol."

"No, you didn't, but there are ways you can handle things better. Especially with the way things are in the streets now," Williams replies, trying to teach his partner. "Murphy, I know I'm just the old veteran waiting to retire, and you're just the young soldier trying to make the world a better place. In a world of camera phones and social media, we gotta take it back a couple notches. Doesn't matter that you followed protocol. What matters is how it looks in the public's eye. If one of these mopes start to push this out there, next thing you know, they're gonna change the way we do things out in the field. Every change they make puts us more and more at risk. This is the political thing I was talking about earlier. Whether you like it or not, this is part of the war. How can you protect and serve if the department neuters you?"

Murphy sighs, nodding his head with agreement.

"Alright, I fucked up," he admits. "The blatant disrespect was getting to me. I couldn't let her talk to you like that. You know you wanted to punch her in the mouth just like I did."

Williams chuckles as he taps his partner on the shoulder.

"I've heard worse from my wife," he jokes as the two get up from their bench. "Knowing that she's going to have to pay those tickets to keep us from arresting her daughter, however, seems to make up for it. Come on, lunch is on you to make up for all that paperwork shit."

Murphy nods his head as he and Williams make their way back towards their police cruiser.

CHAPTER 3

Black and Blue and Red

A few weeks after quietly probing the area, keeping a look at any suspicious characters, and running background checks on those who he deems as a person of interest, Duke is all out of ideas as his investigation is leading nowhere. The people weren't talking to him about anything, even as he regained the trust of those he grew up with. A lot of them see him as nothing more than a cop, and would never fully trust him again, and Duke knew it. With no movement thus far, it was time for Duke to enact a plan he was hoping to avoid. At a local pool hall, normally visited by neighborhood residents, Duke is at a pool table located at the center of the floor engaged in a game, working one of the locals over. After he hits the last ball in, he celebrates as his opponent pays him money from an earlier bet. He's about to start another game when he receives a text on his phone.

"Hey, yo, I'm gonna take a smoke break real quick. I'll be back," he says to his opponent.

He walks off and makes his way out of the bar, passing up a decent size crowd that is hanging outside of the establishment. He lights up a cigarette and looks around the area waiting impatiently. The number of people outside was perfect, and he didn't want to waste an opportunity to raise his street credit. While taking a puff of his cigarette, he looks up as a smile grows on his face. A police cruiser pulls up just on the curb. Reid and Slater hop out of the vehicle wearing patrol uniforms, which is odd for them. The crowd in the area looks on suspiciously as the cops slowly approach them looking around. A few members of the crowd try to go unnoticed as they scurry off not wanting to interact with the officers. Reid looks at Duke and chuckles as he and Slater make their way over to him.

"Now, don't I know you from somewhere?" The sly Reid asks. "I never forget a face, and you look so familiar."

"Nah, I don't think so," Duke says before taking another puff of his cigarette. "You must have me confused with someone else."

Reid acts as though he's thinking before snapping his fingers.

"Last month. We busted you for trying to assault one of my peers," Reid says, purposely making a scene for all to see. "Yeah, you thought you were hot shit, didn't you. I told you I don't forget a face."

"I don't know what you're talking about," Duke says before trying to walk off.

Reid grabs Duke by the arm and turns him around creating tension with the onlooking crowd.

"Well, if I didn't know any better, I'd think you didn't like me," a coy Reid responds, smiling. "How did it feel to get your ass handed to you?"

"Look, I don't want no trouble, okay? I wasn't tryin' to start shit then, and I ain't tryin' to start shit now," Duke replies before jerking his arm from Reid's grasp.

He's about to walk away once more when Reid grabs him and pushes him to the wall, much to the surprise of the bystanders in the area.

"What's your fuckin' problem?" Duke says.

"Thugs like you, that's why my problem is," Reid responds, getting into Duke's face. "You like beating on a cop? Well, here I am! Take your best shot at me! I dare you! Let's see how hard you are when you go up against a real man, not some old ass cop on his final days!"

Duke chuckles before taking a puff of his cigarette and blowing the smoke into Reid's face.

"Go fuck yourself, officer," he says.

An infuriated Reid smacks the cigarette from Duke's lip, causing the ex-cop to push Reid, who trips and falls towards the ground. Slater takes out his nightstick and delivers a blow to the stomach of Duke, sending him to the ground gasping for air. He lands several more blows to the back of Duke before Reid rushes over and stops him.

"That's enough!" He yells to his fellow officer.

Slater stops his assault, as Reid takes out a set of cuffs.

"Well, Mr. Officer Attacker, seems like you bought you some time downtown," he says as he cuffs Duke and raises him off the ground.

Duke is still struggling to breathe as he's lead over to the police cruiser amidst all the onlookers in front of the pool hall. A smiling Reid looks at the crowd, happy to accomplish what he set out to.

Forty minutes later, Duke is sitting in an interrogation room, still feeling the effects of the assault he took earlier. After a few moments, Irvin and Reid make their way into the room infuriating Duke as he leaps up and grabs Reid by his shirt, slamming him on the wall.

"You son of bitch!" He yells. "You were supposed to make a show of the shit! Not have your boy beat my ass!"

"Hey, take it easy! I tripped and fell to the ground! Slater wasn't even supposed to be part of it!" Reid says with his hands up. "I didn't expect you to push me that hard. Damn-"

"He could have killed me!" Duke responds before Irvin breaks the two men up.

"That's enough!" He yells, calming both men down. "The fight is out there, not in here, so settle the fuck down!"

Duke backs away shaking his head as Reid calms down as well. Irvin looks at Reid, seeking answers.

"What happened out there?" He asks.

"Look, we were supposed to make a scene, he was supposed to push me, and I was supposed to arrest him on the spot," Reid explains. "I ended up tripping over a rock or something, and Slater took at as an attack, and responded accordingly."

"Accordingly? Using a nightstick on an unarmed citizen is what you call responding accordingly?!" An angered Duke fires back. "I might have a broken spine or some shit!"

"Slater is not a part of the operation!" Reid responds, becoming irritated looking towards Irvin. "He thought we were there to grab a beer. You told me nobody outside the agreed upon personnel was to know about the operation. It wasn't supposed to go like that! If anything, it's his own fault for pushing me like that!"

"My fault?! My fault?! You must have lost your mind," Duke says as the two men face off once more.

Irvin once again gets in between the two men trying to settle things.

"I said that's enough!" He yells before turning to Duke. "Once we're done here, I want you to file an official complaint against Detective Slater."

"Oh, come on, Deputy! He didn't know what was going on," Reid pleads.

"It doesn't matter if he knew or didn't. This will only help Duke's cover and earn points with the streets," Irvin explains. "It'll look like he's just another citizen with a brutality complaint to whoever's watching. It'll never make it to the review board."

Reid sighs, but nods his head with understanding as Irvin takes a seat. Duke leans on the wall across from the Deputy, refusing to sit for the moment.

"Was there a big enough crowd out to witness this?" Irvin asks.

"Yeah, it was half off Thursdays. There's normally a big crowd always trying to get in," Duke answers. "Enough folks saw it."

"Good, so what's our next move?" The Deputy inquires.

"Well, hopefully with the incident a month ago, and tonight's incident, people will start to loosen up around me,

41

maybe even someone in The Hand of God Crew," Duke says. "Everybody knows the club, the barbershop, and the pool halls are places to gossip about the streets. Word should get around about that lunatic."

Reid frowns as Irvin nods his head with approval. The deputy notices Duke grimacing as he tries to remain loose.

"Do we need to get you checked out?" Irvin asks.

"Nah, I'll be fine," Duke answers. "Besides, I'm trying to sell police neglect. Y'all being all neighborly getting me medical attention would confuse the narrative. I'll get checked out after I'm bailed out."

"Speaking of which, have you arranged bail?" Irvin inquires. "Is there something we can do that won't mess up your street cred?"

"Actually, there is," Duke says as he goes into his pocket, pulls out Terricka's card, and hands it to the deputy.

Irvin frowns as he looks at the card.

"You can't be serious," he responds.

"I'm serious," Duke replies, smirking. "She's a lawyer and close to the streets. She makes enough noise, maybe they'll come looking for me. I mean, it's either that or hope this ass whoopin' draws attention. I've been out there for almost a month and don't have shit to go on so far."

Irvin frowns on the thought of having to deal with Terricka. They have crossed paths several times in the past, and each time came with unwanted attention. He knows the kind of exposure she will bring, and would rather not deal with her. At the moment, he doesn't have any other options at his disposal. He hands the card back to Duke and turns to Reid.

"Give him his phone call," Irvin says before making his way out of the room.

Reid nods his head as he leads Duke out of the interrogation room as if he is a perp to make his phone call to his attorney.

About an hour has gone by as Duke is back in the interrogation room clutching his head, still feeling the effects of the earlier beating. Terricka is led into the room and is stunned to see Duke in the shape he's in.

"Oh my God. What did they do to you?" She asks before taking a seat across from him.

"Just some of that old LAPD hospitality," Duke responds, smiling. "Well, I guess it was worth it to be able to see you. I guess this is our first official date."

"How can you joke at a time like this?" Terricka says as she takes out her note pad and camera. "Do me a favor, take off your shirt."

"Damn, we gonna do this right here in the station?" A sly Duke responds. "I mean, I would prefer somewhere a little more romantic with candle light. I'm not a total heathen."

"Boy, take off your damn shirt so I can document this," Terricka fires back as she holds up her camera.

Duke does what's asked of him as Terricka snaps a photo of him. While snapping her photo, she can't help but notice his rock abs and perfect physic. She snaps out of it, as she takes the required photos she needs before moving on.

"Okay, turn around," she orders.

She's stunned as she notices the bruises across his back and sides. She snaps a couple more pictures, disturbed with the view.

"We need to get you to the hospital," Terricka says before Duke turns around.

"I'm fine," he replies.

"No, you're not! Duke, you could have a broken rib or something! Don't worry, I'll take care of this as soon as I leave," Terricka fires back. "Now, what happened?"

Duke takes a deep breath as he explains the altercation to his lawyer. As he explains every detail, Terricka takes meticulous notes, prepping herself to speak on his behalf. Moments after finishing his tale, Terricka seems as if she's offended with the treatment Duke has received. She drops her pen and sighs, shaking her head.

"This is bullshit," she says, still processing all that's happened. "I can't say I'm surprised. Reid and Slater have been on my hit list for a while now. Just can't get anything to stick on them. Then they gave that bastard his own detail, I think in spite of me. One brutality case after another."

"Yeah, he doesn't seem like the friendly type," Duke says, chuckling. "So, what's up? I'm gonna be able to get out of here, or what?"

"Well, first thing's first, I need to get you seen by a doctor. Let him check you out and make sure there are no internal injuries," Terricka explains as she begins packing her things. "Plus, his testimony might be needed if they decided to fight this and go to trial, which I doubt they will. I'm gonna reach out to the deputy in the morning after I run my investigation. See if I can get this bullshit charge thrown out, and you released."

"Damn, worth every penny," Duke jokes as Terricka smirks.

"Baby, trust me, you're getting me at a discount," she replies. "Don't have me come looking for you for my money when you get out."

"I got you, but if you want me to pay you, you're gonna have to let me take you out," a suave Duke responds. "It's the least I can do to thank you."

"Don't thank me yet. You're not out. Just give me the night. I should have something for you in the morning," Terricka says before rising from her seat.

Duke rises as well as he shakes her hand.

"Real talk, thank you for this," he says.

There is an awkward silence between the two before Terricka smiles and makes her way out of the interrogation room. Duke takes a deep breath before taking a seat once again, waiting for someone to lead him back to the holding area.

The next morning, Deputy Commissioner Irvin is looking outside his office window watching several 'defund the police' protesters chanting on the street below just outside of the precinct property. He frowns as frustration begins to gather inside of him. The protests were starting to get out of control in his mind, but with all the media attention into the protests, his hands are tied for the moment. While he continues to watch the crowd grow peering down from his office, there is a knock on his door, from his assistant.

"Sir, Ms. Terricka Jackson is here to see you," the assistant announces.

"Send her in," Irvin answers as he takes a seat back behind his desk.

A few moments later, Terricka is led in by the assistant, who leaves her and the deputy alone. Terricka, wearing her business skirt with a name tag on the chest, walks in and takes a seat across from Irvin with a smirk on her face.

"Deputy," she greets as she opens her legal case to pull out several documents.

"Ms. Jackson. I'm assume you are the one behind what's going on outside," Irvin deduces.

"No. What's going on outside is behind the mistreatment of black people by your police force daily," Terricka jabs. "But you know that already."

"Bullshit. The protests were finally starting to die down, and all of a sudden, I get a meeting request from you and a gathering outside my precinct. You're telling me it's just all one big coincidence?"

A sly grin enters into Terricka's face, revealing what Irvin knew all along.

"What is it that you want?" A blunt Irvin asks.

Terricka hands the deputy Duke's file as he quickly looks at it as if he wasn't expecting it.

"Says here he attacked one of my officers, and they defended themselves," Irvin says, tossing the file on his desk. "I assume you want him pulled?"

"Yes, with all charges dropped," Terricka replies. "I also want a suspension of both officers involved in the arrest. Your boys Reid and Slater are at it again. It's time to see some action."

"Let me get this straight. Your client attacked my officers, and you want me not only to release him but suspend the officers who were attacked?" Irvin says, chuckling in disbelief. "No disrespect, counselor, but you've got a set of balls. You're asking for too much even for you."

Terricka smiles as she takes out her phone and starts a video she had cued up. The video shows the assault Duke took from Slater the previous day before Reid intervenes. Irvin chuckles once more, getting comfortable in his chair.

"How much did it cost you to get that video?" He says, grinning.

"The truth is always free," Terricka quips.

"Then where's the rest of the video?" Irving fires back. "We both know there's more to it than what you showed me."

"Maybe there is. Maybe there isn't. Look, we both know I can make this go viral by pressing send on my phone to several media contacts. The question is do you want your department on CNN or not?" Terricka says, leaning back in her chair, crossing her legs. "What's it gonna be, Deputy?"

"We both know I'll find the full video and post it just as fast as you will," Irvin points out.

"Yeah, maybe, but by then half of America would have made up their mind, and that crowd you see now out there won't be anything compared to what's to come. Reid and Slater's name will be drug through the dirt, and their history will be broadcast all over television. You willing to go through all that?" A sly Terricka asks.

Irvin's smugness fades as he knew that Terricka has a point. Most people's minds would be made up by the time he'd be able to track down the actual video causing unnecessary riots and placing his officers in more harm's way. He takes a deep breath pondering the lawyer's proposition.

"Your boy walks, but I'm not suspending my officers," he says, negotiating with the attorney. "If Duke wants to make a formal complaint, I'll get IA to look into it. Best I can offer."

"I want an independent panel to review the situation," demands Terricka. "You think for a moment I'm gonna let your people conduct the investigation?"

"Please. For all your marches and speeches, you couldn't get the mayor to agree to an independent review board, so what makes you think I'm going to allow it on my end," Irvin responds.

"Mayors change. So do deputies," Terricka replies, grinning.

"Well, that may be the case, but until there is a new mayor, I'm going to have to decline your request," Irvin says. "IA review board if Duke files a formal complaint. Best I'm going to give you."

Terricka shakes her head, upset she's not getting everything she wants. Eventually, she nods her head with agreement sealing the deal for her client.

"I would say pleasure doing business with you, but we both know that isn't the case," Irvin says. "I'll have your client processed and release within the hour."

"If he's not released in the next fifteen minutes, I'll have the media out front doing interviews bringing your department down further, if that's even possible," Terricka says. "Make the call."

Irvin doesn't feel like adding on to his stress as he picks up the phone to order the release of Duke. Terricka smiles before leaving out of the deputy's office. After he gets off the phone, he leans back in his chair, smirking, knowing the performance went better than expected. Duke would be known as a man who fought the police and won. If this didn't increase his street credentials with the locals, nothing would. Terricka played right into the deputy's hands.

Ten minutes later, Terricka is waiting outside of the precinct checking her phone when Duke makes his way out, being released from the holding area. He notices her and smiles, making his way over towards her.

"You work fast," he says, grabbing her attention. "How'd you pull that off?"

"Me and the Deputy Commissioner came to an understanding," she says, putting her phone away.

"I bet it has something to do with that," Duke says, pointing at the protesting crowd. "This your doing?"

"Alone, they can choose to ignore, but together, they are forced to listen whether they want to or not," Terricka answers. "Their voices scare them in a way their Billy clubs scare us."

"Yeah, but do they know they are protesting the release of a former cop?" Duke inquires.

"They know a black man was mistreated by the police. That's all they needed to know," Terricka replies, smiling. "Anyway, I did my job. Make sure you file a formal complaint against those officers that assaulted you. Now since that's done, how are you gonna pay me for my time?"

"I told you I got you," Duke says. "Why don't we go out tonight, and I'll bring you a check then?"

"Why don't you give me my money now, and we call it even?" Terricka quips.

Duke chuckles as he pulls out his wallet.

"How much do I owe you?" He asks.

"Since I like Ms. Evelyn, I'll only charge you three hundred," Terricka says, surprising Duke.

"Can you break a twenty?" He says, smirking while taking a twenty-dollar bill from his wallet.

Terricka rolls her eyes, looking at her client as a lost cause.

"I'll pass by the store in a few days," she replies before snatching the twenty-dollar bill from Duke's hand. "You owe me two eighty. Borrow it or something. Anyway, I gotta go. You're welcome."

Terricka rushes off, leaving Duke shaking his head at his attorney. The first phase of his plan was done. There is nothing left to do but wait and hope his story floods the neighborhood. After a few moments of pondering his decision, he makes his way off, heading towards a bus stop.

Later that evening, in the notorious Nickerson Garden Housing Projects, Terricka makes her way down the street down the busy sidewalk filled with drug dealers and other project residents. Normally someone of her beauty and appearance is harassed by the men in the area, but Terricka doesn't get a look like most as the people in the area part ways as she passes them. She doesn't acknowledge anyone while making her way into one of the abandoned buildings in the center of the projects. Nickerson Garden is known for its gangs and drug dealings. Several of the project buildings became unlivable and were evacuated due to safety precautions. The city never funded repairs to the buildings in the project, which left them abandoned, and the perfect place for squatters, and people who didn't want to be found. Inside one of the living spaces, Terricka walks into what seems like a sit down between rival gang members. In the center of it all is Damu, who is coordinating discussions with the two factions. She notices Jules observing the discussion from the other side of the room, and quietly makes her way over without disrupting.

"Hey. Isn't that the Bounty Hunters and Grape Street crews?" she whispers to Jules.

"Yeah. Crazy, ain't it?" Jules says with a smirk. "Bet you never thought you'd see the day them crews would sit down and squash the beef."

"Wonders never cease," Terricka replies, smirking.

"For real. Where your ass been all day anyway?" Jules questions. "I know you got my texts."

"Last I checked my dad is over there," Terricka snaps back, referring to Damu. "What I do is my business."

"For now it is," a sly Jules fires back with a smirk. "One of these days you're gonna come to your senses and let me take you out. Then we'll get married, have a couple of kids. I'd break your back a time or two during the week cause lord knows you need it. Basically, you'd be mine, and your business will be my business. So you might as well get used to it."

Terricka shakes her head before slightly giggling at Jules's response. He's been trying to get with her ever since they were kids. Growing up together, he looked after her as if she was his younger sister but always had an attraction to her. Terricka thinks he's cute as well, with him being a highly sought after pretty boy in her eyes. He has the perfect fade, killer smile, and chiseled body that all the women love. She wasn't attracted to light-skinned guys, however, and would never date anyone in her father's organization. Jules is his number one lieutenant that oversees all of the streets keeping Damu in the loop of things. He's down with the cause, which causes some conflict in Terricka's feelings attracting him to her, but she's a woman of discipline and refuses to lower her standards. Terricka and Jules continue to watch in silence as Damu wraps up the meeting between the two rival gangs. Both gang leaders shake hands before making their way out of the room. Damu turns and smiles as he walks over and hugs his daughter.

"I thought that was you I saw sneakin' in," he says.

"Really, dad? Both Bounty Hunters and Grape Street crews in here? Are you trying to get caught?" Terricka asks.

"There was a beef, and I was trying to make sure it was taken care of without bloodshed. What's wrong with that?" Damu inquires.

"What's wrong is you're too exposed here. What if one of the gangs tried to set the other one up? Guess who's in the crossfire?" Terricka explains. "Also, what happens if members of the gang were being investigated? You could have surveillance all over them, and eventually you. Dammit, dad, you can't keep risking yourself like that."

Damu nods his head with agreement as his daughter has made valid points.

"I understand your concern, and I appreciate it," Damu replies. "However, what good is our cause if we can't help out the community? If we're at war with each other, how can we rise above the oppression? Just fighting for police reform doesn't mean anything if our people don't take advantage of it. The cops are armed for war because of the gangs. There will never be a 'defund the police' discussion if the gangs are shooting each other down over some simple beef."

Terricka throws her hands in the air before turning to Jules.

"You wanna chime in here?" She asks.

"You know me, Tee. I'm down for whatever. If Damu thinks it's best for the cause, then I'm cool with it. We need to be a part of the solution on both ends," Jules says, disappointing his childhood friend. "However, maybe it's too early to show our faces. That news story about the cop Stonebrook is still getting heavy rotation. More and more people are starting to know your name."

"By design," Damu fires back. "I want them to know my name."

"I get that too, but maybe Tee is right. Why don't you take a step back for a little bit? Let me take care of shit for a minute. You know I can handle it," Jules says.

Damu sighs as he decides to break some bad news.

"They found Jamal last night," he says, shocking both Terricka and Jules. "Well, I should say they found what's left of his body. He was beaten to death from the looks over it and dumped in the water, just coming to shore last night."

"Any word on who did it?" Terricka asks.

"We know who did it," an angered Jules responds. "I'm tired of lettin' that pig get away with shit, Damu. We need to cancel his ticket quick, fast, and in a hurry."

"We've been trying to get a lead on him for months now," Damu says. "Reid and his crew aren't like the other cops. Nobody in his squad has any family to go home to. They're a kill squad sent to find and eliminate us. He has no known address other than what's on his police file, which he hasn't been to in months. He bunkers in a safe house with his unit from what we can tell, and we don't even know where that is. Just no way to get to him."

"Any nigga can be got," Jules replies. "I say we strap up and start pluckin' his people for information just like he does us. They'll talk, and eventually give up that address. Then we strap up and settle it in the streets."

Damu sighs as he puts his hand on his second in command's arm.

"That's why you're not ready for the top spot," Damu responds. "You would sacrifice our brother's lives just for vengeance. Patience, old friend. That's what they want us to do. Come at them head on. They've been through months of training prepping for that exact outcome. We don't have the type of people who can pull that off."

A sighing Jules nods his head, understanding his leader's words when Terricka grabs her father's attention.

"Speaking of the type of people we need, I just got charges dropped for Evelyn's grandson, Duke," she announces. "According to my sources, and the videos I seen of last night's incident, he took it to Reid head on, before that asshole Slater intervened. I don't know, I think he may be useful to the cause."

"Ain't he the nigga that was an ex-cop in Cleveland or somewhere?" Jules asks.

"Yeah, well Cincinnati, but yeah, that's him," Terricka answers.

"Then fuck him. We don't need no cop rollin' with us, ex or not," Jules rejects.

"This is exactly the type of guy you need. He took it to them pigs and they beat his ass for it. It's also the second time they've arrested his ass over some bullshit. He sees it the same way we do. Plus, he was a Cincinnati cop, not LAPD. He's not associated with anyone in that department. We could use his knowledge of police procedures and shit like that. Tell me it's not a good idea to have someone on our squad like that."

"He may have taken an ass whoppin' or two, but that don't mean he's down for what we do," Jules points out. "Will he pull the trigger on one of his blue buddies if it came down to it? If you ask me, once a pig, always a pig."

"Dad, tell me you don't see this working for us," Terricka says as all attention is on Damu.

Damu ponders his daughter's thoughts and weighs them with his thoughts trying to decide.

"Bring him in for a look," he orders. "I'll see what's truly in his heart. If he's everything you say he is, he would be a wonderful asset to the cause."

Terricka smiles while Jules shakes his head, still not buying into Duke and his past.

"Alright, it's your call, but I think this shit is gonna blow up in all our faces," he says. "Just look what happened to Jamal. You want that shit happening to either of you?"

"It's just a look over, Jules. It'll be fine," Damu replies, reassuring his number two. "Can you give me and Terricka a moment, please?"

Jules nods his head as he exits the room leaving father and daughter alone with each other.

"Are you sure about this guy?" Damu asks. "You know I'll normally don't question your thoughts on subjects, especially in front of others, but this ex-cop. You really think we can trust him?"

"I think we can bring him along with certain aspects of the cause, and leave him out of the more vital issues we deal with," Terricka suggests. "He knows their methods. He could prove invaluable."

Damu thinks for a moment before nodding his head with agreement.

"Alright. I'll let you take care of the specifics," he says.

Both he and his daughter hug once more before making their way out of the room, joining the others who were waiting for them on the outside.

CHAPTER 4

Jamie

Just off Crenshaw Boulevard in the early morning hours is Jamie, a sixteen-year-old high school student hanging with his friends Tony, known on the streets as Big T, and Robert. Big T and Robert were a year older than Jamie, and unlike him, both were involved in local street gangs. The trio has just finished up their fast food meal, hopping back into Big T's car, pulling off down the road. They are on the hunt for a member of a rival street gang, who had an altercation with Jamie a few days earlier. While Jamie isn't a part of their gang officially, his old friends still feel the need to protect his name in the streets. They've been circling the area all night looking for the gang member and are getting restless.

"Aye, let's just call it a night," Jamie says. "I got shit to do tomorrow. We ain't gonna find this nigga no time soon."

"Stop acting like a bitch, Jay," Big T responds as he picks his gold tooth, struggling to dislodge food from it. "Nigga punked you, and you out here actin' scared."

"I ain't acting scared, I'm just sayin' we then been out in this bitch all night, and I ain't seen one nigga from his crew," Jamie fires back. "I still got homework I need to do and shit before Monday."

"Look at this fool talkin' bout homework," Big T says to Robert. "You wonder why niggas always testin' you."

"For real, Jay. You can't let them niggas punk you. You may

not be part of the Deuces, but you represent us. If niggas feel they can fuck with you, that means they feel they can fuck with us. We gonna find this crab ass nigga and fill his ass with some hot ones," Robert says, whipping down his tec-nine. "Niggas gonna learn tonight, for real."

Big T chuckles before turning up his music in his car. Jamie has a look of despair filling his eyes. He didn't want to be in the car with his friends this night but didn't want to look soft in their eyes. Word spread around his school about the altercation he had, and once it reached his friend's ears, he knew what would happen next. He's gotten lucky so far since they have yet to come across anyone, but growing up in LA, he knows that things can change in a heartbeat.

After an hour of driving around, even Robert is getting tired of searching the city as he turns down Big T's radio.

"Aye, I'm gettin' tired, for real," he says. "Look, we can ride on these niggas another time."

"I'm sayin'. Let's call it a night, damn," Jamie supports, causing Big T to shake his head.

"Man, y'all niggas ain't shit," he says, giving up as well. "For real, if it was me who the nigga dissed, I wouldn't stop rollin' 'til I found his ass. Y'all niggas just can't hang."

"We tired nigga, fuck. Don't know how your fat ass can ride around all night. Us normal niggas need a break, shit," Robert fires back. "In fact, pull over at the next gas station. I need to take a piss."

Big T shakes his head but listens as he pulls over at a nearby gas station. Robert hops out of the vehicle and heads inside to see if he can gain access to the bathroom. Big T gets out of the car to the pump and begins to fill his tank. Jamie gets out as well, stretching his legs, happy that this night is over. He's hoping that with a night of rest that his two friends will let the matter go. Moments later, Robert comes out of the store with a bag of chips and a soda in his hand just as Big T finishes pumping his gas. They are all about to get back in the car when Big T notices

Dee, part of the Rollin' 60s Crip gang, and another gang member pull up to the gas station as well. Dee is the gang member that had the altercation with Jamie earlier that week, and the one they were looking for to exact their revenge. Big T points him out to Robert, who immediately drops his bag of chips and pulls out his weapon.

"Yo, what's up, crab ass nigga!" Robert says before opening fire on the gang members.

Dee and his crew member duck behind their car and pull out their weapons to return fire as the gunshots echo throughout the area. A terrified Jamie is in a daze as everything is running in slow motion around him with bullets whizzing past his head just missing him. Big T notices his friend freezing up and quickly pulls him in the car before starting the engine. Robert unloads a few more shots before jumping into the car himself just as it screeches down the road. When the dust settles, Dee is lying on the ground bleeding out after taking several shots. His fellow gang member is crouching over him trying to keep his friend alive, but the wounds are too far gone as the life fades from his eyes.

Speeding down the street, Robert looks back and pumps his fist, happy with the results of their run-in.

"Yo, I got that nigga, for real!" He exclaims with the adrenaline still flowing through him. "Yo, y'all see that?! Tell me y'all saw that!"

"We saw it, nigga. Damn, calm down," Big T responds, slowing down to avoid drawing attention. "Them nigga's shot up my ride though. Your ass payin' for that, best believe."

"What? How you gonna blame me for them niggas?" Robert questions. "We was lookin' out for them! How is that shit my fault?"

Big T and Robert continue to go back and forth with each other as Jamie sits silently in the back seat with his friend's words sounding muffled in his mind. The whole incident has him out of it as he stares blindly into the window, distant from everything going on around him. He repeats the shooting over and over again in his head, torturing himself with the traumatic experience. While continuing to stare out of the window, a blue and red blur catches his attention and snaps him out of his state. A police cruiser is following them, causing Big T and Robert to stop their bickering.

"Oh shit! One-time nigga, one-time," Big T says as he notices the cruiser following them. "Aye, duck that shit under the seat, fool! Hurry up!"

Robert quickly wipes down the gun used in the shooting and quickly positions it under the seat as best he can. Once the gun is put away, Big T slowly pulls his car to the side of the road, keeping his hands on the steering wheel.

"Y'all niggas keep y'all's mouth shut, you hear me," he commands, looking in his rearview mirror, checking on Jamie's status. "Aye, Jamie. You hear me?"

"Y… yeah, I hear you," Jamie utters nervously.

Big T slowly lowers his window as Officer Williams slowly walks up to the vehicle, tapping the vehicle's tail light as per training. He has his hand on his holstered gun taking his time to look into the vehicle to see everyone that's present. His partner Murphy is back in the cruiser running the vehicle's plate, but making sure he kept an eye on his partner. Williams finally makes it towards the driver's side of the vehicle and looks on at Big T.

"Gentlemen. You know you were going ten miles over the limit?" Williams calmly asks.

"Sorry, Officer. I wasn't payin' attention. It's my fault," Big T replies, doing his best proper impersonation.

"Shut the engine please, and I'll need your license and proof of insurance," Williams says.

Big T complies shutting the engine and handing over his license.

"I'm gonna go into the glove to pull my insurance," Big T states, making sure Williams knows his every movement.

Williams nods his head as he goes into the glove box and

pulls out several papers. The veteran cop notices the tattoos on both Big T and Robert signifying their gang affiliations. After Big T locates the insurance, he hands the papers to the officer and places his hands back on the wheel in plain view. Williams looks over the documents and nods his head.

"I'll be back," he says before making his way back to the cruiser.

Big T and Robert are cool, but Jamie is nervous, catching Williams's eyes before getting into the cruiser.

"Anything?" He asks his partner.

"Plates come back clean, but there was a shooting on Crenshaw where this vehicle description came up," Murphy says. "You see anything?"

"The two in the front are gang members," Williams points out while typing Big T's info into the computer. "And according to this Tyrone Mathis, also known as Big T, has a file. Multiple arrests, and he's out on probation right now. No active warrants though."

Murphy nods his head as he continues to monitor the vehicle.

"What are you thinking?" he asks.

"I'm thinking the nervous kid in the back seat says they're hiding something," Williams answers. "Call it in, and take the passenger's side."

Murphy nods his head as he quickly radios in to dispatch. After he's done, both he and Murphy exits their cruiser and cautiously make their way back towards Big T's car. Murphy immediately notices the bullet holes on the passenger's side of the vehicle and signals Williams, who nods his head.

"Can you please step out of the vehicle," Williams orders with his hand on his holstered gun.

"Officer, I don't think that's necessary. We haven't done anything wrong," Big T pleads.

"I need you to step out of the vehicle. All of you," Williams says, being a little sterner than before.

Big T shakes his head in disgust before complying with the

officer's orders, slowly exiting the car. Robert, realizing they were caught, also complies as Murphy keeps an eye on him. Jamie, knowing that the gun would be found in the car, starts to panic. He's never been arrested before and is terrified of what awaits him once the officers find the hidden gun. He slowly opens the door to exit the vehicle, noticing that Murphy was searching Robert, who is being patted down. Noticing the officer is distracted, Jamie darts out of the vehicle and makes his way down the block.

"Hey! Stop!" Murphy yells, and he quickly pursues the runaway.

Robert looks to run as well amidst all the ruckus but is quickly stopped by Williams, who pulls his gun out.

"Hey! Hey! You stay right there!" Williams warns as Robert gives up his attempt to run.

Williams subdues Big T before ordering Robert on the other side of the vehicle to subdue him as well. Down the block, Jamie has ducked off down a darkened alley trying to evade Murphy, who remains in hot pursuit of him. With his gun drawn, Murphy cautiously makes his way down the alley making sure to check every corner before proceeding. There's very little light in the area, but Murphy can tell it was a dead-end area. Several discarded items fill the area making it difficult to see throughout the space.

"Okay, kid, come on out. There's no way out of here," Murphy says, trying to reason with Jamie. "It doesn't have to go down like this. We already got your friends, no need to make things worse."

Ducked down behind a trash container at the furthest end of the alley is Jamie, praying and hoping the officer doesn't locate him. He is scared of what might happen to him, thinking about how his mother would react. He shakes at the very thought of not being able to see her.

"Come on, kid! Don't make me have to get the dogs in here to sniff you out," Murphy threatens, hoping to strike fear in the youngster.

The light is almost non-existent as Murphy makes his way deeper into the abyss. He stops for a moment to check for his flashlight before realizing he left it in the cruiser. He takes a deep breath as he continues to make his way down the alley, with his gun pointed.

"Look, I know you're scared, and to be honest, I would be too in your position," Murphy says, going with the more relatable approach. "Things go wrong and it isn't your fault. Your friends back there seem to be about this life. It's not for everyone, kid. What I can and I can't do depends on you coming out right now and turning yourself if. I can't help you if you don't. Let's get together so we can talk this thing out."

Murphy's words are influencing Jamie as a few tears start to fall from his eyes. He wants everything to be over. He wants to go home to his mother and be done with everything that happened earlier. He slowly rises from his hiding space and is about to walk towards Murphy. Before the officer can notice him, Jamie stumbles on a bottle causing him to lunge forward. Murphy quickly reacts by firing a shot into the youth's chest, sending him falling to the ground. Murphy quickly checks to make sure there is no weapon in sight before taking out his cell phone and using the flashlight to give him some sort of view. The light quickly shines on Jamie, who is coughing up blood after the shot hit him in his heart.

"Oh my god!" Murphy exclaims, kneeling next to the fallen juvenile.

He quickly grabs his radio to request an ambulance down towards his location before turning towards Jamie, who is fading fast.

"Hang in there, kid. Don't you die on me," Murphy says, trying to compress the youth's chest to stop the bleeding.

His attempt fails as a coughing Jamie dies, tears still flowing from his eyes.

"No, no, no!" Murphy exclaims as he tries to revive Jamie to no avail.

He continues to try and revive the fallen youngster screaming out for help to anyone in the area. Moments later, he realizes that the youth is gone, filling him with grief.

Forty minutes later, the once dark grimy alley is now lit up with police lights as officers work tapping off the area, and the coroners getting ready to move Jamie's body. On a stoop just outside of the alleyway, Murphy sits silently, hands still bloodied from his resuscitation attempts. In his eyes, the blood fills the hands of a killer. As long as he's been on the force, he's never needed to fire his gun on anyone, let alone kill someone. He couldn't believe Jamie died by his hand and is struggling to process everything that's going on. Williams wraps up his conversation with a few investigating officers when he notices a distraught Murphy sitting alone. He makes his way over towards his partner, trying to put his mind at ease.

"Well, it seems they were the kids that started that firefight at the gas station," Williams says. "Once ballistics matches the gun to the casings, it'll be an open and shut case. Don't lose any sleep over this."

"I... I killed that kid," a somber Murphy responds. "I took his life. He wasn't even armed."

"But he lunged at you, right?" Williams asks for clarification. "It was dark. He could have been coming at you with anything."

"He was just a kid, Williams. A kid. Maybe, I could have done, I don't know. Something different," Murphy replies, replaying the event over in his head. "I could have shot him in the leg, or better yet used the taser. I could have taken him down a million other ways."

"Hindsight is twenty-twenty," Williams reminds his partner. "You did what you had to do. Sure, he didn't have anything, but what if he did? Would you know? I mean, it was dark as shit back there. If he did have something, a gun, knife, or whatever, and lunged at you. You didn't do what you did, your wife and kids would be without a father. He and his crew just lit up an entire gas station, killing a rival gang member. As tragic as this is, I think we did some good here tonight."

Murphy shakes his head in disagreement, feeling this could have been prevented if he could have just done some things differently. Williams continues to try and comfort his partner when Commissioner Billick arrives at the scene. He asks one of the officers the whereabouts of Murphy, who points him out. Billick quickly makes his way over, surprising both Williams and Murphy, who quickly jumps up from the stoop.

"Commissioner, sir," Murphy says before Billick waves him off.

"At ease, son. At ease," he says with a hint of a smirk on his face. "I heard you had quite the night."

"Yes, sir. I guess you could say that," Murphy responds.

Billick nods his head before looking towards Williams.

"And you are?" He questions.

"Officer Williams, sir."

"Oh, right, Murphy's partner," Billick responds, shaking Williams's hand. "Good work tonight taking care of those bangers. With the video from the station and the gun found in the vehicle, I'm sure we're going to be able to put them away for a very long time."

Williams nods his head with agreement as Billick looks around the crime scene from a distance.

"Williams, you mind giving me and your partner a moment?" He requests.

"Sure, sir," Williams replies before patting Murphy on the shoulder and walking off.

Billick offers Murphy a seat back on the stoop as the two take a seat, observing everything going on in the area.

"I know how you feel, son," Billick says. "You don't know how to feel when you kill your first perp. They don't teach you that in the academy. When I killed my first perp, I couldn't sleep for days. Just kept replaying it over and over in my head trying to see if I could have done anything differently."

Murphy is stunned hearing the commissioner's words mirroring his exact thoughts.

"How did you overcome it?" He asks, seeking answers.

"Well, you're a little too deep into it now to think about it," Billick points out. "It's too soon to think about overcoming. It'll take a few days, maybe even a week, but you will eventually get over it. The one thing you can't do is blame yourself if you followed all the guidelines. The body cam will tell the tale, but if there is something that you believe you did that was outside of guidelines, let me know now. Maybe we can talk it through so we can gain clarity before IA gets to questioning you."

Murphy processes his thoughts once more, trying to make sure that everything had been done by the book. He shakes his head, taking a deep breath.

"My flashlight," Murphy utters. "I should have had my flashlight with me."

"Flashlight? That's it?" Billick asks.

Murphy nods his head, causing the commissioner to laugh.

"Son, if that's all that was wrong here, you're fine," he says with a chuckle. "Just say you lost it in the pursuit, and you'll be fine."

"But, I didn't lose it in pursuit. I left it in the car," Murphy admits. "It was a little bulky, and I had taken it off to get a little more comfortable. When we stopped the suspects, I didn't think to put it back on, and-"

"Officer Murphy, let me be clear about something. You're about to face an Internal Affairs investigation. An investigation taking place in a time where everyone hates cops, I might add," Billick explains. "They are about to drag your name through the dirt, son. Whether wrong or right, everyone is going to have an opinion about you before they even learn the facts. IA has been pressured by the administration to make examples out of police brutality and shooting cases. You're going to be news now, so every little thing from your past and your family will be investigated by the media. Do you really want the fact that you didn't have your standard issued flashlight be the thing that gets you fired or brought up on charges?"

Billick's scare tactics work on Murphy, as he hadn't even begun to think about the outcome of the shooting, and how it's going to look.

"Br... brought up on charges?" Murphy stutters.

"Yes, son. We're living in dangerous times now where we are the enemies in the public's eye," Billick points out. "Every little thing we do will be challenged by those who have no idea what it's like to wear that badge. You killed a banger who shot up a gas station before you pulled them over. This wasn't an innocent child, but you can be damn sure that's how they are going to portray him. He participated in a violent crime and suffered a violent death. That's their code. That's how they live. So I'll ask you again, Officer Murphy, are you going to let a standard issued flashlight be the thing that gets you in the spotlight, or are you going to make sure the light stays where it should be, on the violent gangster who killed earlier tonight, and who could have killed again had it not been for your bravery and resilience?"

Murphy ponders silently for a moment taking into account everything Billick has told him. He didn't want to be in the spotlight over this incident, but even he was aware enough to know with everything going on he's going to need support from his fellow peers to survive the charges. He slowly nods his head with agreement, much to Billick's delight.

"You're right, sir. He got what he deserved," Murphy responds.

"That he did, son. That he did," Billick says, rising from the stoop. "Tell you what, take the rest of the night off. IA is going to want to talk to you, but I'll hold them off for the night. First thing tomorrow, report in and meet with your union representative. IA is going to play hardball, but don't worry, we'll make sure everything goes accordingly for you."

Murphy nods once again before rising from the stoop and shaking the commissioner's hand.

"Thank you, sir," he says.

He's about to walk off when Billick pulls him back.

"Make sure you ditch the flashlight," he tells the officer.

"Yes, sir. I'll take care of it," Murphy responds.

Billick smiles as he lets Murphy go on his way. The commissioner takes one more look around the crime scene as sighs with frustration, knowing what's to come in the following days. After a few moments, he makes his way back towards the investigating officers, questioning their findings thus far with the case.

The next day, Duke is walking down the street after his shift working the corner store. He's about to head towards the bus stop when he passes a local resident begging for spare change. Duke waves him off initially but remembers the few dollars he came across earlier that day that someone dropped in the store. He goes into his back pocket and approaches the man with the dollars in his hand.

"Yo, my man. Here," he says trying to get the resident's attention.

"Bless you, sir," the resident says before pulling a gun out from his waist strap. "But I'm gonna need you to come with me!"

A confused Duke raises his hands.

"Yo, what the fuck is this?" Duke asks. "I just drop some funds on you and you gonna rob me like that?"

"Not robbin' you brotha. You've been summoned. Don't make me have to clap you," the resident says before motioning over to the curb where a van is sitting. "Let's go."

Duke hesitates until the resident pulls back the hammer on the gun, leaving the ex-cop no other choice but to comply. He slowly makes his way towards the van thinking about several ways he can disarm his current captor. He's about to make his move when the van door suddenly opens with Terricka inside, stunning Duke.

"Terricka?" He says in confusion. "What's going on?"

"You wanted a date, right? Well, here it is," Terricka says with a smirk. "You comin' or not?"

The resident lowers his gun as Duke looks around the area. Inside the vehicle with Terricka is a man who is wearing a ghost-like mask covering his face with a gun in his hand looking towards Duke.

"What the fuck is this?" Duke says calmly.

"If you don't get in, you'll never know," Terricka responds with a wink.

Duke hesitates until he notices the reassuring look on Terricka's face. He sighs before agreeing to join her in the truck. Once he's in, the door is slammed shut as the masked gunman hands Terricka a mask to cover Duke's face.

"Are you serious?" Duke asks when Terricka offers the mask.

"Trust me," Terricka says, once again reassuring the former cop.

Duke sighs once again as he puts on the mask and leans back in the van. A smiling Terricka nods her head as the masked gunman knocks on the van, letting the driver know they can pull off. All of the passengers remain silent as the van begins making its way down the street to an unknown location.

CHAPTER 5

First Contact

Sitting alone in a room, still with his head covered denying him a view of his surroundings, Duke tries to make out what he can listening to the background sounds of the empty room. He can hear what he believes is a TV playing in another room of the location, and can make out several voices, but can't make out what's being said. After a few moments, he's about to remove his mask, when he hears a voice in the room with him.

"Ain't nobody told you to remove your mask," the voice says as Duke freezes.

"Is anybody gonna tell me what this is about?" Duke asks. "Where's Terricka?"

The voice doesn't respond as Duke shakes his head and crosses his arms waiting to see what's in store for him. After a few more moments, he hears a door opening and several footsteps making their way towards him. His hood is quickly removed, and once his eyes can adjust, he makes out Terricka, the masked man who was riding in the van with earlier, and Damu, who is cautiously looking him over. Duke remains silent as Damu continues to try to read the former cop. He turns to Terricka as if he's unimpressed.

"So this is your guy?" Damu asks his daughter. "Doesn't seem like much."

"Give him a chance. I think he'll impress you," Terricka responds.

Damu chuckles as he turns his attention back to Duke, who is trying to read his captor as well.

"Terricka here seems to think you're someone who could benefit the cause?" Damu says.

"And what cause would that be?" Inquires Duke.

"Police reform," a chuckling Damu responds. "In LA, what other cause would there be? I heard you've had a rough stretch since becoming a citizen with your former brothers at arms. I heard that the LAPD has been a pain in your ass as much as they have been in mine. Not too fun being one of the locals, is it?"

Duke doesn't respond, not wanting to give his hand away as Damu walks around him.

"I'm curious, how does that feel?" Damu inquires. "How does it feel to go from beating folks, to taking a beating from your former fraternity?"

"I never beat on anybody," Duke fires back. "I had an impeccable record within the department while I was there until-"

"Until your brothers turned on you, and sold you out," Damu says, cutting Duke off. "If anyone knows the corruption of the police force, it's you. Especially with your recent run-ins. Still, from what I was able to gather, you never turned against your old unit. I guess there's always something good to be said about loyalty, but even you must admit if there was ever a time to talk, that would have been it."

"Seems like you know a lot about me," Duke points out. "Mind telling me who you are, and why have I been dragged in the middle of nowhere?"

Damu stops circling Duke, coming to face him with a hardened look in his eyes.

"You know who I am," he responds to the former cop. "My name is in the streets, and I'm sure everyone's talkin' about me. So cut the 'who am I act' and say my name."

Duke pauses before responding, trying to decide if he should admit he knows who Damu is or not. Would he look more guilty if he acts like he's never heard Damu, or is this a trick to make him admit he knows more than what he's letting on?

"Damu," Duke responds.

Damu is silent for a moment before chuckling once more, looking back at his daughter.

"I like him," he says, smirking. "So, you know who I am, and you know what I'm capable of. How do you feel about that?"

"I don't know how to feel. I mean, I'm just walkin' to the bus stop before I'm kidnapped in broad daylight. How would you feel if some shit like that happened to you?" Duke replies.

"It's not exactly kidnapping," Terricka points out, going into lawyer mode. "I asked you to come; you came. You didn't have to get into the van. You came on your own accord."

Duke shoots Terricka an evil look, annoyed with her lawyer lingo.

"Whatever the case may be, I'm still here, so you mind getting to the point," A direct Duke responds.

Damu nods his head, impressed with Duke's straight to the point attitude.

"As I said, Terricka seems to think you'd be willing to support the cause, given your recent interactions with the LAPD. She seems to think with your police background, you might be able to help us with this war," Damu says.

"A war? Is that what you're calling it?" Duke asks.

"What would you call it?" Damu inquires.

"I mean, when you're sayin' war, you're talking like you're soldiers," Duke points out. "This isn't the middle east, or whatever. This is LA. You can't possibly think you can win against a well-organized police force with that type of mentality. All you're doing is escalating the violence, and I promise you their funding is a lot more than what you're bringing to the table. This isn't a war that you can win. Too organized, too equipped, and too well funded."

"I'm working on getting the police defunded," Terricka chimes in. "As far as the organization is concerned, you'll be surprised with death among the black community can do for motivation. We didn't start this. It's been going on for far too long. It's time we make a stand. One unarmed black life killed by the police is one too many. Seriously, Duke, I know you were once a part of their little gang. How many more of our people have to die before you take it seriously? You see how they treated you. You were only spared because you used to be one of them. We don't have that luxury. We don't want to go this route, but what other options have they left us?"

A silent Duke sighs as though he's considering Terricka's words. He didn't want to look too eager to join the outfit as it may blow his cover, but he also isn't so dense to realize that Terricka has a point.

"Killing cops, though? I just think that is going to bring them down harder on us?" Duke retorts. "It causes escalation which could end up being the National Guard or some off the wall shit like that. There's gotta be a better way. No, I don't have the answers, but trading blood for blood... I just can't see us winning that way."

"So does the fact you're saying *us* means that you're interested in joining the cause?" Damu asks.

"I... I don't know," Duke replies. "I don't know if I can be down with folks killin' others."

"Wouldn't be the first time, now would it?" Damu responds with a smile, referring to Duke's past as a cop. "It's okay. I need to sleep on it too. Terricka will be in touch."

"Hey, wait, I-"

Damu quickly walks off leaving Duke speechless as the masked male in the room puts the mask back over his head to lead him back out to the van. Terricka follows her father into the other room as he un-pauses a video he was viewing prior to his meeting with Duke. It's a newscast covering the protests after the Jamie shooting. One of the images shows Terricka leading the charge of the protests down the city streets, which causes Damu to smile.

"You did well out there today," he says as Terricka joins him by the TV.

"So, what do you think?" She asks her father.

"I think the deputy will be ringing your line shortly, hoping to come to an agreement to contain the protests," Damu answers. "He knows who has the power. Don't let up until this officer is trialed and convicted."

"I mean, what do you think about Duke?" Terricka says.

"Oh. *That* what do you mean," Damu replies, smirking as he pauses the TV. "Well, it's obvious you've taken a liking to him."

Damu hinting that Terricka seems to like Duke a little more than she's letting on offends her.

"It's all about the cause, dad! Come on, you know me better than that," Terricka fires back, causing her father to chuckle.

"That I do," he responds. "I don't think he has what it takes to do what's necessary. He talks about a better way but has no idea how to achieve it. He doesn't have the vision. He couldn't get past the cop killings as if that's all we do."

"That's because that's all he knows," Terricka points out. "Hell, that's all anyone knows about you. The problem is you're so quick to announce yourself killing cops that you don't take the time to announce yourself with all the good you've done. You need to show him, and everyone else all the good you do too."

Damu ponders his daughter's words when she gives him a look he can never turn down. Terricka has always been a daddy's girl, especially after her mother passed. There is a face that she's been doing since she was an infant that Damu could never turn down. It was a gaze of innocence that a father couldn't help but love. After a few moments, he eventually nods his head agreeing with his daughter, much to her delight.

"Alright. I'll show him the goods. Still, I don't want him knowing too much. Not right now anyway. He's your responsibility to keep an eye on," Damu warns. "I want to know how these procedures go on the inside once an officer is accused of something like what went on yesterday. The best way to defeat an enemy is to learn about them. I know it's still early, but I want to find out exactly what happens. Let's see if we can trip up Jamie's shooter peacefully, as your friend would say. If not, we have another target."

Terricka nods her head before sharing a quick hug with her father. She quickly makes her way out of the room as Damu goes back to watching the protest coverage on TV with a smile on his face. A plan is forming in his head, and he thinks it may be time to start getting things together for its execution.

Forty minutes later, Duke is dropped off at the place he was picked up earlier. Terricka takes the mask off from his head as he struggles to get his eyes to adjust.

"Hey, keep close, okay?" She says to her newfound friend.

"I will. Looks like you're in some deep shit over there," Duke replies while rubbing his eyes. "You sure you cool in a life like that?"

Terricka chuckles as she hands Duke back his cell phone, which she had taken from him earlier.

"Are you sure you're cool living in the world we live in?" Terricka fires back. "I'll get with you in a few days. Try not to get into trouble."

Duke chuckles as Terricka winks at him and hops back into the van. He watches as the van pulls down the street while waiting for his phone to cut back on. As soon as the van is out of sight, he dials Reid's number, excited with what just happened.

"Yeah, it's me. I made contact," Duke says when Reid answers the line.

He starts walking down the street as Reid gives him a location to meet.

"Yeah, I know where that is... Alright, cool," Duke replies before hanging up the line.

He looks around to make sure he's not being followed before continuing towards his destination.

Later that night, at her Mid-City Home in the Los Angeles suburbs, Shannon sits on her couch nervously awaiting the arrival of her husband. After the Jamie shooting news broke, her life changed as media members were just outside her property looking for any quote from blonde-haired, blue-eyed, petite wife of Officer Murphy. After about an hour of struggling, she finally was able to put her kids to sleep, who had questions about what's going on with their father. She reassured them that it wasn't anything for them to be worried about, but truth be told, she is also worried. Hearing her husband's name being blasted on the news and her social media being filled with people labeling him as a racist and killer makes her sick to her stomach. She didn't believe the things they were saying about the man she loves. When he arrived home the prior night, she knew something had happened since he was home earlier than he normally was. He tried to explain what had happened as best he could, but she could tell that he wasn't himself. He left early in the morning before she had a chance to speak with him again. By noon, her once silent neighborhood was flooded with media members looking for comments about an incident she knows nothing about. As she waits for her husband, she hears an uproar of media noise coming from outside and gets up to peek outside her front window to see what the fuss is about. She's relieved to see Murphy exit his vehicle and quickly making his way to the front entrance. She makes her way over and opens the door for him, and quickly shuts it once he's inside.

"Dave, thank god," she says, sharing a hug. "I didn't know if you were coming back or not."

"Shit, I didn't know if I would be coming back either," he replies as Shannon releases her embrace of the love of her life.

She looks into his eyes and can tell that he's gone through a lot this day.

"I take it things didn't go well," she states based on Murphy's look.

"It was like a trial in there. IA was all over my ass all day," Murphy answers before making his way over to the living room couch.

He notices the TV is on discussing the incident, and quickly reaches for the remote, turning the TV off. Shannon takes a seat next to her frustrated husband, seeking answers.

"So what's gonna happen now?" She inquires. "I've been

watching the news all day, and they are talking about criminal charges. Is this true?"

"Look, don't believe everything you see on TV," an irritated Murphy quips. "All they are looking for is the next cause to rally behind. They don't care about the truth or anything involved in what actually happened. It's just a modern day witch hunt."

"So the department is going to back you, right?" A hopeful Shannon asks.

"I don't know, to be honest," Murphy replies. "With all the press with police-involved shootings recently, it's a little hard to tell. Right now, I'm officially on administrative leave until IA has a chance to run their investigation. It's with pay, but Shan, I'll be honest with you, I don't know where we go from here."

Shannon can see the exhaustion in her husband's eyes. He's normally a confident man, which is what made her fall in love with him in the first place. The look she sees now frightens her.

"I pulled the kids from school today," she says, trying to ease her husband's mind. "I didn't want to have them bothered with all of this just in case news started to get out. I'm probably going to call out of work tomorrow and keep them home for the week until this all blows over."

"I don't want you to do that," Murphy says, looking into his wife's eyes. "This isn't going to go away anytime soon, and we need to keep things going as ordinary as possible. You can't keep calling out, and the kids can't keep missing school."

Shannon nods her head, slightly disappointed in Murphy's decision. He notices her mood and changes his stance slightly.

"I wouldn't mind you and the kids staying home tomorrow though," he says, smirking. "It's been so long since I've actually been home at a decent hour. I think I'm overdue some family time."

A smile slowly grows on Shannon's face as she leans in and kisses her husband.

"I know this might not be the time or place, but there's something else we're overdue for," Shannon replies, referring to sex. "If you're not in the mood, I-"

"No. You're right; we are overdue," Murphy replies. "Anything to get my mind of that kid. I can't believe this shit is happening to me, Shan. I really can't. I'm starting to doubt myself now. Did I shoot too quickly? Did I do everything I could to avoid it? I don't know if-"

"Shhh," Shannon interrupts by placing her finger on her husband's lips before quickly mounting him. "You did what you needed to do to come home to me and the kids. That's all that matters."

Murphy sighs, still concerned if he did the right thing, but slowly nods his head, reassuring his wife. She leans in to kiss him once more as the two start to get hot and heavy with each other. She carefully unbuttons his uniform shirt, opening it up to his muscle shirt he wears underneath it. After Shannon runs her hands down his chest, she unbuttons his pants, and takes a firm grasp of his manhood, pulling it through his underwear. Murphy, who is in a state of bliss, quickly removes his wife's panties from under her sundress before inserting himself inside his wife, causing her to gasp. The two begin having sex on the couch with the problems of tomorrow still in the back of their minds but put to the side for a moment of passion.

At a bar deep in the heart of South Central, Duke sits on a barstool enjoying beer watching sports highlights on a TV from a distance. It's a typical bar area, equipped with pool tables and a booth area where couples can be alone. The bar has a decent amount of people in it, but nowhere nears its full capacity. It is a perfect meeting place for those who want to go unnoticed.

"You look a little lonely," a female says to Duke, breaking his attention from the TV. "You mind if I keep you company."

Duke turns and notices the Hispanic female with booty shorts and heels on, and a top that seems painted on, grabbing all the nearby male's attention. She smiles with her dark brown hair flowing towards her back and a hint of lip gloss upon her lips.

"Sure," Duke replies, going into flirt mode as the female takes a seat next to him. "Can I get you a drink?"

"Sure," she says as she waves the bartender over. "Vodka double, straight. And none of that cheap shit. I want the top shelf brand."

The bartender nods his head and walks off to fill her order as the female turns her attention back towards Duke.

"Damn, I see you don't play," he says, turning towards her. "Vodka double. Must have had a rough night."

"Trust me, you wouldn't believe me if I told you," the smirking female responds as her drink arrives. "So what's your story? Why you sitting here all alone like you lost your best friend?"

"Damn, I look that bad?" Questions Duke with a chuckle. "Just tryin' to piece some shit together. What's up with you and this rough night though? What could have happened to you so bad that you ended up in a place like this?"

"I'm here meeting someone," the female says before downing her first vodka quickly, grimacing at the strength of the drink. "Damn, he really did hit me up with the top shelf shit."

"Who you meeting? One of your girlfriends?" Duke inquires.

"A guy actually," she answers back, letting Duke down.

"A guy? Then I gotta ask why are you over here with me?" he questions as the female plays it safe with her second drink, sipping it slightly. "I mean, what if your dude walk in here and see you talkin' to me? I ain't tryin' to start no shit with another man's girl."

"Relax. I'm sure he doesn't mind me talkin' to you," the females quips. "I mean I'm with a cop right now, so I think I'm about as safe as I can be. Isn't that right?"

A confused Duke looks around before questioning the female.

"Who the fuck are you?" an intimidating Duke replies. "What's your game, lady?"

"I have no game. The man who I am meeting here is sitting right in front of me," the female replies. "Detective Valentina Martinez, at your service."

Duke calms down slightly, confused thinking that his contact Martinez is supposed to be a guy.

"Wait a minute, you're part of Reid's squad?" He questions, scratching his head. "Reid never mentioned you were a... well, he didn't give me a head's up, and-"

"Yes, Officer Mitchell, I am a woman," Martinez points out. "Look, let's take this party to a place a little more private."

A still stunned Duke nods his head as he drops some cash on the bar and walks off towards an unoccupied booth. He's distracted by her beauty as she stumbles a bit heading into the booth. The two officers take a seat across from each other as Martinez gets down to business.

"So, you made contact I heard. What did you find out?" She asks.

"How are you in Reid's outfit?" Duke responds, ignoring Martinez's question. "I mean, don't get me wrong, this isn't a female cop question. It's a *you and Reid's crew* question."

Martinez sighs, knowing she's not going to get anywhere with Duke without an explanation.

"I'm part of Reid's crew the same way you are part of his crew. Only difference is I did the right thing when it came down to it," she quips, confusing Duke.

"Like me?" he replies, almost with a chuckle. "I seriously doubt you're here like me."

"You'd be surprised," Martinez fires back with a smirk. "I was part of a tactical unit just like you, where I noticed dirty cops doing dirty things. Unlike you, I reported it to my CO only to find out he was part of the issue too. He tried to sweet talk me and shit, talking all that loyalty foolishness, but in the end, I did what needed to be done. I was the good cop, so to speak, and other commanders commended me for what I did, saying it took courage to come forward."

Duke nods his head, getting more comfortable as Martinez continues.

"You'd think that would be my ticket to career accolades and whatnot, but it was the exact opposite," Martinez says with her mood changing. "Nobody wants to work with a snitch cop.

No unit would take me in, and the ones that did take me were forced to. You ever been forced into a situation that you weren't welcomed to? It's sickening, and to top it all off, nobody wants to partner up with you. I was on my own in every post."

"That's messed up. Even doing right you can't win," Duke points out, relating to the officer's struggle.

"Yeah. IA offered me a post, but I didn't become a cop to investigate cops. I wanted to be in the streets. I want to career progress, you know. Anyway, Reid and his band of outlaws were just cleared of their latest IA investigation, and part of the deal was that someone on the outside be assigned to his crew to be the voice of reasoning within the bunch. I heard of his hard nose tactics and noticed there was a lack of color in his detail," Martinez explains. "IA reached out to me to see if I'd be interested in the post. I didn't wanna do it, but they said a year or two here I'd make rank, and open a lot more doors for myself. So I said fuck it, and went with it."

Duke nods his head, impressed with his fellow officer's story.

"So, how long have you been in?" He asks.

"Going on seven months," Martinez answers. "Reid is particular though. He has me out on the streets constantly. I'm either in a hot ass van all day, or in this get-up trying to find one person or the next. It's apparent he doesn't trust me, and I don't really care honestly. Just trying to do my time and make rank. I don't even know where he and his headhunters' base of operation is. He keeps me out of the loop of everything, just giving me jobs that he doesn't wanna waste time on. We came to an agreement. I won't complain to the brass, and he will give me nothing but positive performance reviews to help with my career path."

"So, I guess you are like me. More than what you want to admit," a cryptic Duke points out. "I mean, I haven't been around the man but a handful of times, and even I can tell the son of a bitch is dirty. The worst kind of dirty. You being quiet just to make rank is no worse than me not rattin' on my old detail for some of the shit they were doing."

"You forget one thing though, I don't know what they are

doing since I'm out on the streets all day, every day," Martinez quips. "Hard to tell who is doing what when you're not around."

"You don't know what they're doing, or you don't care? Seems to me it's the latter," Duke fires back with a smile.

Martinez giggles, shaking her head in disbelief that a man she's just meeting is talking down to her.

"This coming from a guy who was basically forced into this assignment to avoid spending the rest of his life running a corner store," she blasts back, catching Duke off guard. "I'm just sayin', you are the last person who should be talking about who did what in the department after what you let go."

Duke chuckles to himself, nodding his head in agreement.

"Fair enough," he responds. "I didn't mean to offend you. My bad. It's just I see Reid, Slater, and the other officers like them, and with everything going on with the protests and whatnot… I don't know, I just thought with your background you would have found a way to get in their shit, you know."

"You're right about that. Reid and his crew are definitely a problem," agrees Martinez. "But right now, he has the backing of the commissioner, and there's not much anyone can do about it without ending their career. Not yet anyway."

The tense mood fades as both Duke and Martinez relax for a moment.

"Anyway, now that we've discussed my life and history, why don't you tell me about your contact with our target," Martinez says, getting back down to business.

"It wasn't long. He's about six-two, six-three, around one-eighty if that. Age, upper fifties, lower sixties. Has that old pimped out permed hair down to his shoulders with gray hair mixed in with the black. Appearance wise, this guy looks as harmless as they come," Duke describes. "When he talks though, you can tell there's force behind his words. Apparently, with my run ins with Reid and the other incident, he's looking to recruit me to their cause."

"Look at you. Moving up in the world," Martinez responds, smirking. "Where did you meet up with him?"

"Don't know. They bum rushed me while I was walking to the bus stop," Duke explains. "Loaded me in a van, took my cell phone, patted me down, and put a mask on so I couldn't see anything. We drove about forty-five minutes before they led me into a room. By the time they removed my mask, there I was with the man himself."

Martinez looks disappointed with the information she's getting as Duke continues with his story.

"I do know I was in the projects somewhere," he points out, piquing Martinez's interest.

"The projects?"

"Yeah. Grew up in this area and spend a lot of time in the jects. I don't know which one, but they're pretty much all the same. My guess is they're using vacants to conduct their business. Doesn't mean that's where he's laying his head, but we were definitely in the jects somewhere."

"So, we pinpoint where they picked you up, check forty-five minutes in all directions, see what projects fall into that limited area, and start our search there," pitches Martinez. "At least that gives us something to work with."

"Yeah, but the only problem is when they dropped me back off, it only took around thirty minutes," Duke points out. "I think the drive was them just going round and round trying to throw me off the path. Hell, for all I know, I could have been right across the street from where they picked me up. It was a little sloppy, if we're being honest, or they wanted me to know that the drive was bullshit. Either way, in that area, there are a lot of projects to sweep, and could be a lot of wasted man hours. I say we hold off for now until I'm sure."

Martinez nods her head, agreeing with Duke's plan.

"Okay, those that abducted you, what can you tell me about them?" Martinez asks.

Duke acts as though he's trying to remember his captors, hoping to keep Terricka's name out of the investigation for now.

"Not much. They all wore masks as well," Duke answers. "I didn't see their faces."

"Interesting," Martinez replies. "So masked men just all of a sudden approach you and loaded you into a van? In broad daylight?"

"Yes. Well, not exactly. There was a woman there too. I can tell by her voice, but she was masked as well," Duke tries to explain. "I mean, they did have guns and shit."

Martinez chuckles to herself, trying to figure out the undercover cop's story.

"Well, they certainly are a bold bunch, aren't they?" She says slyly. "I'm just saying, a cop, former cop, or whatever you're calling yourself these days lets a bunch of masked assailants get the drop on you? It's just odd."

"My job was to make contact, and I did just that," Duke fires back, becoming irritated with his contact. "I figured that's what it was, so I went along with it."

"If you say so," Martinez says, smirking. "So what's next? You're on the cop kill team, or what?"

"They said they'd make contact with me in a few days, so I guess we'll see then," Duke replies.

"Alright then. Looks like we have our first big lead on this thing. Awesome," Martinez says when she notices the look of frustration filling Duke's face. "Hey, don't take things so personal. I was just messin' with you. You did good work here so far. With you in their organization, we'll finally be able to connect the dots and hopefully avoid more of our own taking one in the line of duty. If they are as cautious as you say they are, bugging you is probably out of the question. I'll report back to Reid and the others, and follow up with you hopefully before your next contact."

Martinez rises from her seat, straightening herself out as Duke looks on with admiration once more.

"Be honest, you enjoy the attention that outfit gets you," he says, smirking.

"I do, actually," Martinez replies. "It lets me know which men are dogs, which I would say is about ninety-nine percent of y'all. This image isn't real, but go ahead and get your look in now.

Hope it keeps you warm on those lonely nights. See ya, Mitchell."

Duke chuckles, admiring his contact as she makes her way towards the exit. He sighs, shaking his head, paying particular attention to her legs before she exits the bar.

"Nice calves," he says to himself before leaning back.

Keeping Terricka out of the conversations is starting to weigh on him, as having her in custody could lead to the whereabouts of Damu and his top lieutenants. He didn't trust Reid, however, and didn't want her in their clutches for interrogation. He wants to hear her side of the story before turning her in and realizes he needs to be patient for the moment.

CHAPTER 6

Hidden Realities

In a mid-city local grocery store, the customers are scarce which is the perfect time for Murphy and his wife to go shopping, avoiding the paparazzi that tend to follow them around the last few days. Interview requests and constant phone calls have made the last few days unbearable in the Murphy household. With everything going on, this is the first real time Murphy and Shannon have had alone. Murphy is pushing the shopping cart down the aisle with Shannon stopping every so often selecting items. They are in the cereal aisle when Shannon stops him to check out the selection.

"Anything in particular you want?" She asks.

"You know I'm not too big on cereal," Murphy replies. "Just get the normal raisin bran that you normally get."

"I know you're not big on cereal, Dave, and normally given the circumstances I wouldn't ask, but we don't know how long this part of our life is going to continue like it is," Shannon explains. "I don't really like leaving the kids alone with all those reporters outside of the house. I want to take the bare minimum trips to the store, so we need to load up on everything we can right now."

"I know, but cereal? Really, Shan?" Murphy questions, smirking. "I mean, we can be in the house for the next twenty years, and I wouldn't eat that stuff."

"Well, you better start because I'm not cooking every morning," Shannon warns, smiling back at her husband. "You're going to need something quick in the morning to help out with the kids. Especially with Junior. He's in the pissy teenage mood phase, and getting him to focus on anything other than video games is a challenge. Eventually, I have to head back to work, and it's going to be your responsibility to make sure he's doing his work. Speaking of which, have you sat down with him and talked about what's going on?"

Murphy sighs as he starts making his way down the aisle once again, much to Shannon's surprise.

"You haven't spoken to him about it yet?" She asks, scurrying next to him.

"With social media today, I'm sure he knows," Murphy replies. "Kids today have more access to information than we did nowadays. If he had questions, I'm sure he would have asked by now."

"Dave, you know as good as do that the media doesn't tell the whole story, just the narrative they are trying to push for ratings," Shannon points out. "Your son needs to hear from you, not the TV, social media, or whatever. He may have questions that he's scared to ask you."

Murphy sighs, ashamed that he has to discuss the shooting with his thirteen-year-old. He has been purposely avoiding this discussion for the past few days. Having to explain to his son why he shot and killed a kid three years his senior is difficult to process for him, especially since he's been struggling himself trying to come to terms with it. As the couple makes it to the end of the aisle, Shannon sighs, looking back towards the front.

"Shoot, I forgot the syrup," she says, tapping herself on the head. "I'll be right back."

Murphy nods his head watching as his wife makes her way back towards the front of the store. He's checking a couple of items in his basket when he's suddenly distracted by someone making their way through the area.

"Murderer!" The black female yells, surprising Murphy. "I know who you are! You should be ashamed of what you did to that young boy! Shootin' an unarmed black boy down in the street!"

"Ma'am, look, I know you're upset, but that's not what happened," Murphy responds, trying to explain.

"Yeah, it's never what happened according to y'all!" The female fires back. "Just killin' niggas, so it's cool, isn't it?! What if that woulda' been your kid? How would you feel then? Bet you wouldn't want the killer wanderin' through the store doin' grocery shopping and shit like it's all good would you?"

The black female's voice is carrying causing others to take notice of Murphy.

"We're sick of all you cops killin' our kids! I hope they put your ass under the jail!" The black female says, gaining support from others who have gathered in the area as well. "Don't worry though, the streets will be coming for you, best believe that! Karma is gonna eat your ass alive!"

Shannon makes it back by her husband's side and notices the crowd getting rowdy as they begin chanting 'No justice, no peace' repeatedly.

"Dave, let's go," Shannon says, trying to pull her husband away from the crowd.

Murphy struggles as he wants to explain to the crowd what really happened that night, but the crowd becomes increasingly agitated. For the safety of his wife, he had no choice but to back away, abandoning their shopping cart and quickly heading out of the store. The crowd continues to follow him out to his car, chanting all the way. Murphy and his wife are able to jump into the car and pull off before the crowd has a chance to block their exit. Tears being to flow down Shannon's face as a frustrated Murphy slams his fist on the dashboard. He looks at his wife and notices the fear in her eyes before taking a deep breath.

"I'm sorry, Shan," he says, trying to calm his wife's nerves.

"It's not your fault," she responds, wiping the tears from her face. "I can't believe that just happened."

"Believe me, it's not gonna happen again," Murphy says, still upset over the altercation. "From now on, we shop online. Put it in your mother's name just so there's no tampering issue. I could have choked that loudmouth bitch, I swear!"

"Dave, calm down. People are just afraid right now, I'm sure once-"

"They're afraid?! I'm the one who is getting dragged through the dirt here! What the fuck do they have to be afraid of?!" Murphy exclaims, overloaded with emotions. "I don't deserve this! All I did was my job! And... and..."

He stops in midsentence, filling with hurt as he notices his wife's glare towards him. These emotions have been building in him for the last few days, and it's the first time he's had to face it. Shannon rubs on her husband's shoulder trying to help relax him. The show of affection works as the anger in his eyes starts to fade.

"I'm... I'm sorry, Shan. I didn't mean to blow up like that," Murphy says to his wife.

"I'm here for you, Dave. Always and forever will be," Shannon responds. "We're going to get through this, I promise you."

Murphy takes a deep breath before nodding his head with agreement. He continues to make his way down the street, heading for home.

A few hours later, outside of Evelyn's corner store, Duke walks out waving by to his grandmother before noticing Terricka at the side of the curb waiting for him. He looks around the area before cautiously approaching her.

"Hey, what's up?" He asks.

"It's been three days, and I'm here checking in on you," she replies with a smirk.

"Well, it's about time. I left you like five messages," Duke quips.

"I've been busy with the Jamie protests," Terricka points out. "Besides, I told you we'd check back with you in a few days. So I'm here today to take you somewhere and show you something. That is if you're still interested."

"In the back of a van, blindfolded again?" Duke asks, looking around the area, causing Terricka to giggle.

"Not yet, hotshot. For this, we're gonna catch the bus. Come on," Terricka says, waving Duke over.

Duke hesitates for a moment, but eventually follows Terricka to a nearby bus stop bench, which the two take a seat next to each other. After a few moments of silence, Duke looks towards Terricka wanting answers to something that is bugging him.

"Hey, I know you're down for the cause and all, but do you really agree with what's going on with your organization?" He inquires, looking around to make sure his words aren't leaking to bystanders. "Killing cops, Terricka? Seriously?"

"The problem is that you think that's all we're about. I'm here to show you that we're about more than that," Terricka replies. "Besides, we didn't start this. They did. They started it when they thought they could get away killing unarmed black folks for no apparent reason, then hiding behind the badge when it came time for consequences. Seriously, Duke, I know you're down with the back the blue bullshit, but what did you expect to happen? You keep pushing folks to the corner, and eventually, those folks are gonna fight back."

"Doesn't make it right," Duke points out. "Blood for blood will backfire. These people are trained for this shit."

"*We shall overcome* didn't work in the sixties," Terricka fires back. "They won't give, so we'll take by any means necessary."

Before Duke can reply, the bus pulls up to disrupt their conversation. He takes a deep breath as he and Terricka both get on the bus to an unknown destination in his eyes.

About thirty minutes and a couple of transfers later, Terricka and Duke exit the bus in what looks like an almost abandoned area. It was a city slum falling apart with mostly condemned buildings flooding Duke's view. There isn't much life as it seems like the neighborhood is that land that time forgot with trash everywhere and stray animals abound. Duke is confused as Terricka leads him towards one of the main buildings in the area.

"Girl, what the fuck is this?" Duke says while continuing to take the area in.

"What's the matter? You scared?" Terricka quips with a smile.

"No, it's just... what could you possibly show me up in this dump?" Duke responds, hiding the fact that he is nervous.

"Not all people can afford the best, Duke. You think The Hand is all about killin' cops and shit. I want to show you the good we're doing to see if I can change your mind," Terricka responds just as the two make it into the building's entrance.

Terricka knocks on the door several times, almost in a coded pattern. The door slowly opens as a burly figure answers the door.

"Clean, what's up, baby doll," Terricka says, greeting the doorman with a hug and a kiss before turning towards Duke. "Duke, this is Mr. Clean. He works at this establishment making sure things are safe for the public."

Duke reaches out his hand to shake Mr. Clean's hand but is rejected by the doorman.

"Don't sweat it. He's like that until you get to know him," Terricka says to Duke, referring to Mr. Clean's attitude. "Come on, let me show you around."

Duke nods his head, keeping an eye on Mr. Clean before making his way into the building behind Terricka. As they make their way through the hallways of the building, Duke is stunned to see lower-income residents in the building receiving health care in the makeshift hospital. One of the child patients runs over and hugs Terricka.

"Hey, Sarah. How are you feeling today?" A smiling Terricka asks.

"Much better," Sarah responds with a giggle.

Terricka waves at Sarah's mother as the little girl runs back over to join her parent. Duke is confused as hell as he notices a couple of rooms down, full medical beds, and heart machines monitoring a patient.

"Quite remarkable, isn't it?" Damu says, surprising Duke from behind.

"How is this possible?" Duke asks as he continues to take the hospital in.

"Well, it's not technically sanctioned," Damu responds with a smile. "Our people are tired, Duke. They're tired of medical bills they can't afford, with treatments that are just as bad as the illness. What we've created here is a sanctuary for lower-income residents to be treated properly, thanks to the many volunteers from the neighborhood. We heal folks the right way. None of that 'keep you on the medication for profits BS the real world does. It's not a business here; it's humanity."

Duke watches as a doctor walks over and checks on a patient that's laying in the bed. Damu can tell his guest is full of questions.

"She's a real doctor, in case you were wondering," Damu says, looking at the doctor as well. "Graduated with an accredited degree, and is licensed to provide healthcare in the state of California."

"But how?" Duke asks. "How are you able to afford this?"

Damu chuckles as he and Duke slowly make their way down the hall, followed closely by Terricka and one of Damu's bodyguards.

"Not all people are heartless as the world would lead you to believe," Damu points out as they look at treatments in different areas of the building. "The doctors all have day jobs, mostly, but spend extra time giving back to the community. As far as funding, we have a few big-time athletes, entertainers, and business execs who cut us a chunk of change every now and then, along with several of the local gangs."

"Gangs? You mean this place is supported by drug money?" Inquires Duke. "You're running a hospital off drug money. You don't see any issues with that?"

Damu sighs as he stops and turns to his guest.

"If more people like yourself would take in interest in their own people, we wouldn't have to use the criminal element for funding," he explains. "Officer, what you have to understand is we do what we need to ensure the betterment of our race. Those sanctioned hospitals charge eight dollars an aspirin and thousands of dollars of medical bills that burden our people daily. Most of the people who come here can't afford that type of treatment, and they shouldn't have to. I know, it's not perfect, but tell me, Officer, what have you done to uplift and support your people?"

Duke is silent as he continues to observe the work going on around him. He's still stunned to see such work taking place without anyone knowing, and he did agree with various points Damu is making. Still, he has doubts about what he's witnessing.

"I mean, what about staph infections?" Duke quips. "What about the constant equipment updates? How safe is this really?"

"It's as safe as going to the old Killer King Hospital back in the day before it closed down." Terricka chimes in. "Some folks say we're better than the new one too, but it all depends on who you ask."

"In any case, we're providing the public with options," Damu says, building off his daughter's point. "We take every precaution as a normal hospital would. This is just one of the many things the Hand of God does in our neighborhoods. We help find funding for afterschool programs, work with future political parties to provide funding for their campaigns, and fundraise to feed struggling families. We also sit down with the local gangs and negotiate peace terms and boundaries to drive down the violence."

"Drive down the violence? Hate to spoil it, Brotha Damu, but the violence is on an uptick as of late," Duke replies.

Damu chuckles and nods his head.

"Well, we can't control everything, now can we?" He fires back. "There will always be some form of criminal element in the world no matter what we do. Answer me this, out of all the things that I told you that we do, why are you focusing on the one negative thing in the bunch?"

Once again, Duke is speechless, having no answer for the

Hand of God leader.

"I think that we're more alike than you care to admit, Duke," Damu says, smirking. "I think deep down, you agree with me, and if it wasn't for that one thing you have a problem with, you would join our cause with no hesitation."

"The cop killings," Duke brings up, causing Damu to nod with agreement.

"Yes. The cop killings. I'm going to be honest with you, it's something I'm not proud of. We've tried every avenue before taking the battle to them. We've tried to get the commissioner to sanction an independent council for investigations, and were turned down. We suggested more police and neighborhood interactions and were turned down. We tried peaceful protests and got nowhere. They weren't willing to meet us even half-way. Meanwhile, our people are getting shot down day after day after day with no consequences. They continued to ignore us until one of their own was taken out. Now, our voices are being heard."

"But at what cost?" Duke asks. "You think this is gonna bring about change? You're just hardening their stance and putting more of our people in the line of fire."

"Then help me, Duke. Help me find a better way. Help me understand. Right now, this is the only way I know. It's why I'm offering to bring you in. Now that you see we're not the vicious animals they believe us to be, maybe you'd be willing to help us close the gap to enact real change?"

Damu extends his hand, waiting for Duke to seal his membership request with a handshake. Duke hesitates momentarily, taking a look at Terricka seeking guidance. She smiles at him and nods her head, urging him to take her father up on his offer. After a few more moments, Duke shakes the Hand of God's leader, much to Damu's delight.

"You've made a wise decision," Dame replies.

"I guess we'll see about that, won't we?" Duke quips, causing Damu to chuckle.

"Well, in any case, I need to get into the mind of an accused officer, and as it happens, I have one right in front of me," Damu says, smirking as he starts to make his way down the hallway once again. "I'm sure you've heard about the Jamie Powell shooting that happened recently."

Duke nods his head as he, Damu, and the others all enter an unoccupied room. Damu offers Duke a seat as the two sit across from each other. Terricka and Damu's bodyguard take their positions behind their leader, preferring to stand during the questioning.

"This detective, this David Murphy, is going through an internal investigation right now. Tell me about the process and how it works. Well, not necessarily from a process standpoint, but the mentality of someone accused. What's going on in Officer Murphy's mind?" Damu questions.

Duke takes a deep breath as he thinks about his time under the microscope back in Cincinnati.

"Well, if he has a family for starters, that's going to be his main concern," Duke explains. "I can't vouch for that because I don't have a wife or kids, but if I did, that's where my thought process would be. He's probably already gone through the questioning at this point, and depending on what they find, I'm sure he's on some sort of paid leave."

Damu nods his head as Duke continues.

"Now, the next part is tricky. If he's guilty, he may feel the guilt creepin' up on him, or if he's one of those types who gets off on doin' shit like that, he won't feel anything. He'd just be looking to get back on the street and fight the good fight, so to speak. If he's not guilty, he's probably going over the incident in his head daily, wondering what he could have done to avoid it," Duke points out. "Right now, he's getting adjusted with being a household name. He'll figure out the new normal quickly as he tries to continue with his day to day. He's a face now, and people will recognize him wherever he goes. After an altercation or two, he'll lock himself in his home. Probably keep his wife and kids home as well, avoiding the public unless it's absolutely necessary."

"Is that what happened to you?" A curious Terricka asks.

"Well, news travels fast in Cincinnati," Duke answers, smirking. "Even after everything was done, folks would still recognize me in the streets. It's the only reason I came back home."

Damu nods his head, taking everything in when Duke decides to question his new leader.

"You're thinking about going after Murphy, aren't you?" He asks.

"We're not what you think we are, Duke," Damu responds. "We are a fair organization. We'll let the legal process work its way through the investigation. Depending on what we find…,"

Damu shrugs, signaling they will do what they need to do to find their own justice. Before Duke can reply, Jules walks in with a few members of God's Hand.

"Damu, glad I caught you before you headed back to Imperial," he says, approaching his leader. "You got a minute?"

"Sure," a smiling Damu says before turning Jules's attention towards Duke. "Jules, meet our newest member, Duke."

"Hey, what's up," Duke says, trying to greet Damu's second in command.

Jules ignores Duke, turning his attention back towards Damu.

"Brother, please, I gotta get with you," Jules says once again.

Damu nods his head, signaling Duke to give them space. Duke rises from his chair and makes his way out of the room. The other members also walk out of the room, leaving Terricka, Jules, and Damu as the only ones left.

"You did good," Damu replies. "Let's see where this goes."

"The thing is I really did need to holla at you," admits Jules. "I heard that Murphy was seen in a grocery store earlier. Seems like a few folks scared him off, but we need to be on his ass in case he shows his face again. We may not get another shot."

"Patience, Jules. We don't even have the bodycam footage or anything to go by yet," Damu preaches. "We need to let the legal system run its course."

"Damu, come on! You know this pig is guilty as fuck," Jules

fires back. "Why do we need to wait for some shit that we already know?"

"Because we're not a hit squad, Jules. You know that," Damu replies. "It's not the right time right now. However, since you're so eager for blood, I am sanctioning the job on Officer Williams."

Jules's mood changes as he's been waiting to take out Officer Williams, who has been known to apply an illegal chokehold on his victims, killing a black male a few months prior.

"Williams, huh?" A smirking Jules responds. "You coming along?"

"No. My daughter thinks I need to focus more on the good, so I'm gonna sit this one out, blood," Damu responds, satisfying Terricka. "Get in and out, and watch your back."

Jules nods his head as he and Damu dap each other off.

"I got you," Jules responds before making his way out of the room, full of excitement.

Terricka is about to walk off when Damu pulls her back.

"A moment," he says, offering his daughter a seat across from him.

"What's up?" She asks.

"I want you to keep an eye on him," Damu replies.

"I know, you said, remember?" Terricka reminds her father. "I told you that Duke is on me. I got you."

"I wasn't talking about, Duke," Damu corrects, confusing his daughter. "I'm talking about Jules."

"Jules? Why?"

"Because I never trust anyone who is in a hurry to kill," Damu explains. "And lately, our friend seems real eager."

"He just believes in the cause, dad. He's ready to make these cops pay just like we all are," Terricka responds.

"To kill without evidence, that's their way, not ours," reminds Damu. "If we go off all half-cocked killing cops, we'll be at war, just like your friend Duke said. Once that happens, the message will be lost between bloodshed on both ends. That is not the cause. Not one I'm comfortable with."

Terricka shakes her head in disbelief before giggling.

"Well, I'm sure he'll get it out his system with Williams," she says. "I want you to get some rest. You've been doing too much lately. It causes you to be paranoid."

"My paranoia is what keeps us alive," Damu reminds his daughter as they both rise from their seats. "I may not be around to see us win this war, but I'm damn sure gonna leave my imprint on it. You're good at the camera life, and being front and center where it counts, but the cause, the real cause, happens on a playing field you're still green in."

"That's because daddy dearest won't let me make my bones," Terricka quips.

"And as long as I live, you never will," Damu replies before hugging his daughter. "I carry this so you don't have to. Something happens to me, I'm just some OG banger. You, you're more important to the cause than I could ever be."

"I've heard this all before, dad. I may not agree with it, but I know why you're against it. I'll do whatever you need me to do," Terricka says, causing her father to kiss her on her forehead.

The two continue to embrace one another, before making their way out of the room as well, planning their next move.

Later that night, Duke is sitting at the bar that he and Martinez met at before. He's surfing on his phone when he notices Martinez walking in. He notices she's not in a skimpy outfit as she was during their first meet, electing to wear blue jeans, a short sleeve top, and a ball cap covering her ponytailed hair. She notices him and quickly makes her way over, taking a seat next to him.

"Not what I expected," Duke says, joking with her.

"What?"

"Where is the girl with the booty shorts that I met a few days ago?" Duke says, chuckling to himself.

"Fuck you," a playful Martinez responds. "So, what did you call me out here for? I don't like to be on this side of town unless I have to."

"I told you that you didn't need to come," Duke reminds her.

"We could have had this conversation on the phone."

"You know the routine. Face to face with undercovers. I need to look you in your eyes to make sure you're still good," Martinez points out. "You know that, so quit wastin' time and tell me what you got."

"I got their next target. Murphy, the one who shot and killed that Jamie Powell kid. They're looking into him hard," Duke informs. "They are asking me questions, trying to get into his mind, or some shit."

"Well, we figured that's the next place they'd go," Martinez replies. "It's getting a lot of press lately."

"Put some security on him and his family. The kind they don't see," Duke says, "The last thing we need is for this shit to go sideways."

"On it."

"Something else. One of Damu's subordinates mentioned something about needing to get with him before he went back to Imperial. I assume he meant Imperial Courts," Duke deduces. "I'm not for certain, but that may be where he's laying his head."

"Right, cause you said you was in a project last time, didn't you?" Martinez replies, pulling out her cell phone. "That might be the spot. I can get on the horn with Reid and tell him to set up shop out there, and maybe we'll catch him-"

"No, wait!" Duke says, stopping Martinez from calling anyone on her phone. "It could be a trick."

Martinez looks at him strangely before dropping her phone on the table.

"A trick? Explain," she says.

Duke thinks for a minute, trying to remember the entire conversation from earlier. In his memory, he tries to focus his vision on the outside of the room and has Jules standing just outside of the room before entering in.

"Son of a bitch," he says, smiling. "He's testing me. Can't believe I didn't catch it before."

Martinez is confused as Duke begins to explain.

"His guy came in just to say Imperial, hoping I'd pick it up,"

Duke explains. "These guys have been so careful with me in the beginning, but today I'm seeing more folks without masks and everything. They dropped this on my lap to see if I'm working with the police, feds, or whoever. They're nowhere in Imperial, and if we go charging the area, they'll know it was me that leaked the location and become ghost on my ass."

Martinez bursts into laughter, confusing her undercover partner.

"You sound loco," she says. "These are just some better than normal organized street thugs. You're acting like they're Double-O-Bond or some shit."

"It's Double-O-Seven, James Bond," Duke corrects. "And trust me, you don't kill multiple cops and get away with it unless you're on point. We may be underestimating these cats."

"So I guess the whole Murphy target thing is a hoax too," theorizes Martinez. "I mean, if they're going out their way to throw you off on where they're staying, why wouldn't they throw you off the track on their next target as well?"

Duke sighs as he thinks for a few moments.

"That part of the conversation sounded real," he replies. "You don't get that deep into it unless you're trying to make a move. Let's... let's hang back on the Imperial thing right now. I need a little more time."

Martinez nods her head as she puts her phone back into her pocket.

"So, back in there, I see," she says, smiling. "Where'd y'all meet up this time since it wasn't the projects?"

Duke sighs as if he's in deep thought.

"It was an abandoned roadhouse in Inglewood," Duke answers, lying to cover up the hospital. "I can tell they've never been there before, so it's a non-factor."

"Okay?" A confused Martinez responds. "You said something about them not being in masks this time around?"

"No, well, yeah. Some of them were, I guess," Duke answers.

"You don't sound too sure," Martinez deduces as if she's suspicious. "You sure you're okay with this? I know it hasn't been that long, but if I gotta pull you, that's what I'll do if I need to."

"I'm fine, I'm fine. Just tryin' to figure this shit out, that's all," Duke responds with confidence. "Besides, you can't pull me now. We don't have enough to go on. I need more evidence. Pull me now, and more officers could die."

Martinez thinks for a moment as she tries to decide the next course of action. Duke is acting strangely to her, and she doesn't want him to get in too deep and lose himself. Still, this is the furthest they've gotten within the Hand of God, and losing Duke would mean losing their target.

"Alright, Duke, I'm gonna let you ride for now," she says, relieving the undercover officer. "I'll get on adding security on Murphy. In the meantime, keep your head down. I don't want to end up finding you dead on the street somewhere."

Duke smiles and nods his head before getting up and walking out of the bar. Martinez sighs hoping she's making the right decision with her counterpart. She pulls her phone out, and sends a text to Reid, requesting more security on Officer Murphy just as Duke had requested.

CHAPTER 7

Dissension Within the Ranks

On a cool Los Angeles night in an Inglewood neighborhood, Officer Williams is sitting in his police cruiser with his partner, Officer Jacobs, patrolling the area looking for anything suspicious like they normally do. Williams is happy to be back on the streets after a lengthy battle with Internal Affairs, and other investigative departments. Being behind a desk makes him feel weak, as he believes in order to stay on top of his game, he has to be out on the frontline. He's still fighting public backlash as his acquittal caused a surge of protests, and eventually riots. He didn't care as he is back on the streets doing what he loves.

"Quiet night," Jacobs says, looking around the area as they stop at an intersection.

"What do you expect? Half of them are out there rioting, tearing up their own neighborhood like a bunch of savages," Williams remarks.

"It ain't all that bad," Jacobs responds. "I mean, it's bullshit, but it's peaceful protests. What do I care if they wanna waste their time spreading their agenda?"

"Tell that to the shop owners on Manchester," Williams fires back. "Honest, hard-working people whose lives have been turned upside down on this bullshit. You would think they would at least take care of their own down there, but I guess a spade is just a spade, know what I'm saying?"

Jacob nods his head as the police cruiser pulls up at a stoplight. The two are silent when a sudden radio dispatch call comes through, seeking assistance several blocks away from Williams and Jacob's position.

"That's a 10-4 copy. We're en route," Williams says before turning on his emergency lights.

He's about to pull off when a black van blocks his position.

"What the fuck is this?" Williams questions, honking his horn.

Before he can back away, several Hand of God members jump out of the van, all wearing masks, surprising the officers. Jules, also wearing a mask, walks out as well, aiming his automatic weapon at the two officer's cruiser.

"Waste them," Jules orders, causing his members to open fire towards the cruiser.

Williams and Jacobs don't have time to react as they are quickly riddled with bullets that light up the night with each trigger pull. After several moments, Jules holds his hand up, signaling the shooters to stop with their attack. He calmly walks over towards the driver's side where Williams is sitting and confirms the officer's death, much to his satisfaction. He does notice that Jacobs is still breathing, although faintly. He slowly walks over to the passenger's side of the vehicle and smiles watching the cop choking on his own blood. He removes his mask to take the moment in, waving one of the other gunmen in to witness the event.

"Hey, yo, Fatboy, take a look at this shit," he says.

Fatboy, who earned the name due to his obese weight, makes his way over and laughs as Jacobs looks on to his attackers while bleeding out.

"Man, that nigga done for," Fatboy says with a smile. "I thought we was supposed to only kill that Williams nigga?"

"Fuck that," Jules replies, showing how different he and Damu are. "He was ridin' with this fool. Probably a nigga killer in training and shit."

Fatboy laughs as both he and Jules watch Officer Jacobs

breathe his last breath. Jules shakes his head as he turns to the rest of the crew.

"Alright, let's roll," he says, quickly making his way back to their van.

Fatboy and the others quickly join him as the van pulls off leaving the two dead officers in their cruiser with their lights still flashing.

Early the next morning, Duke is preparing to start his day as he walks out of his second-floor apartment. He's making his way down the apartment steps when he's suddenly bum rushed once he gets to the base by Slater. He drags Duke over to a nearby car as Reid lowers his window on the passenger's side with a smile on his face.

"Good morning, sunshine," he says to a confused Duke. "Get in."

Duke, still confused, follows orders as he gets into the back of the unmarked vehicle. Slater gets into the driver's side, quickly starts the vehicle, and pulls off.

About thirty minutes later, Duke is led to the Venice dock area, which is pretty quiet for the early morning, with the exception of a few bums that have set up around the area talking with each other. Under one of the main docks is both Billick and Irvin, who are waiting for their undercover's arrival, surprising Duke.

"Sir? What's going on?" He asks Billick, who looks him over quickly.

"Officer Mitchell, it was told to me, by Sargent Reid there that the Hand's next target would be officer Murphy, is that correct?" Inquires Billick.

"Yes, sir. That's what I heard," Duke responds.

Billick nods his head before taking a deep breath.

"Then why, Officer Mitchell, was I informed that late last night, two different officers, Williams and Jacobs, were found shot to death in Inglewood in their police cruiser?" A smug Billick responds, shocking Duke. "Why am I'm on my way to meet with the family of another one of my fucking cops?! Your job is to prevent this from happening!"

A stunned Duke tries to respond, but he's left speechless as a cooler headed Irvin steps up.

"Duke, did you hear anything about this?" He calmly asks.

"I… I didn't know," Duke replies nervously. "Everything they asked me led me to believe they were going after Murphy. I don't even know who Williams and Jacobs are."

Irvin nods his head, turning his attention towards Billick.

"Sir, I believe him," Irvin says.

"I don't give a fuck!" Billick snaps back, getting into Duke's face. "You do realize the nature of your job is to bring results, right? It's over a month since you signed on with us, and what do you have to show for it? Maybe you're a mole working us now!"

"Sir, all due respect, but I just made contact with the man about a week ago," Duke points out, not backing down from the commissioner trying to bully him. "It's not like they opened their books to me on the first day. Hell, maybe they already had a plan for this or maybe they don't trust me enough to let me in on their schemes. Sir, I would never let a fellow officer die in the line of duty. You know that!"

"Then what happened?! How the fuck did this happen?" Billick snaps back, scaring the others with his demeanor.

"Are you sure The Hand even did it?" Inquires Duke. "You got anything that I can check on from my end?"

"No," Irvin replies. "We're checking traffic cams in all directions, but that's hit or miss."

"So we're not even sure they are the ones who did this?" Duke asks before an irritated Billick turns his attention towards him.

"Don't you even think about it!" He fires back. "Don't you dare think about calling this a copycat case."

"Sir, I'm not saying that. What I'm saying is there's nothing to link them to anything, so we can't be sure it's them who did the killing. Hell, it might be, but until we have evidence, we don't know for sure. Doesn't Damu normally leave someone alive to tell the tale?" Duke asks. "That's like his trademark. He wants people to know it's him. And two officers at once? According to his file work, he's never done two officers together. Where both of the officers indicted together?

"Williams was the one that was targeted," Billick responds. "Jacobs hasn't had so much as a parking ticket on his record."

"Then there you go. It's not Damu's style to be that sloppy," Duke points out. "I'll see what I can find out, but it doesn't sound like it's them to me. Let me do my thing, and I promise I'll get to the bottom of this."

Billick thinks for a few moments before approaching Duke.

"See that you do," he responds, poking Duke in the chest before walking off.

Irvin sighs as he walks over and pats Duke on his shoulder.

"Sorry about that. He's just been under a lot of stress lately," Irvin explains. "He'll come around."

"Deputy, this could have all been done with a phone call," Duke fires back. "That's the type of shit that can get me killed on this OP."

Irvin nods his head with agreement.

"I'll talk to him," he replies before making his way off as well.

Reid and Slater both approach Duke, who shoots them a vicious scowl.

"Don't ever come at me like that again," Duke growls as both he and Slater stand toe to toe.

"What's the matter? We're supposed to make it look real. Relax, champ," an arrogant Slater responds, smirking.

"Why the fuck are you even here?" Duke responds to Slater before turning towards Reid. "I thought that the only one of your group who knows about this operation is Martinez?"

"I convinced the commissioner that I needed a little more help, and he ok'd my man Slate here," Reid replies, smirking. "I hope that's not a problem."

"If he puts his hands on me again, oh it's most certainly gonna be a problem," Duke responds, sizing Slater up.

Duke and Slater continue to face off with each other with

tension continuing to build. Reid sighs as he gets between both men, pushing Slater back.

"Ease up, gents. We're all on the same team here," Reid says with a smile. "Sorry about earlier, but like the man said, we wanted to make it look real just in case someone was watching. Come on, we'll drop you off a little closer to home."

"I'll walk," Duke begrudgingly says before walking off towards the main road.

Reid chuckles, shaking his head while watching Duke make his way off.

"He's got a fuckin' attitude problem," he says.

"A real bad one," Slater replies. "I'm gonna get in his shit real soon."

"No, not now. He's in that gang, and until we take those assholes out, we need him happy," Reid says. "Once we take care of them, and you feel the need to have a one on one conversation with the man, by all means, have that conversation."

A sinister grin grows on the face of Slater as he nods his head with agreement. The two begin to make it back to their unmarked car to officially start their day off as they plot their next move hoping to finally get a break in their case.

Later that evening at the hidden hospital, Duke is sitting with Terricka sharing lunch with her in an empty sizable room that was converted to a makeshift cafeteria area with several tables scattered throughout the area. Several other hospital visitors were occupying the room as well as eating and conversing with one another. Terricka notices that Duke has been picking at his food, not really eating. He seems distant to her because his mind is still on his earlier meeting with the commissioner.

"Where are you right now?" Terricka asks.

"Huh?"

"You seem, I don't know, somewhere else or something," she clarifies. "You're just pickin' at that burger, eyes hazed like you got a lot on your mind."

"It's nothing, it's just...," a hesitating Duke says, trying to come up with the right words. "Did you see the news today? About those two officers who got shot last night? I know y'all are behind that, Terricka. How does that sit with you? Really?"

Terricka shakes her head in denial before taking a quick bite of her burger.

"I don't know what you're talking about," she replies, her mouth full of food. "I saw the story, yeah but that had nothing to do with us."

Duke looks at her unconvinced, shaking his head with disbelief.

"I know you think I'm an idiot, but at least do me the favor of not lying," Duke quips. "Officer Matt Williams, charged and cleared of manslaughter charges. Just released back on the streets not too long ago. This fits The Hand's motive."

"Even if we did, and that's not an admission, it was justified, believe me," Terricka fires back with an attitude. "What do you care anyway? You're not even a part of that side of things if it happened. Williams was a dirty cop, plain and simple. He got what he deserved.

Duke is stunned by Terricka's narrow-minded view of the situation and continues to argue his point with her just as Jules and a few others walk into the room. He notices the two sitting with each other and frowns. A hint of jealously hits him as he and his followers make their way over and interrupts their discussion.

"Well, what do we have here?" Jules says with a smile. "Terricka, I thought you didn't eat pork."

"I don't," she replies.

"Then why you over here messin' with this pig?" Jules responds, causing his group to chuckle. "I'm just sayin' you could be having a whole better conversation if you ditched the pig, and stuck to your own kind."

"Excuse me, we're trying to have a peaceful meal over here, so if you don't mind…" an irritated Duke replies.

"I don't mind," Jules replies as he takes a seat at the table next to Terricka. "So, what were y'all talkin' about?"

Duke grunts as Terricka looks to calm the situation.

"Nothing, just talking about that police shooting last night, that's all," she says, causing Jules to smile.

"Oh, I see. Hard seeing your people gettin' shot up, isn't it?" Jules says, mocking Duke. "I'm sure that shit must have hurt."

"Not at all," Duke calmly responds. "All I was saying is that shooting a dirty cop down is one thing, but the other guy, Jacobs I think was his name, that guy had an impeccable record. No brutality cases, or anything that would show he's a threat. He's just an innocent family man that got gunned down!"

"Fuck him! He's ridin' with Williams, so you know he's just crooked as the letter S," Jules responds with a chuckle. "Besides, he's part of the problem too. If he's a good cop as you said he was, and he didn't drop a dime about his partner, he's part of the problem."

Duke looks at his adversary with confusion in his eyes.

"So let's assume that he knew about what Williams had did. In fact, let's say he was there to witness the whole thing. He didn't participate, but he had firsthand knowledge of the issue. You're telling me his death is worth starting a war over? You're telling me he deserved to get shot?" He asks.

"You damn right he did," Jules says. "Let's be real, that's what makes y'all cops dirty. Heard you was in that position and didn't rat out your partners either. You can't talk about it like it's one thing, and still don't pay attention to the fact that your so called good cops are just as bad as the assholes because they don't step up."

Duke chuckle as he takes a sip of his drink before responding.

"I'm gonna go out on a limb here, and say that you didn't grow up in Beverly Hills," he responds, smirking. "No, I'm gonna assume you grew up like the rest of us in the projects and shit."

"Fuckin' right. Imperial here," Jules proudly replies.

"Ah, yes. Imperial thug. Let me guess, you and several of your family members, y'all were on the block servin' the fiends at times, weren't y'all?" Duke asks, causing Jules to nod his head with confirmation.

"No doubt, we had a few folks doin' dirt, but that was then. We're not like that anymore. All we care about is the cause. What does any of that shit have to do with anything?" An impatient Jules asks.

"Well, the street code is not to snitch, am I right? No snitchin' to cops about nothing that does around on your block. Now you say you're down with the cause now, and I get that, but I'm sure there's a lot of other family members and friends who are out on those corners doing the dirt," Duke says, making his way to his point. "Now, in all your time in Imperial, did you ever once call the cops and snitch out your homie?"

Jules shakes his head, finally seeing where Duke is going with the conversation.

"That ain't the same thing," he replies.

"Hold up, how is it not the same thing?" Duke inquires. "Both of us see things that are wrong with certain aspects, for me my old job, and for you the neighborhood. You turn a blind eye to your cousins, uncles, or whoever abiding by the no snitching street guidelines. They're dirty, but you overlook it. It's funny how the police get shitted on about that, but people like you allow the dope to flow through the neighborhoods without doin' a damn thing about it. One could even argue that what you're doing is worse, allowing folks like that to sell that shit to our own community."

Terricka laughs, which irritates Jules.

"He got you there, Jules," she responds, giggling.

"Please. With all the shit your dad then did, you can't even talk," Jules snaps back, piquing Duke's interest.

"That's enough!" Damu exclaims, after observing the discussion from the doorway.

He slowly makes his way in, nodding to one of his bodyguards, who starts clearing the room of non-Hand members. Duke is about to exit when Damu motions to him to stay. He slowly walks over, his tall frame intimidating Jules as he stands over him.

"You crossed the line, Jules," Damu says, berating his second in command. "You had a simple task, and because of your carelessness, you've created a voice against the cause."

"Damu, all due respect, but I don't think we should be talking about that in front of him," Jules points out, referring to Duke.

"He's part of the team now. He deserves to know what he's in to," Damu responds. "You were supposed to take out Williams, and only Williams."

"Fuck that," a defiant Jules fires back as he rises from his seat. "Wasn't you the one that told me the only good cop is a dead one? You preach about the cause, but as of late, it seems like you're fallin' back on us. First asking us to chill on that cop responsible for the Jamie shooting, and now this shit. Maybe your heart isn't into it like it once was."

"First of all, remember who the fuck you're talkin' to," an intimidating Damu says, getting into Jules's face. "I've been down with the cause while you were still suckin' on your mama's tit, so don't you ever question my heart in this game. Secondly, killing a corrupt cop is the one thing that gives a voice to our cause. It lets the pigs know if they continue to fuck with us, we will fuck with them. Killing a cop who has no prior investigations, no brutality cases, or not so much as a slap on the wrist silences our cause making us look like random thugs and uniting all the 'back the blue' folks and police personnel together. He was a family man, and best believe the media is going to use his story to exploit our cause!"

Damu's words cause Jules to back down. While Damu's thoughts make sense to him, he didn't care. In his eyes, all cops deserve to die, even ex-cops like Duke. He's never been on board bringing him in and is upset his leader is letting him sit in on the discussion.

"Look, I get what you're sayin' and all, but there wasn't nothing we could do. It just happened real quick," Jules says, choosing to go the excuse route. "If you don't believe me, ask Fatboy. He'll tell you."

Fatboy, who is standing by the entrance, is caught off guard that Jules would throw his name out there. Damu isn't buying it.

"If you made a plan, and someone else was with him, you walk away," Damu fires back. "If I wanted Fatboy in charge, I would have told him to do it. You fucked up, Jules, and because of that, a lot of our brothers are gonna suffer. I'll let you live with that."

A frustrated Jules storms out of the room, refusing to settle his differences with his leader. Damu nods everyone out of the room, holding Duke back for the moment. Terricka stays as well but is motioned out of the room herself.

"Really?" She says as if she's offended.

Damu slowly nods to her, causing her to roll her eyes before exiting the room as well. As soon as the room is clear, Damu takes a seat across from Duke, sizing him up. He didn't know if he could fully trust the ex-cop but decides to be honest with him.

"I'm sorry you had to hear that," he says to Duke. "I figured since you've seen the good, you might as well know about the ugly as well."

"Here's what I don't get, you have all this. The hospital, the rallies, the training. You've made a bigger difference than most people will ever make in their lifetime, but there's this whole killing cops thing that you just can't let go. Walk away. Just do this shit, instead of that shit," Duke pleas to The Hand's leader.

Damu takes a deep breath and nods his head with agreement.

"It's true, I'm not getting better with time," he replies, smirking. "But until there is justice for our people in the streets, I'll continue to make my presence felt with the law. Kumbaya wasn't working for us."

"And this is?" Duke questions. "I don't know if you noticed, but your number two there is about to go off the deep end. You know him better than I do, obviously, but it looks like you might have a mutiny on your hands one day. A number two that wants to be number one."

Damu chuckles, thinking that Duke has seen too many movies.

"Jules has always been passionate, which is why I like him," he explains. "This back and forth between us has been going on for years. It's true, his passion sometimes makes him unpredictable, but there is nobody who is more down for the cause than him. You don't know what he's been through. I will always trust him with my life."

Duke isn't convinced that Jules has Damu's well-being in his best interest, but knowing that Jules and Fatboy were involved in the Williams' shooting is enough intel for him for the day.

"Well, that's on you. Watch your back though," Duke replies. "Anyway, Terricka said you wanted to see me. What's up?"

Damu smiles as both he and Duke rise from their chairs.

"I have a job for you. One that will give you a purpose and more importantly, help out the cause," Damu says. "I have a lot of youngsters that are looking to leave the gangbanging life alone and make a difference in their community. They are a little rough around the edges as you might expect, so I think you'd be the perfect person to talk with them. Let them know how to go unnoticed by the police, and things they can do to blend in. These youngsters are going to need to enter the workforce, but they need to be civilized first."

Duke looks at Damu suspiciously as the two begin making their way towards the exit.

"You're not trying to set up some strike team sleeper cell shit, are you?" He asks, causing Damu to burst into laughter.

"You do like watching movies, don't you?" The Hand of God Leader replies.

Duke chuckles with Damu leading the conversation on his vision for the youngsters in the neighborhood.

Later that night, Duke walks into his apartment, exhausted after spending most of his day in the hospital, preaching to the inner city youths. He makes his way to his bed and completely collapses face first into his pillow. After a few moments of silence, he pulls out his cell phone and dials Martinez's number.

"Hey, it's me," he says while rubbing his eyes. "Yeah, I think I might have a lead on the Williams's shooting... nah, it wasn't

Damu who rode on this one. It's his number two, Jules, and his sidekick, a cat that goes by the name Fatboy... Yes, the name describes him perfectly."

Duke chuckles before taking a look at the time on the clock on his nightstand.

"Yeah, look, I'm worn out today. Why don't we get together tomorrow? I can text you the description of the two perps, but I don't have a last name or anything to go by. Run it through the facial recognition software, and see if we can get lucky... Yeah... No, I'll text you here in a minute... okay... yeah, that works. Cool. Hey, wait a second," Duke says as he's conflicted about the next bit of information he's thinking about sharing. "Hey, you know that lawyer Terricka Jackson?... Yeah, the one with the loudmouth. Can you do me a favor? Can you run her background?... No, it's nothing like that. I'm specifically looking for anything in regards to her parents... yeah... I just have a hunch about something, and I wanna make sure before I act on it... yeah... yeah, bring it tomorrow with you... Alright, that works. Hey, so tomorrow, are you gonna wear your street walkin' outfits again?... Hello? Hello?"

Duke chuckles as his flirting runs Martinez off the line. Jules's comment about Terricka's father has Duke curious as he still is trying to figure things out. Police killing aside, Duke is starting to warm up to the cause that The Hand of God is involved with. Between working at the corner store, his involvement with Damu and his crew, and dealing with the undercover case, Duke is drained. He quickly undresses and turns in for the night with his allegiances to both Damu and the police firmly in the back of his mind.

CHAPTER 8

The Life and Times of Jules Thompson

Officer Murphy is nervously waiting outside of the Deputy Commissioner's office in the early morning hours. He's been summoned and knows that his professional career is at stake. He thought it would take months to come back with a verdict, like most major cases with this type of spotlight on it, and didn't know whether or not his early summons is a good thing or a bad thing. With everything racing in his mind, he didn't hear the Deputy Commissioner's secretary calling out his name.

"Officer Murphy," she says, finally getting his attention.

"Oh, yeah. I'm sorry," Murphy replies as he rises from his chair.

"He's ready to see you now. You can go in," the secretary says to a nervous Murphy.

Murphy nods his head and takes a deep breath before entering Irvin's office. Irvin is sitting behind his desk looking over a few work-related items on his computer when Murphy finally makes his way in.

"Officer Murphy. Please, have a seat," Irvin says with a smile on his face. "I have some good news for you."

Murphy is relieved as he takes a seat across from Irvin, anticipating the Deputy Commissioners' news.

"The review board has looked over your file and the evidence, and based on their findings, they have come to the conclusion that the shooting was justified," Irvin announces.

The news removes a huge burden from Murphy's shoulders as he breathes a sigh of relief, happy to have won the board's favor.

"That's... Deputy, sir, that's great news," he replies, struggling to find his words. "You have no idea how much I've stressed over this for the past few days."

"Well, it's not official just yet, but it's a step in the right direction," Irvin replies. "We're going to keep you in-house for the next month or so until things die down. An official announcement won't come till then."

"Why so long, sir?" A curious Murphy asks.

"In these times, and the publicity we're facing with this case, we need to be delicate on the way we address things such as your absolvement," warns Irvin. "This case has a lot of traction, so once they find out that you're off the hook, riots may arise. Our hope is that after a month or so, we can announce it. It'll look like we're doing a thorough job, and maybe the public would have moved on by then."

Murphy sighs, disappointed he has to wait so long for his name to get cleared, but understands what the department is trying to do in order to protect him, and more importantly, his family.

"Understood, sir," he says with Irvin noticing his enthusiasm has diminished.

"I know it's hard, officer, but it's all about protecting both you and the brand," Irvin explains. "Right now, you're a celebrity. Everyone who turns on the TV knows your face, and to announce it now, assuming it doesn't leak to the press, could be catastrophic for both you and your family."

"I know, sir. I had an incident in a grocery store not too long ago. Couldn't even finish my shopping because of this," Murphy admits. "Still, this is... It's a bit much, sir. I know you're trying to protect me and my family, but being a desk jockey wasn't what I signed up to be. Before this incident, I had my choice of posts. As crazy as it sounds though, I still feel like I'm getting away with murder here."

Irvin nods his head and leans back in his chair. He can see the

113

guilt in his officer's eyes and can tell that Murphy is struggling with his feelings.

"You seem like you're not sleeping," Irvin observes. "I've never been in your position before with a shooting case like this, so I know this may not mean much coming from me, but I've watched the body cam footage over a hundred times. You did what you had to do, and it's probably the same decision I would have made had I been in your situation. What you can't do is blame yourself for what happened. The kid was involved in a shooting earlier. I know the media is selling him like he's a saint, but at the end of the day, he went down that path. You did what needed to be done, and you shouldn't feel any guilt over it."

Murphy nods his head, still conflicted about the incident. He isn't sleeping well at night, just as the Deputy Commissioner has pointed out.

"I don't know, sir. I've... I've just had a lot on my mind dealing with this," Murphy admits. "I've tried to move past it, but when you're a prisoner in your own home, all you have is time to think about what you could have done to avoid this. I know what the kid was, and that does feel a little better knowing that he wasn't some innocent victim in all this, but death is still death."

Murphy becomes emotional as the thoughts he's fighting with constantly is starting to come to the forefront of his mind. Irvin walks over and takes a seat next to the struggling officer, trying to calm him down.

"Look, why don't you take another week off to clear your mind," he suggests. "I'll approve the leave extension. Have you had a psych meeting yet?"

Murphy shakes his head, as he didn't believe that meeting with a psychiatrist would help him with his issues.

"I mean, I had that brief mandatory meeting with him after the shooting, but that's about it," Murphy admits. "I don't think that will-"

"Make an appointment. That's an order," Irvin injects. "You

may not think you need it, Officer, but trust me, it's the best thing to get over events like this. I'm surprised they didn't mandate it to begin with."

Murphy sighs and nods his head with agreement as both he and Irvin rise from their seats and shake hands.

"Thank you, sir," Murphy says before making his way out of the Deputy's office.

Irvin sighs as he makes his way back behind his desk. After a few moments of pondering Murphy's mindset, he picks up his desk phone and makes a few calls hoping that the department hasn't lost yet another officer.

Just outside of their normal bar meeting place, Duke is waiting for his contact patiently in the parking lot. As he scrolls through his phone, he notices Martinez pulling up in an unmarked vehicle on the curb. While approaching her, a smile grows on his face when he notices the skimpy outfit she's wearing. He opens the door and hops in, still checking his colleague out.

"Well, I was about to trip out on you for having me wait here for forty minutes, but seeing that outfit on you has me feelin' some type of way," Duke says, smirking.

"LA traffic, what can I tell you," Martinez says before reaching for a couple of files on the dashboard. "I have a couple of line ups for you to check out. First, here's our Jules suspects, based on your description."

Duke looks through several pages of line ups until he notices Jules's picture.

"Boom, right there," he says, handing the file back to Martinez.

She pulls out her computer tablet from her side door and enters the lineup picture's information from the page into the police database system.

"Jules Thompson. Not much to him. Petty theft when he was younger. We brought him in for a couple of disturbing the peace charges, but let him go. No history of violence, or anything gang associated. He was related to a James Thompson, AKA Gutta Rat. Colorful name. Other than that, your man is clean," Martinez says, continuing to read the file before something catches her eyes. "Oh shit! Seems like Gutta Rat got caught up with a police altercation and was shot seventeen times. There was a civil case, but it was settled by the department out of court. No charges were ever filed."

"Let me see that," Duke asks, amazed at what he's hearing.

He looks over the tablet reading into Jules's brother's case file. According to the record, Gutta Rat was unarmed when the police pulled him over. The arresting police pulled him out of the car and claimed they were fearful for their lives, thinking that the gang banger had a weapon on him. The two officers opened fire on Gutta Rat, emptying their clips, and striking him seventeen times in the process, killing him. The city settled with the family for an undisclosed amount to move forward and dismiss the case against the officers involved. Duke shakes his head with disbelief.

"Un-fucking-believable!" Duke exclaims, handing the tablet back to Martinez. "Well, at least now I know why he's running with The Hand of God. Are there any cops in the LAPD that aren't corrupt?"

"Well, I'm not, and so far neither are you," Martinez points out. "Sometimes two people is all we need to make things right."

An unmoved Duke sighs, wondering what's the point of the job after reading Jules's profile.

"What about the other one? Fatboy?" He asks.

"Now that one is a little harder," Martinez says, handing a big file to a confused Duke.

"What's all this?" He inquires.

"Your description came back with a lot of hits. Apparently, there are a lot of fat black guys going by the name Fatboy," she answers with a smirk. "Unless you got something else to give me, that's with the search came back with. About a thousand perps in that file that all look hungry."

Duke laughs as he puts the file to the side.

"What about that other thing I asked for?" He questions.

"What other thing?" Martinez replies, knowing what Duke wants but toying with him.

Duke shoots her a look, realizing that she's playing with him waiting for what he asked for. Martinez eventually gives in as she pulls one more file from her side door. Duke is about to take the file from her when Martinez jerks it back at the last moment.

"What do you want this for?" She suspiciously asks. "She's not a part of the case, right?"

"Huh? No, she's… I don't know. I'm just curious, that's all," Duke replies, hiding his true intentions. "She got me out of a jam the first time around, and I'm tryin' to see who she really is."

"I thought you said you had a hunch about something?" Martinez reminds her colleague. "Something about her parents that you wanted to be sure about."

"It's… it's nothing. I'm just curious, that's all," Duke stutters to an unconvinced Martinez.

"Yeah, that sounds convincing," Martinez sarcastically fires back before handing the file to Duke. "You're not gonna find much there though. Her father died ten years ago, and her mother died four years after that. She has been arrested thirty-two times though."

Duke is reading the file, surprised at the number of times Terricka has been arrested.

"Jesus," he says, reviewing the file.

"Yeah, mostly disorderly conduct and shit associated with protests," Martinez explains. "Every last one of them have been dismissed, which I find very odd. I mean, the number of times she's been held, you would think we'd be able to make one thing stick. Must be one hell of a lawyer. Guess she feels like she's the modern day Martin Luther King Jr."

Duke is silent as he continues to view her file. He notices a list of perps she's been able to get off and is surprised to see Jules's name on the list.

"Says here she represented our man Jules way back when,"

Duke says to an unimpressed Martinez.

"Yeah, I saw that too. Those disturbing the peace charges. Are you saying our girl here is representing all members of the Hand of God?" Martinez asks.

"Not sure," Duke answers as he closes the files and hands it back to Martinez.

"So, what's the plan? You wanna put out an APB on this Jules guy?" Martinez asks.

Duke thinks for a minute before shaking his head with disagreement.

"Nah. I don't know who I can trust down there," Duke responds. "I know where he hangs out. I say let's case the spot, and as soon as we see him, we let Reid and his band earn their paychecks and pull him in. I'm sure they won't mind the extra work."

Martinez looks at Duke strangely before nodding her head with agreement.

"Alright, so that means stakeout? Me and you?" She says, smirking.

"Yeah. Unless you got something better to do," Duke replies.

"Sure. Let me work the block for leads that don't go nowhere while every guy who passes me pinches or smacks my ass for fun," Martinez responds sarcastically. "Shit, I'll do the job just to be off my feet. You have no idea how it feels to walk in heels for eight hours a day."

Martinez looks at Duke strangely once more, before smiling.

"Then again, maybe you do," she jokes, causing Duke to burst into laughter.

"Fuck you," he playfully responds. "Alright, meet me here around three. I'll get off the day job early, and we can case the spot this evening."

"Sounds like a plan," Martinez says as she puts all her files up. "You gonna peep out the Fatboy file?"

"Nah, you hold on to it. I'll check it out when we're at the spot," Duke says before opening the car door. "By the way, you look very nice, Officer Martinez. Once we're done here, care to

THIS IS AMERICA

meet for an off duty drink? Just you and me."

A smiling Duke is hanging, waiting on Martinez's response as she considers his proposal.

"Tell you what, why don't you do me a favor," she says seductively, leaning towards him. "And get the fuck out of my car!"

Duke is slightly disappointed but expects such a response from the brown-haired beauty.

"Alright, I hope someone pulls you by your thong today," Duke responds before getting out of the car to a laughing Martinez.

He closes the door and looks around the area before making his way down the block. Martinez watches him from behind in her rearview mirror with a smirk before pulling out her phone and pulling her car off from the side of the curb.

In the perfect weather in The Valley, all is quiet on a back road leading to a Calabasas neighborhood when a speeding motorcycle comes streaking through the area. The bike blurs down the road, not slowing down at any intersections along the way before coming to a complete stop in front of a gorgeous home tucked away in a cul-de-sac. The biker parks their motorcycle at the end of the driveway before removing their helmet, revealing themselves to be Jules. He looks around the area, almost as if he's disgusted by it before making his way up the sloped driveway, and to the front door. He rings the doorbell taking a deep breath while waiting for someone to answer. After a few moments, the door opens as Janelle is stunned to see her son, Jules, standing in her doorway. Jules shakes his head at his mother's appearance as she's wearing a bathrobe with her hair tied up in a scarf.

"Is this how you answer the door in this neighborhood?" He jokingly asks, smirking.

Janelle, however, isn't in the mood, shooting him a look of disgust out of her ferret-like eyes.

"What you then did now?" She asks in her gravelly voice with an attitude, folding her frail arms.

119

"What? Why I gotta always have done something when I come see you?" Jules replies. "Can't I just come see my mother to see what she's up to? Damn."

Janelle is suspicious of her son as she looks him over for several moments.

"Your ass only come to see me when you then did something," she points out.

"I promise you, mom, I'm not in any trouble. I… I just needed to get away for a while," Jules responds with a look of defeat on his face.

His mother sighs, waving her son in.

"I was just about to get me some red beans. You want a plate?" She asks.

Jules nods his head as the two make their way through the lavish home towards the kitchen. There is black art scattered throughout the household, especially in the hallway and main living area. It's an updated open concept home that really brings attention to the fine details, from the marble flooring to the crown molding. Jules shakes his head looking at the house, almost as if he's disturbed by it. They make it to the kitchen as Jules takes a seat at the high-end table.

"So you coming all the way out from the city because you need to get away?" Janelle says as she walks over by the stove and stirs her beans. "I've been seeing all the coverage on that Jamie Powell shooting. Protests breakin' out every which way it can. You apart of that?"

"Not really," Jules says as Janelle prepares a plate for both her and her son.

"Sad what happened to that kid. Look like they settin' us up to announce they lettin' another police off with murder. These times we're living in, I swear," she says as she walks over, places a plate in front of her son, and takes a seat next to him.

Jules is about to dig in when Janelle shoots him a look. He lowers his fork and lowers his head for prayer. Jules knows that his mother is deeply religious, especially after the death of his brother. The shooting had a different effect on him as he turned away from religion and God after the shooting, upset that his brother was taken from him. He did respect his mother, however, and would only pray in her presence. After a few moments, he gives the traditional sign of the cross, raising his head and digging into his food finally.

"So, since you're not involved in making the news lately, what are you up to?" Janelle asks before taking a bite of her food.

"I'm still out there trying to wake folks up. It's just… I don't know. People love to stay sleep it seems. Feels like I'm not getting anything done," Jules says in between bites.

"Ignorance is bliss," Janelle reminds her son. "Some people don't wanna see the world for what it is. Why ruin their fantasy with reality? It's easier to live in the dark than it is in the light."

"Tell me about it," Jules replies. "I've been doing work with this organization that I thought was on the same page as me. Now it seems they want to switch up their views giving the cops some slack. I just don't see how anyone can trust the police with all this foolishness going on."

"Cause it's normal to them," Janelle points out. "They get away with it because we're too busy killin' each other over bullshit. Jules, and I mean this with the utmost respect, but you're wasting your time, baby. You can't even get them street thugs to stop killin' each other, so what makes you think you're gonna be able to change things out in those streets?"

Jules doesn't respond, choosing to take a few bites of his meal instead. At times, he did feel like he's fighting a losing battle, but he refuses to think his cause is a waste.

"Black folks can't get together for shit," Janelle continues. "As long as we remain silent, and stay in our lane, nothing will change."

"That's just it, we're not staying silent anymore! We have to start somewhere," Jules fires back. "If we stand still, the same old same will happen. I choose to keep moving and keep fighting for the cause. Eventually, they're going to hear our voices. And for the record, me and my organization sat down with a couple of gang leaders the other day trying to keep the peace. There's a lot of good going on out there, mom. The media only presents the bad because that's what they're programmed to do. Nobody cares about progress. They only care about division amongst us all."

Janelle chuckles to herself before taking a few bites of her food once again. She feels her son is naïve to think anything that he's doing matters. She was born in the sixties and lived through the bulk of the Civil Rights Movement as a child. She felt the progress made during that time frame was a pacifier to keep the blacks in line while the whites continued to grow their wealth. Seeing that they weren't going to see eye to eye in this discussion, she decides to change the subject.

"You've been to see your sister lately?" She asks.

"You know Jameka is too busy for me," Jules quips. "Besides, she got that uppity husband who don't like me. I don't have time to be dealing with all of that."

"Yeah, he's a bit snobbish for my taste too," Janelle agrees with a smile. "Still, he treats her right and takes care of her, which is all I could ask for. Sure wish you'd find you someone to settle down with. Stop all this street stuff and build you a family."

Jules chuckles, dropping his fork on his plate after quickly downing the meal.

"Here you go," he says, smiling back at his mother. "Every time you see me, you have to bring that up."

"I just wanna see you happy, baby. You can't keep running these streets forever. Eventually, you're gonna need to settle down with someone and build a family," Janelle preaches. "I don't never see you with a girl. There's gotta be someone out there that has your eye. Unless you sittin' in the house every day not gettin' any."

Jules cringes at the thought of his mother commenting on his sex life.

"In what world do you think I'd want to talk to you about my sex life?" He quips. "Come on, mom, you know that's not appropriate!"

"I'm just sayin', I haven't seen you with a young lady in a while," Janelle replies with a giggle. "Figured we're grown adults now and can talk about such things. I don't want you or your sister to end up like me. This is a lonely life, Jules, and the only thing that will get you through these times is the loving of a good woman, believe me."

Jules nods his head with understanding as Janelle continues.

"So for real now, you don't have any girl who has your eye?"

Thinking of Terricka, Jules sighs and leans back in his chair.

"Yeah, there's one," he responds, smirking. "She's everything I've ever wanted. Problem is that it's unrequited."

"Un-re-who?" A confused Janelle inquires.

"Meaning she doesn't feel the same way I do about her. It's a one way thing," Jules explains.

"Maybe she doesn't know what she has yet," his mother points out. "Maybe if you give her a little time, she'll come around."

"Maybe," Jules repeats.

"You know, the last girl I remember you dating was that Hispanic girl. I always liked her and saw y'all two as a cute couple. The one who became a security guard, a cop, or somethin'. Whatever happened to her?" Janelle asks.

"A long story, mom. An extremely long story," Jules responds while shaking his head as he and his mother continue their conversation, catching up for lost time.

About an hour has gone by, as Jules and Janelle have made their way into the back yard area, both smoking a cigarette to ease the mood a bit. Jules looks around at the massive back yard and notices how well kept it is with a pool, and high-end yard furniture perfect for entertaining. As he takes a puff of his cigarette once more, he looks towards his mother, filled with curiosity.

"You know, there's always something I've been meaning to ask you," Jules builds up, piquing his mother's interest. "I never wanted to go there with you, but it's always been in the back of my mind, and since we're talking about the past and all earlier,

I figured this is good as a time as any to get it off my chest. You ever regret all this?"

"All what?" A confused Janelle asks before Jules points out the house and the amenities around them.

"All of this. The house, the neighborhood. The settlement that made you rich letting the officers who killed James off the hook. Don't get me wrong, seven million dollars is a lot of money, but don't you ever feel guilty accepting that?" Jules asks while basking in his surroundings.

Janelle is quiet, initially looking as if she's offended. After a few moments, and a couple more puffs of her cigarette, she decides to finally answer her son.

"I knew you'd come here one day askin' about all this," she quips. "The problem is that you only see through current eyes, not the past. We didn't have all these cell phones and social media showin' the world of our struggle back then. Back then, it was all about them versus us. Their word versus out word. It's all about what you could prove, and back then, we couldn't prove a damn thing."

Jules shakes his head in disbelief with Janelle noticing his reaction.

"Oh, you don't believe me?!" Janelle fires off with an attitude. "Boy, you must not remember, we had just left the projects on section eight back when all this happened. We didn't have no money to fight shit. Hell, the one lawyer I was thinkin' about hiring wanted ten thousand just to sit down. Now I'm on section eight, barely able to scrape money together to feed y'all asses. Where you think the money was gonna come from?"

Jules sighs, backing down from his mother, realizing she's making sense. Janelle backs down to taking another puff of her cigarette.

"Nowadays, you could probably get a 'go fund me' account or somethin' to help out. I didn't want it to be like this, but it's a fight I knew I was gonna lose. When the city approached me with the money, I didn't look at it like sellin' out. I looked at it like I'm saving the two children I had left," Janelle responds as she starts getting emotional. "I tell you what, I'd give it all back if it would bring James back to us. Every last penny. I'll let the Lord deal with those cops."

"Let the lord deal with them? Stop it," Jules quips with a chuckle. "Wasn't it the lord that took your son in the first place? I just don't understand how you still going for that hustle."

Janelle shakes her head, ashamed of her son's thoughts on religion.

"I knew you turned your back on the lord after James's death. I pray every night that you'd release that hatred in your heart and come back to him before things get out of hand," Janelle admits, putting out her butt in a nearby ashtray. "Yes, the lord took James, but maybe he was tryin' to save both of you in a way."

"Save both of us? How?"

"You followed your brother everywhere. If James jumped in the pool, you would jump right in the water with him, not knowing how to swim, mind you," Janelle replies with a giggle. "He was performing at a school play when you were four once, and I lost track of your ass. Why you ended up on stage trying to dance with him and his class?"

Jules chuckles as he and his mother reminisce.

"I remember that. Damn, you tore my ass up that night," Jules says with a chuckle.

"Yeah, you would do whatever James did. It started concernin' me when James got caught up in those gangs though," Janelle says, shifting her mood. "It was only a matter of time before you followed him into that life too."

"Come on, mom. Me and James was close and all, but I wasn't like him in that way," defends Jules. "We was like two different people."

"You say that now because of how you turned out, but don't forget I had to pick up your ass for stealing skittles from the store," Janelle points out. "I'm like, seriously, who steals skittles?"

Jules burst into laughter, remembering that day well. He remembers the look on his mother's face that day in the police station and quietly wished that the police would keep him in custody, being fearful of what she was going to do to him once she got him home. Just as he'd thought, she whipped him good that night.

"Yeah, that was a crazy night," he responds with a smirk.

"Well, your skittles fiasco had me thinkin' that you were maybe a year or two from joinin' the gang yourself. I told James not to bring that foolishness to my house, but he didn't listen. I knew he was gonna end up just like y'all daddy, spendin' the rest of his life behind bars because he had to rep his hood," Janelle says, rolling her eyes at the very thought of her children's father. "I was about to put him out completely before the shooting happened. After that, I just knew I had to get you outta there before you went down the same path as him. Go figure you'd still end up in a gang."

"What are you talking about? I never joined no gang," a confused Jules responds.

"Oh yeah? So what's the cop killin' gang you running with now?" Janelle fires back, stunning her son.

"I… I… what are you talking about?" Jules says, trying to save face.

"Boy, don't look at me like I'm stupid," an irritated Janelle fires back. "Just cause I don't live in the hood doesn't mean I'm not in the hood. I know what you're up to, and what you've been doing. I always said I would work up the nerve to ask you myself, but I could never do it. Seems like we're both gettin' answers today, aren't we?"

A stunned Jules remains silent, trying to figure out how his mother knew what she knew. A disappointed Janelle looks at her son in the eyes with shame.

"Boy, don't you know these people are gonna catch up with you one day and kill your black ass?" She says. "There's not gonna be no trial or anything. These cops are gonna find you, and they will settle the shit out in the streets."

"It's… it's not even like that," Jules quietly responds. "We're not at all what you think we are."

"Negro, please. So you and your group aren't out there killin' cops? Everything I'm hearin' is bullshit? Is that what you're tryin' to tell me?" Janelle asks her son. "Cause that look you givin' me right now is tellin' me otherwise."

Jules is silent, not having the courage to look his mother in the eyes. Janelle lights up another cigarette, stressing seeing her son in this light.

"How did you find out?" Jules asks.

"Like I said, I'm still hood. I hear shit all the time," Janelle admits. "I didn't want to believe my own son would be behind that foolishness. I don't even wanna know if you've killed someone before, Jules. What I want you to do is look at yourself and realize nothing lasts forever. Leading protests for social injustice is one thing but my god, Jules, do you realize what will happen when they catch you?"

"It's a chance I'm willing to take," Jules quips, finally working up the nerve to look her in her eyes. "We're making changes in the city. When it's all said and done, our voices will be heard!"

"Baby, no they won't," Janelle replies. "They are going to kill you. Plain and simple. Every time a black man, or black cause gets the power, they shoot them down. Every damn time. They bought down the Black Panthers, the Crips, Martin Luther King, and Malcolm X. And I don't wanna hear that shit about The Nation killin' Malcolm. If they did, it was because the government set it up. A black man who can influence other black men to rise up is the most dangerous thing in America, and you best believe they will do their best to suppress any voice like that. They even took out Tupac."

Jules looks at his mother strangely.

"Alright, I was with you until you said Pac," Jules replies with a chuckle. "That didn't have nothing to do with the government."

"Didn't it? They tried to silence the brother by sending him jail, and when that didn't humble him, they killed him," Janelle replies to her unbelieving son. "See, he became a threat because a lot of black folks were starting to listen to him. Every time we get a voice that can organize us, they silence it. They wanna keep us in the streets fighting over territory that we don't even own. I know you think I'm crazy with conspiracy theories but look at your history. They don't want us to thrive. Just look at Tulsa. Power doesn't want black excellence. They want to keep us fighting with each other so they can control us. If we're too busy fighting each other, we'll never unite and take the fight to them."

"But that's what we're doing now! We're taking the fight to them for a change! We're on the cusp of-"

Jules becomes silent as his mother turns away from him. He could tell there would be no convincing her of his point as she's made up her mind. He knew she had his best interest at heart, but he isn't about to back down from the cause because others failed to achieve what they have.

"I pray for you every night, Jules. I really do. I hope you find peace someday before they take it from you," Janelle says once more before getting up from her chair and walking back into the house.

Jules sighs, shaking his head, trying to gather his thoughts. His mother's words made him question his path. He leans back in the chair and relaxes, closing his eyes to feel the cool breeze flowing through the yard.

CHAPTER 9

Terricka's Song

Just after three in the afternoon, Duke is once again waiting for the arrival of Martinez in their normal meeting spot's parking lot. He left his corner store job early, telling his grandmother he isn't feeling well to maintain his cover from her. To say he's struggling with his decision to bring in Jules, Fatboy, and any other of The Hand of God's associates who were involved with the police shooting from a few days back is an understatement. He knows just as they did what they did to make a statement to the cops that the LAPD will want to make a statement back towards the group, which could lead to fatalities on both sides. Still, someone needs to go down for the shooting, and Billick is getting impatient with his undercover efforts. He needed results and in a hurry. He's also confused with Terricka and her relationship with Damu. The file states her father is dead, but Duke feels otherwise as he wants to continue digging on that end as well. With all those thoughts racing through his head, he doesn't see Martinez pulling up to the curb waving at him. After several honks, she finally catches his attention. He starts making his way towards her when his cell phone suddenly rings. He takes a look at his caller Id and notices Terricka is calling. He stops in his tracks and motions to Martinez to give him a moment before answering the line.

"Hey, what's up?" He answers.

"Hey, Duke. Thank god I got a hold of you. Look, I know it's last minute and everything, but I really need you to do me a favor," she says.

"Okay, what's up?"

"So, I have to give a little speech down in front of the Crenshaw Community Health Center for a protest rally. It's nothing too big and all, but normally Jules is there keeping watch over things to make sure nothing pops off, but I haven't heard from him since he left the other day."

"Haven't heard from him? He's not at the hospital?" Duke inquires, trying to see if his stakeout plan is still relevant.

"No. It's not the first time he's done this. When him and Damu get into it, he normally disappears for a few days or a week to clear his head. Anyway, Damu told me to contact you and see if you can cover for him," Terricka requests. "I'll have a couple of bodyguards by the stage, but he always wants someone in the crowd to cover me just in case. Someone who has a keen eye I guess. Anyway, if you don't do it, he's not gonna let me do the speech, and that would suck since I'm the protest organizer. Please, Duke. I need you on this."

"Well, I... well I had something going on and-"

"Duke, please. I'm begging you. Do me this favor and I'll owe you one," Terricka pleas.

Duke thinks for a moment looking towards Martinez, who looks back at him, wondering what's the holdup.

"Alright, I'm in," Duke says. "What time?"

"At five. Thank you so much, Duke. I owe you one for real," an excited Terricka replies. "I'll see you then."

"Yeah, see you then," Duke says before hanging up the line.

After a few moments, he makes his way over towards Martinez's car, and motions for her to lower the window.

"Hey. What's up?" She asks.

"Yeah, look, something came up. We're gonna have to push this back," Duke says, hoping Martinez wouldn't press him. "I got word our target isn't where I thought he is right now, and he's kinda out of pocket at the moment."

"Out of pocket?" A confused Martinez asks. "What do you

mean he's out of pocket? Who were you just talking to?"

"Nobody. Look, I don't want to waste both of our time on this, so for now, we're gonna chill until I hear otherwise," Duke answers.

Martinez becomes suspicious as she tries to get a read on her colleague.

"What are you not telling me?" She inquires.

"Nothing. The guy isn't where I thought he is, and until I can get an exact location, we'd be wasting time," Duke reaffirms. "Trust me, you'll be the first to know when I hear something."

Martinez still isn't buying Duke's excuse but goes along with it for the moment.

"Alright. Well, I guess I'll be hearing from you?" She says before raising her window and pulling off.

Duke watches as she turns on the corner before making her way over towards the bus stop and taking a seat at the bench waiting for his ride to arrive.

Just after five, the rally has begun as hundreds of protesters holding signs supporting Jamie and putting down the LAPD cheer on the current speaker who is on a makeshift stage located in front of the Crenshaw Community Health Center. Duke comes running down the street from the bus station knowing he's running late and didn't want to disappoint Terricka. As he makes his way through the crowd, he notices Terricka in the front looking around for him. He walks up to her out of breath as she giggles.

"You alright?" She asks as he leans over, gasping for air.

"Yeah… I'm… the buses… ran… ran into… traffic," Duke says in between pants. "Am I late?"

'No, you're actually right on time," Terricka answers with a smirk. "Just keep a lookout for anything suspicious. Do your cop thing."

Duke, still hunched over trying to catch his breath, nods his head and waves her off, causing his friend to burst into laughter before heading towards the stage. As Duke continues to recover, in the distance, Martinez, who has been following Duke the entire time, unbeknownst to him, looks on from a distance trying to figure out what's going on with her undercover partner. Both Duke and Martinez watch as Terricka takes center attention on the stage to start her speech, much to the crowd's delight. She's a hero in the people's eyes and receives an ovation from all those in attendance. She waves her hands trying to quiet the group.

"Thank you, thank you," she says into the microphone with a big smile on her face. "I want to thank each and every one of you who came out today. It shows me that there are people in this city who aren't afraid to voice their opposition to the Los Angeles Police Department and their racists and dated beliefs. For years, the LAPD has been able to force its will upon us with immunity. They've made killing black males, Hispanic males, and other minority figures look normal in most of the public's eyes, which is sad. Well, I'm here to tell you that no more will we stand idly by and watch our men and women gunned down for no apparent reason! No more will we allow them to get by with the 'I feared for my life excuse'! If you can take a white suspect who's shot up a theatre with an automatic weapon alive, you should be able to take down an unarmed minority suspect with just as much ease!"

The crowd erupts with cheers as a recovered Duke checks out the area briefly before turning his attention towards Terricka. Her energy flows through into them hyping them up as she continues with her speech.

"I know today's rally is for Jamie Powell, and I know his family is here with us today in support of what we're here to do," Terricka continues, pointing out Jamie's mother and other family members who are standing behind her. "I know we're here about Jamie, and it is a tragedy, make no mistake, but even his mother will tell you this is bigger than Jamie. This is about years of mistreatment coming from the law enforcement side, not just here in LA, but all over the United States, if you wanna call it that! Jamie is just the latest victim in the social justice battle, and we're not going to rest until there are actual changes in police department procedures! We want to make sure they are held accountable for their actions!

You've seen the videos where police are able to take down threatening white victims, many of who have weapons, without any issues. All we're asking is the same thing. All we want is to live in a place where a minority isn't killed for selling CDs, walking with a bag of skittles, sleeping in their own house, or because the officers claim they're 'resisting arrest' because I've seen the footage of the police able to do their jobs when it comes to white suspects. We're not buying the lies anymore! We want police reform, an independent investigative panel who can give their unbiased ruling on brutality and police shooting cases! No more officers getting off with administrative leave! No more of their internal investigations that don't go anywhere! No more!

The crowd feeds into Terricka's energy once more as they begin chanting 'no more' in unison. Terricka chants with the people as an impressed Duke shakes his head with approval.

After the speech, the crowd is beginning to disburse as Terricka wraps up her meeting with Jamie's mother, sharing a hug with her. She notices Duke and makes her way over to him with a smile on her face.

"So? What did you think?" She asks, looking for feedback.

"You were incredible," Duke admits. "Up there like a female Malcolm X and shit."

"Whatever," Terricka replies, giggling.

"Nah, I'm serious. That was some deep shit you said up there. I can see why Damu wanted eyes on you. These people love you. They need you," Duke affirms. "I can say, it even moved me."

"Well, thank you," a humbled Terricka responds. "I'm glad I got the Duke seal of approval. You really bailed me out today. I owe you one for real."

"How about have dinner with me, and we'll call it even?" Duke flirts, causing Terricka to laugh.

"You see, I knew it! I knew it! I knew your ass was gonna bring that up," Terricka quips.

She takes a look at Duke for a moment, checking him out before slowly nodding her head, accepting his invitation.

"Alright. I guess I do owe you one, and a deal is a deal," Terricka answers. "You wanna do this right now, or what?"

"I'm free," Duke says as he reaches out his hand.

Terricka sighs as she takes his hand.

"Alright, let's do it. We'll take my car," Terricka says, surprising Duke.

"Wait a minute? You have a car?" He asks. "Why the hell you're always on the bus then?"

Terricka giggles as the two start walking towards the corner.

"For the people to respect you, you have to live like the people," Terricka explains. "You can't understand their struggle if you're not willing to put yourself in their shoes. Besides, it's a nice way to meet folks. I only drove my car today cause I had planned to head back home and unwind, but since some fool decides to hustle a dinner date out of me, I guess that's out of the question."

Duke laughs and is about to respond to Terricka's jab when a voice from the distance quickly ruins the mood.

"Duke?! Duke, is that you?!" Both he and Terricka hears from a distance.

They turn around and notice Martinez smiling and waving, quickly making her way through the remaining crowd members with an excited look on her face. Duke is stunned as she quickly hugs him, and kissing him on his cheek, breaking him and Terricka's connection for the moment.

"Oh my god, I can't believe it's you! I hadn't seen you in forever, baby!" She exclaims in her most campy rachet dialect.

"H… hey you," Duke replies nervously. "What are you doing here?"

"Same as you, for the rally," Martinez answers with a smile before taking a look at Terricka. "Please excuse his rude ass, I'm Angela, and I assume you're his new boo?"

"Terricka, and no, we're just friends, that's all," Terricka replies, looking at Martinez in her scantily dressed booty shorts and tight top.

"Well, y'all sure look like a little more than friends walking around all coupled up," an insinuating Martinez says.

"Okay, so how do you two know each other?" A curious Terricka asks. "Y'all seem like the dating type too."

"Us? Dating? No, we're-"

"Oh, Duke is just shy about it," Martinez says, cutting Duke off. "We dated a long time ago, before he went to, where was it, Chicago?"

Duke sighs, grabbing his heading, frustration unsure what Martinez is trying to do.

"Cincinnati," he softly replies.

"Yeah! That's it. I knew it was one of them cities that start with C," Martinez replies with a chuckle, noticing Duke's displeasure with her presence. "Anyways, I didn't wanna hold y'all up. I just saw him and thought he'd wanna at least talk to me, but he seems like he's over dealin' with my ass. Let me give you a little advice. I know y'all just friends and all, but he gonna try and slide up in there eventually. The dick ain't worth it, girl. He's a premie, so make sure if you do decide to dip, that you have you some plans afterward cause, baby, he's gonna be like the movie 'Gone in Sixty Seconds'."

Both Terricka and Duke are stunned at Martinez's comments, with Terricka bursting into laughter.

"See ya, boo," Martinez says before walking off down the street.

A speechless Duke shakes his head with embarrassment as Terricka grabs his arm once more.

"So, a premie, huh?" She jokes, leading him down the curb. "Well, at least I know your type. Like 'em rachet, I see."

"No, I don't! That... that was a long time ago," Duke replies, trying to stick to the story.

"Apparently not too long. According to her anyway," Terricka jokingly says, causing Duke to lower his head with shame.

As they get to the end of the block, Terricka takes out her keys and unlocks her car, a silver Lexus, which stuns Duke.

"This is your car?" He asks, checking it out.

"Well, I am a lawyer, remember?" Terricka responds as she gets into the driver's seat.

Before closing her door, she turns and looks at Duke, who is still in awe over the vehicle.

"Hey. You coming or what?" she says, snapping Duke from his thoughts.

"Oh. Yeah," he replies before hurrying into the passenger's side.

As soon as the two are buckled in, Terricka starts the car and screeches her way down the block at full speed.

Later that evening, Terricka and Duke are enjoying their sit down meal at the luxurious Fleur Dis Lis restaurant, located just outside of Beverly Hills. It's a swanky place with an upscale clientele that makes Duke feel a little out of place. Unlike the other customers, most of who are wearing a shirt and tie or dinner gowns, Duke and Terricka are wearing t-shirts and jeans, with tennis shoes. As he takes a sip of his drink, Duke notices several of the other customers looking at them almost in disgust.

"Why did you pick this joint?" He asks. "I mean, we're certainly not dressed for the spot, and these white people looking at us like it's back in the sixties or some shit."

"Fuck them," a nonchalant Terricka replies. "Let them stare. Probably the only time they've ever seen black people in person. It'll be a great story they can tell their circle one day. I like it here, so why would I let these folks run me off?"

"Could be the fact that they're all dressed up, and we're looking like we're looking," Duke points out before taking another sip of his wine. "Surprised they even let us in."

"I helped the owner out of a legal jam a while ago. Since then, I've been able to come here, however, and whenever I want," Terricka explains. "Don't need a reservation or anything. Just show up, and I'm seated right away."

"I saw that shit," Duke says with a chuckle. "It's like I'm dating Henry Hill or some bullshit. Very emasculating."

"Well, I'm sorry I'm treating you like a Karen," Terricka jokes, referring to the same Goodfellas movie Duke had. "Where would you have taken me if the choice was yours?"

"Red Lobster, or somewhere where there's black folks," a smirking Duke says, causing Terricka to burst into laughter.

"Naw, you see, you need to bring your ratchet girl Angela there," a laughing Terricka says. "I'm just saying, if you want to impress me, you need to go big. Red Lobster ain't it."

"So much for being part of the people," Duke says, using Terricka's words against her. "I mean this spot speaks 'common folks'."

"Whatever. Keep talking, and I'm gonna leave you with the bill," Terricka fires back.

"Then you gonna have to come bail me out because ain't no way I can afford all this," Duke replies causing Terricka to burst into laughter once more.

After a few moments, Duke decides to get some answers from his date.

"So, I have a question for you," he says, piquing Terricka's attention. "When we first met, you had mentioned your dad and mine had ran with the Pirus way back when. I'm gonna be real, I don't remember him. Is he still around?"

The smile on Terricka's face slowly starts to fade.

"No. He died a while back," she says. "Why are you asking me about that?"

"I don't know. Just trying to remember that's all," Duke answers.

"Well, I don't like to talk about it, so can we please not go there," Terricka says, causing Duke to nod his head.

"Sure, my bad, I didn't mean to bring up painful shit," Duke says before taking a sip of his wine. "Just so I don't fuck up again, I'll let you lead the next subject."

Terricka thinks for a moment before a smile grows on her face.

"Tell me about Angela," she says to a confused Duke.

"Who?"

"Angela. Your ex we met earlier today," Terricka responds, jogging Duke's memory of Martinez's lie from earlier.

"Oh, Angie... she's... I mean, what do you wanna know?" Duke responds.

"I don't know. How did you two meet? How long were you together, and what happened. All the tea," Terricka replies, smirking. "Give it up."

Duke chuckles as he finishes his glass of wine before going into his story.

"I don't know, we met at a party about a couple of years after graduation," Duke tells, trying to come up with his best lie. "Honestly, I was drunk as fuck, one thing led to another, and we hooked up."

"So after that thirty-second marathon, what happened?" Terricka asks, smirking.

"Well, first of all, it wasn't no thirty seconds," Duke fires back. "After that, I mean we kicked it for a minute, but she's not my type. Maybe ten years ago, she was, but as you get older, you see it's not all about looks. You need a woman who can bring something to the table other than sex."

"And did you find such a woman who could quench your thirsty not only sexually but mentally as well?" A smiling Terricka asks.

Duke hesitates as he looks on at Terricka.

"I don't know. I'll tell you after dinner," he flirts causing his date to giggle. "What about you? We all in my tea, let's talk about you and Jules."

"Me and Jules? What are you talking about?" Terricka fires back. "There ain't no me and Jules."

"Maybe not to you, but in his head, I can tell he's interested in you. Tell me he didn't try to hook up with you before," Duke quips as Terricka shakes her head in denial.

"You trippin' for real," she responds, waving Duke off.

"You never answered me though. Did Jules try and knock that?" Duke pushes, awaiting Terricka's response.

Terricka doesn't say anything, as she drinks her wine silently. She notices the look Duke is throwing at her and finally bursts into laughter, revealing that he was right about her.

"I mean, of course, he did. All y'all men want is a piece of ass, so don't think he's the only in the crew that's tried to holla at me," Terricka admits. "Hell, you sittin' here trying to holla at me now after your ex told me you have erectile dysfunction and shit."

"That girl was lying," an offended Duke replies. "You know how y'all women are. The more pissed you are with a guy, the more his dick gets smaller and smaller when you tell your stories. Not to mention the fact that me and her slept together multiple times and shit. If it wasn't all that, she would have left, and why the fuck are we back on me?"

Both Duke and Terricka burst into laughter as Duke refills both of their glasses with the wine bottle that's on the table.

"You tryin' to get me drunk, aren't you?" A tipsy Terricka notices. "Don't think you gonna give me that thirty-second dick by getting me drunk."

"Anyway, so fine, you and Jules aren't hookin' up. What's up with you then? Haven't found a dude that can rattle them drawers yet?"

Terricka chuckles to herself, deflecting the fact that she's lived a pretty lonely life the years past.

"Honestly, I just have been focused on the work," she admits. "I haven't had time to develop anything with anyone. There's just so much to accomplish to worry about all that."

"Yeah, I get that, but we all need someone in our life to kind of keep us going," Duke points out. "Can't be healthy living like that."

"Perhaps," Terricka replies before taking a quick sip of her wine. "Or, perhaps it's worth it if we can see real change come about and not have to see another mother crying her eyes out because of their dead child. I know you think what we do is extreme at times, and truthfully, I feel like that at times. I find myself thinking there has to be a better way than doing, well you know."

Duke nods his head while a few thoughts race into Terricka's mind.

"The thing is, when I look into someone's eyes like Jamie's mother, all my doubts and questions go out the window. This woman has lost a child that she'll never see again. He was only sixteen. He never voted, went to college, paid his first bill, or worse yet, graduated high school. He'll never know those things because some dumb ass officer felt it was his time to go. They are killing us, Duke. They really are. You ask me how can I live life this lonely life fighting for the cause? I ask you, how can you live your life knowing all this shit is going on?"

A silent Duke nods his head as he never thought about it that way. He can see the passion in her eyes is only for her work. While he empathizes with her, he also respects her for doing what she's doing, sacrificing everything for her beliefs.

"That's deep," he says. "Sorry if I offended you."

"Apology accepted," Terricka says as she finishes her drink. "So, my question to you is if it's not thirty seconds, how long is it really?"

Duke bursts into laughter as the two share a moment with each other.

"I don't know. I've never timed it," he responds.

"Maybe I can time it for you," a flirty Terricka responds, catching Duke off guard.

"You sure that ain't the alcohol talking?" A curious Duke asks.

"You sure that you care if it's the alcohol or not?" Terricka fires back with a smile.

After admiring her for a few moments, he raises his hand to call over the waiter.

"Check please," he says with a big smile on his face causing Terricka to laugh once more.

About an hour later, Terricka and Duke walk into her luxury apartment located just outside of the downtown Los Angeles area. Duke is quickly taken aback by the high rise apartment's view of the downtown area flicking in the background. The apartment itself was pretty plain jane, with just the basic necessities such as a couch, TV, appliances for the kitchen, and bedroom furniture. Terricka tosses her keys on a nearby table and joins Duke, who is blown away by the city view.

"Yeah, this is really living with the people," he sarcastically says, looking at the amazing scenery through her window.

His view is short-lived, as an aggressive Terricka surprises him, pushing him down to the nearby couch and mounting him. She starts to unbutton her pants with Duke quickly joining her. She leans in and starts kissing Duke before inserting him inside of her. She is in total control as she starts grinding on him, making sure every thrust is felt between both of them. After a few more passionate thrusts, she stops for a moment, confusing Duke.

"What?" He asks. "What's wrong?"

"Hmm, I guess ol' girl was lying," Terricka says with a smirk. "You've passed the thirty second mark."

"Are you serious?!" Duke exclaims before reversing the position, lying Terricka on her back, with him on top. "I'll show you thirty seconds!"

Duke begins punishing Terricka, sending her body to a state of bliss, causing her to moan after every thrust. With her eyes closed and her body not under her control, she gives in to Duke's touch with a big smile on her face. The two continue their passionate night of sex with Terricka's moans and screams filling the apartment throughout the night.

CHAPTER 10

Collateral Damage

The school day has barely started at Palm Middle School as Officer Murphy finds himself sitting in the waiting area to see the school's principal, Mr. Warren. Murphy's wife, Shannon, had received a call from the school earlier that morning notifying her that their son, David, had been in a fight with another student. Since she has returned to work, Murphy volunteered to meet with the principal. As he waits, he looks around the school, which looks much different from what he remembers when he attended years back. A lot of technology with computers and cameras were the biggest differences he notices. The school seems much more secure as he remembers the times he would duck authority figures in order to cut class. He chuckles, reminiscing about better days, wishing he were back then now. His nostalgia is short-lived, as the principal's assistant approaches him, and leads him into Mr. Warren's office. Once he arrives, he notices his son is already in the office and takes a seat after shaking Mr. Warren's hand.

"Mr. Murphy, glad you can make it," Mr. Warren says, with his glasses on the edge of his nose. "I'm sorry to have to disturb you today, but with today's unfortunate events, I feel we needed to sit down and discuss David's incident personally."

"No problem, sir. Thank you for contacting us," Murphy responds, looking on to his son, who has his arms folded, avoiding eye contact.

"Let's get down to it then. Before school started, David had an altercation with another student. According to witnesses, the two begin shouting at each other when David threw a punch, which started the fight," Mr. Warren explains.

"David, is this true?" Murphy asks his defiant son, who refuses to speak.

Murphy grabs his head with frustration before turning his attention back towards Mr. Warren.

"Mr. Warren, I'm sorry for all of this. David's normally not a disruptive child. I'm not sure what got into him. Is the other child alright?" Murphy inquires.

"Yes, nothing but a few scrapes and bruises. He's already been sent home for the day," Mr. Warren answers while removing his glasses. "As you know, the school's policy is a no-tolerance policy when it comes to fighting. David will be sent home with you today and suspended tomorrow as well. He will be able to rejoin class on Thursday. Any more altercations such as this can lead to further suspension or expulsion."

Murphy nods his head, turning to his son once again, trying to get anything out of him. Mr. Warren can tell Murphy is struggling to connect with his son.

"David, you mind giving me and your father a moment alone, please?" He politely asks.

David grunts as he quickly makes his way out of the office leaving his father and principal alone. Mr. Warren takes a deep breath before explaining David's altercation in more detail.

"Look, Mr. Murphy, I've seen the news, and read all the articles about the shooting," Mr. Warren explains. "As a black man, I'll be honest, I'm not happy to have you in my school right now. I would ask that any further contact with the school be with your wife instead of you."

"Say what?" A confused Murphy reacts. "You're telling me I'm not allowed on the school grounds?"

"No, Mr. Murphy, what I am telling you is that if there is a need for school contact in the future, it would be wise to send your wife instead," Mr. Warren repeats. "I'm still gathering the details, but the altercation in the yard seems to have started because of you."

Murphy is stunned as Mr. Warren wipes his glasses off.

"Apparently, the classmate David had the altercation with, who is black, was criticizing you to your son when the exchange became heated. Your son threw the first punch, defending your honor, I suppose," Mr. Warren explains to a stunned Murphy. "My only concern is for David's wellbeing, but this probably won't be the first time he's going to hear hurtful things about his father."

"Look, Mr. Warren, I'm sorry David did what he did, and I'll discuss that with him, believe me, but you can't ban me from coming to the school in support of my son," Murphy fires back.

"No, I don't suppose we can. Why not embarrass him further so all the kids start to distance themselves from him," Mr. Warren fires back. "In case you were wondering, this is a majority minority-based campus, and with the way things are going now with the protests and whatnot, who's to say this won't happen again?"

Mr. Warren can see the anger in Murphy's eyes growing before he starts to pull back.

"All I'm saying, Mr. Murphy, kids today with their social media look for reasons to pick at a child. We're doing our best to battle cyberbullying, but kids are going to do what kids do. You being here only adds to it."

An upset Murphy wants to respond, but being that he's in enough hot water over the shooting, he decides to let it go.

"You have a nice day," Murphy says with his eyes full of anger as he walks out of the office.

Just outside of the office in the waiting area, Murphy looks over towards David and waves him over.

"Let's go," he says, frustratingly.

David sighs before following his father out of the school and into his truck.

Halfway into their drive, Murphy has calmed down a bit,

looking towards his son, who hasn't said a word the entire drive thus far. Murphy keeps hearing his wife's voice in the back of his head, begging him to talk with his son over the incident. He tried a couple of times to approach him but never had the right words to say. After the fight, he knows it's time to let go, and discuss what happened that night when the world changed for him and his family.

"So, you wanna talk about it?" He asks David, who is still avoiding eye contact, and remains silent. "Mr. Warren told me what you were fighting about. David, I don't want you getting into altercations because of me. You could have hurt that kid."

"What am I supposed to do when they're crackin' on me?!" David exclaims, finally breaking his silence. "I'm being told by all my friends that my father is a racist, and kills black people! They said I'm probably a racist too! Everyone treating me like I'm some KKK member!"

A stunned Murphy tries to maintain his composure as he continues to navigate down the street.

"So is that what you think? That I'm a racist?" Murphy questions.

"I didn't say that. You did kill that unarmed black kid though," David points out. "It's all over the news. The news wouldn't lie about that."

Murphy has heard enough as he slowly pulls off to the side of the road. David looks around confused as his father tries to gather his thoughts.

"Dad, what are you doing?" David asks.

"Son, I should have talked with you about this a long time ago," Murphy starts off. "First, I'll admit it, I did shoot that kid. I didn't go out there to maliciously kill someone, but I did it. It was dark, and he lunged at me. I thought he had a weapon, and I shot him. I didn't shoot him because he's black. I shot him because I felt I was under attack."

The car is silent for a few moments, with David seeing his father in a new light.

"I keep replaying the event in my head over and over again

wondering what I could have done differently," Murphy explains. "All I can think about is that he was only a few years older than you. It's something that has haunted me since that day, and will probably haunt me for the rest of my life."

An emotional Murphy fights back his tears as speaking about the shooting to his son has been more therapeutic than all the psychiatrists he's spoken to.

"The media is going to say what they're going to say because they have an agenda," Murphy says, shaking his head. "I know it can get frustrating, but you can't go out there fighting people over it. I've always told you that words don't mean anything! As long as nobody puts their hands on you, you walk away. David, I've arrested kids your age and even younger with weapons charges. If you attack the wrong kid, they won't hesitate to pull out their guns and shoot. I bust my ass to get you into a school like this in order for you not to have to face things like that, but nothing is guaranteed. I want you to promise me that you won't start fights, especially over this!"

"But dad, they are treating me like I'm a racist too! There's this girl in my class, Shalonda that I kinda like. We've been kickin' it and stuff, and everything was going well until the story started to make its way through the school," David explains, hoping his father will understand. "Now she's looking at me like the rest of the kids there. It's not fair! I'm being judged for things that's not even my fault!"

An agitated David turns away from his father, upset that his job has hurt his social status amongst his friends, especially Shalonda. Murphy sighs, realizing just how much his job impacts his son's daily life.

"I'm sorry, David," he apologizes. "I'm sorry my job has brought this on to you. I'm sure it's going to get worse before it gets better. This girl, this Shalonda, if she likes you, she'll see that real you, and not what the rest of the world sees."

Murphy's words fall on deaf ears, saddening the father.

"If you want, we can try another school maybe," Murphy offers. "I'll stay away, let your mother do all the school stuff so we can keep as much of the attention as we can off of you."

"No, dad. I'll be fine," David replies, finally looking towards his father. "I still have friends there who are cool no matter what people are saying about me. Like you said, if Shalonda really likes me, she'll come around. If not, oh well. I'm sorry I've been such a jerk. With the news stories and everything, I didn't know what to think about the shooting. I didn't think you were one of those types of cops, but maybe I bought into it a little with everyone else talking about it. I knew you weren't like that, and I'm sorry I acted like I did."

Murphy smiles as he leans over and hugs his son, with tears flowing down both of their faces. His son having his back meant the world to him, and with everything going on in his life, Murphy needed the love and support of his family more than ever. After a few moments, Murphy straightens himself out as he looks to continue down the road towards his house.

"Look, let me handle your mother on this," Murphy suggests. "She's going to flip her lid when she hears that you've been suspended. Let me talk to her first when she gets home so I can battle the drama for you. Sounds good?"

David chuckles and nods his head with agreement knowing his father is right about his mother's reaction. Clearing the air has been good for both Murphy and David, and while they don't know what the future may hold, they have each other and an understanding of what's to come. For now, that's all they need.

Back at Terricka's apartment, the lawyer has just awakened, still half nude from the night of pleasure that started on her couch and made its way into her room in the early morning hours. As she yawns, she looks towards the left of her bed and notices Duke is nowhere to be found. It's been a long time since she's let someone in close to her like she did the night prior, and she's a little stunned that Duke isn't there. Her thoughts are put to rest when she smells food throughout her room. She smiles as she makes her way to the bathroom to freshen up.

Ten minutes later, Terricka, wearing some sweat pants with

her pajama top, walks in and notices Duke cooking breakfast. She's impressed seeing sausage, grits, eggs, and pancakes all prepared by her lover.

"What's all this?" She asks, smiling as she takes a seat at the bar area.

"This is breakfast," Duke replies as he finishes the eggs.

"Shit, I didn't know I had all this stuff here," Terricka responds.

"Yeah, well I did have to make a quick trip to the store," Duke admits. "Had to pay the doorman to remember me so I could get back in."

Duke fixes Terricka a plate and hands it to her before heading to the fridge and getting her a glass of orange juice. She takes a bite of her food and is surprised at how good it is.

"Wow, you put your foot in this, I see," she responds before taking several more bites. "Shit, I may have to hire you full time as my personal chef."

"Well, before you go breaking out the checkbook, be aware that breakfast is the only thing that I know how to cook well," Duke says with a chuckle, fixing himself a plate. "When I was growing up, mom wouldn't play. Said if I wanted eggs, grits, and shit that I need to make it myself cause she's wasn't no chef. Surprised the hell out of her when I learned to do this on my own."

"My mom was the same way. My dad though, would take time out of his busy day to cook for his little princess," a smirking Terricka says. "Half the time, he'd just be getting in from running the streets before I headed out to school. He made sure I was taken care of, so I can never knock him for that."

Duke nods as he takes a seat next to her and starts in on his food as well. He can tell Terricka is being very cautious about what she says to him about her father.

"Sounds like he cares for you very much," he responds, hoping that she will open up.

"Yeah, he did," she replies, making sure to emphasize the 'did.'

As much as she likes Duke, Terricka isn't ready to open up to him about her secrets just yet. Damu always told her to distance herself from him to all others. It keeps her safe from any retaliation from his rivals, mainly the LAPD. She can tell that Duke has his suspicions, but for now, she decides to keep quiet.

"So, about last night," she says, changing the subject. "I can say that you're definitely not a thirty-second guy."

Duke chuckles as he takes a quick bite of his food.

"Thank you. Told you she was full of shit," he replies, referring to Martinez's alter ego, Angela.

"Yeah, well don't get all big head on me," Terricka quips with a giggle. "It felt nice to let go last night. It's been so long since I've had a night like that."

"Well, you should have them more often," Duke points out. "I mean, I don't mind being used for a sex buddy. Whenever you need to let loose, hit me up, and I'll be over in a heartbeat."

Duke's jokes cause Terricka to burst into laughter, giving her a sense of freedom she so yearned for. Her mood slightly changes as she knows that she can't continue to see Duke in that way.

"Listen, what happened last night was amazing, I'll admit that, but we can't continue on like that," she says, surprising Duke. "Duke, you're an amazing guy, but the second you walk out of that door, my mind is back on the cause. Truth be told, last night shouldn't have even happened, but with the wine and everything, I wasn't exactly myself."

Duke nods his head as if he knew this was coming.

"I get it. The cause is the cause, but when will it end?" He inquires. "I'm just saying, you gonna do this till you're old and gray? What about life? Family and kids? You're gonna just sacrifice all that for the cause?"

"Would you really wanna raise kids in a world like this?" Terricka asks. "All I can think about is what if one of my kids were killed on the streets by a cop? I wouldn't know what to do with myself. The cause is too important. I fight so another mother, father, sister, or brother don't have to worry about that."

"But at what cost?" Duke asks. "Terricka, the cause is what it is, but in between that, there's a thing called life. Life is love, sex, passion, fun, travel, and living. I understand you have a job to do, and it's important no doubt, but you need something else in life to remind you why you fight. Even the great ones, Martin, Malcolm, and Angela all had lives outside of their fights. It's okay, trust me."

Seemingly touched by Duke's words for a moment, Terricka sighs before shaking her head with disagreement, believing the fight is all there is for her.

"We'll agree to disagree on that point," she says before quickly finishing up her food.

A disappointed Duke sighs, disappointed in himself for not being able to get Terricka to see the full picture. He can tell she at least considered what he had said, but her stubbornness wouldn't allow her to budge from her stance. After finishing up his meal, he starts to grab their plates, when Terricka suddenly stops him.

"Leave it. I'll take care of it," she says. "It's the least I can do."

Duke nods his head as he rises from his stool and is about to walk off when Terricka pulls him back in, much to his surprise.

"Hey, I thought you said this can't happen again?" Duke says with a smile.

"What I said is once you walk out of that door, my mind is back to the cause," she corrects. "As far as I can tell, you haven't walked out of that door just yet."

An aggressive Terricka pulls him in close and unbuttons Duke's pants slightly before reaching her hand in and grasping his shaft. She slowly begins rubbing him, getting the reaction she is looking for as his manhood begins to harden quickly.

"There it is," she says with a smile. "Shall we dance once more?"

Duke shakes his head, smirking with disbelief. He quickly picks her up and walks to the bedroom. The two enjoy another lovemaking session before parting ways later that day.

Outside of their normal meeting spot is Martinez, looking on as the roles have been reversed with her being the one waiting for Duke's arrival. She impatiently looks around the area when she notices Duke making his way towards her. Martinez looks at him with an attitude as he hops into the car.

"Where the fuck were you?" She asks. "I've been out here for like forty-five minutes."

"Serves you right after that shit you pulled yesterday," Duke fires back, grinning. "You know you're dirty for real. Why would you tell that girl we dated, and I'm some thirty-second dude? Why were you even there?"

"I was there to see what weren't you telling me about your boo. It's my job to make sure you're not in over your head, remember?" Martinez reminds him. "As far as the thirty-second thing, I was hoping to run Ms. Loud Mouth off."

Martinez checks out Duke's chipper demeanor and shakes her head.

"However, I can tell that didn't work," she quips.

"Run her off? Why would you run her off? Unless you're trying to shoot your shot," Duke says with a cryptic smile.

"Please, I was just trying to do you a favor," Martinez fires back. "You're sleeping with the enemy. Her name is shit amongst cops, and if they find out y'all two are fucking... I don't even wanna go there."

"Hold up. Back up a second. Who said me and her were sleeping together?" Duke asks as Martinez starts the car.

"Well, the fact that you seemed to take offense with the term fucking by saying sleeping together is one sign," Martinez points out. "Also, you seem to be in a much chipper mood that suggests that you got rid of some frustration today, and finally, you smell strongly of soap as if you just took a shower not too long ago. All that points toward sex, but keep hiding it if you want. Moving on, are we gonna go check out this spot for your boy or what?"

Duke shakes his head, laughing in disbelief over Martinez's assessment of him. It shows that she has great detective skills, which he takes note of.

"I haven't heard anything, but I guess we can go stake out

the spot," Duke answers. "For the record, you forgot one other reason why you think I slept with her. The fact that your ass is jealous cause you missed your window. I'm not admitting nor denying I slept with her, but what I will say is that window is still open if you're interested."

Martinez rolls her eyes, giving her colleague a 'whatever' look before putting the car in drive and screeching down the street.

Hours later, Martinez and Duke are parked a few blocks away from the hospital that Damu and the rest of his crew run. He knew the hospital's location was in the middle of the surrounding area and took note knowing the path Jules and the others take when they leave. He didn't want to reveal the hospital's whereabouts and decided to instruct his partner to park several blocks away in order to maintain its secrecy. While Martinez is keeping a lookout in the area, Duke is in the back seat of the car keeping a low profile as he frustratingly checks out Fatboy lineup files, trying to identify the correct person. He grunts as he moves on to the next page.

"Un-fucking-believable!" He exclaims. "I swear to god half these fat bastards need to spend the rest of their life on a fucking treadmill! I'm gonna be all night looking through this shit!"

"Well, get comfortable because we may be here a while," Martinez replies, giggling at her partner's frustration. "Seems pretty quiet so far. Are you sure we're in the right spot?"

"Yeah, we've met out here a few times. I'm sure if he's back around, he'll show up soon," Duke says, turning to the next page of suspects.

The car goes quiet for a moment before a curious Martinez decides to break her silence.

"So, how was it hooking up with the other side?" she asks, confusing Duke.

"The other side?"

"Yeah, your lawyer friend, Terricka. I mean, she's on the other side when it comes to us and them, so I'm just wondering how was it?" A cryptic Martinez asks.

"Her again? Damn, you won't let shit die, will you?" Duke quips.

"Nah, I'm just bored," she points out. "We are gonna be here for a while, so I guess we might as well talk about something."

Duke sighs, and he closes the suspect file for a few moments. He thinks back to his and Terricka's night together, which puts a smile on his face. He then remembers that she's not looking for anything special right now, and the smile slowly fades away.

"Well?" An impatient Martinez pushes.

"I don't know. I mean, I didn't see the other side of her when we were together, allegedly," Duke replies, throwing the allegedly in there to avoid admitting he and Terricka slept together. "Well, I did, but I didn't if that makes sense. It's true, she's really passionate about her cause, and everything that comes with it. Kinda reminds me of you, a little."

Martinez looks at Duke as if she's offended being compared to Terricka.

"Reminds you of me?" She quips. "What could me and her possibly have in common?"

"Neither one of y'all like dirty cops, for starters," Duke points out. "She's willing to go to bat for what she believes in just as you did when you brought those dirty cops to justice. And allegedly, she screams while in bed, just like you."

Martinez looks at her counterpart strangely before bursting into laughter.

"You're a sick asshole, you know that right?" She says before turning her attention back towards the streets. "Doesn't surprise me that she's a screamer. She's loud enough for it. Figured it would bleed over to the sex life."

Duke shakes his head as he goes back into the file once more. Martinez thinks for a moment that she might have offended him with her comments.

"My bad, Duke. I don't wanna talk bad about the girl if y'all got something going on," she says.

"It's cool. There's nothing there to apologize for. Her cause is the only thing she's capable of giving herself to," Duke replies, almost as if he's disappointed by it. "Nobody's gonna challenge that."

"Don't sell yourself short. You never know. Maybe she'll come around and see the type of guy you are. Maybe you'll end up being enough," Martinez responds, surprising Duke with her kind words. "Either that or her cause will become your cause."

Duke nods his head understanding what his partner is trying to get him to understand.

"Yeah, well, I guess we'll see," he says, flipping to the next page of the file he is sorting through.

"I guess we will," a smirking Martinez quips. "Change of subject, I'm hungry as hell right now. There's a McDonalds a few blocks down. You mind if I step out and get me something?"

"Nah, I can use a break from looking at this damn file," Duke says, closing the document.

"You want anything?" Martinez asks before handing her binoculars to Duke.

"Hell nah, I don't eat that shit," Duke replies.

"You sure? I hear that it comes with a side of Terricka," teases Martinez.

"Girl, get the fuck outta here!" Duke fires back to his giggling partner as she steps out of the car.

After Martinez is gone, he repositions himself to get a good view of the area, looking through the binoculars hoping to locate their target.

About twenty minutes have gone by as Duke grabs his weary eyes, exhausted after trying to maintain tabs on the area. He yawns as fatigue starts to set in when he notices a familiar presence from the distance. He quickly takes out the binoculars and peers in, noticing Fatboy and several other Hand of God members walking down the street. Duke looks around for Martinez but doesn't see any sign of her. He watches as Fatboy and his crew get into a nearby vehicle. Fearing he's going to lose his lead, Duke picks up the radio and calls out looking for Reid.

"Six eight four zero, you copy? Six eight four zero, you

copy?" he says, waiting for a response.

"I got you, copy," Reid responds.

"Hey, have a suspect, male in his twenties, six-foot, roughly three hundred fifty pounds getting into a vehicle with friends here in Nickerson Gardens, looks to be a white Hyundai, license plate number lima, three, lima, lima, zero, whiskey, copy," Duke says verifying the plates through the binoculars.

"Roger that, white Hyundai, plates lima, three, lima, lima, zero, whiskey in Nickerson Garden. Which direction are they heading?" Reid inquires.

"Looks to be heading towards East One Fourteenth Street. Repeat, heading towards East One Fourteenth Street, over," Duke says, watching the vehicle make its way down the street.

"Ten-four, we'll have eyes on the suspect momentarily. Meet me on channel twenty one, channel twenty-one," Reid responds.

Duke quickly changes the channel on his radio as instructed.

"Yeah, it's me," he says.

"Is this who I think it is?" Reid asks.

"He's one of two parties that were involved with the Williams shooting," Duke explains. "He's not the main guy, but he can lead us to the main guy."

"Alright, sit tight. We'll take care of it," Reid responds.

"Negative. This is my collar. Need the suspect in custody to question," Duke replies.

"And I'm tellin' you to hang back! We'll take it from here. Six eight four zero out!" Reid says, frustrating Duke. He slams down the radio and quickly jumps into the driver's seat, reeving up the car, ready for pursuit. He's about to pull off when he notices Martinez making her way down the block. He quickly pulls the car up to his confused partner and lowers his window.

"Get in!" he yells.

Martinez quickly jumps into the passenger side of the vehicle as best she can while holding her food and drink in her hands. As soon as her door closes, Duke puts the pedal to the metal screeching his tires before making his way down the street, trying to make up ground on Fatboy.

"What the fuck is going on?" A confused Martinez asks.

"I had eyes on Fatboy," Duke explains. "I'm trying to catch up to him before Reid does!"

Martinez is stunned as she puts her meal down.

"You called Reid on this?" She questions.

"Yeah! I didn't want to, but you were nowhere around, and I didn't wanna lose him!" Duke points out. "After talking with him though, it seems like he's trying to cut me out of my collar! Said he would handle it."

Martinez seems worried as she looks around the area.

"Alright, what am I looking for?" She asks.

"White Hyundai with a three hundred fifty pound black man driving it," Duke says, continuing to speed his way down the block.

After a few minutes, Duke spots the vehicle making its way down the street.

"Shit, that's it right there!" He yells, pointing it out to Martinez.

The car is in the far right lane and is turning, much to Duke's disgust. He's in the far left lane with two cars in-between him and is unable to maneuver around them. Martinez quickly writes a description of the vehicle down and the plate number.

"Shit!" Duke yells as he tries to get over as fast as he can.

"Careful, Duke! You're gonna get us killed!" Martinez says, holding on for dear life in the car.

Duke maneuvers the car right two blocks away from where Fatboy had turned. He tries to make his way back towards the street Fat Boy was on, but is unable to at his position since the connecting street is a one-way street going the opposite direction. A frustrated Duke pulls over to the side of the road and bangs his fist on the dashboard.

"Son of a bitch," he yells out in frustration.

Martinez thinks for several minutes before picking up the radio and changing the dial to a different channel.

"Seventy-Six, this is Zero Nine, come in," she says to the

radio, confusing Duke.

"Zero nine, I got you, copy," a dispatcher's voice says on the other side of the radio.

"Hey, I need a twenty on six-eight four zero, can you copy," she says, awaiting a response.

"Stand by," the dispatcher replies as Duke continues to look at his partner strangely.

"Who are you talking to?" He asks.

"I told you I was sent here to keep tabs on Reid and his thugs. In certain circumstances, I'm allowed to reach out and find out their location if I think something illegal is going on," she explains. "It's a secure IA channel that very few know about. If we don't get to the suspect first, he's dead. Trust me."

Duke is stunned as the two officers wait patiently for a response from the dispatcher. After a few moments, Martinez is about to lose hope until the radio chirps.

"Zero nine, I have six-eight four zero's car at the Hacienda Village area. Close to the corner of Compton Avenue and One-O-Fourth street. You copy?" the dispatcher responds.

"Ten-four, Compton ave, and one-o-fourth street. Thank you," Martinez says as Duke quickly heads off towards the direction given to them.

Ten minutes later, Duke pulls up to the location, which stuns him and Martinez, who are at a loss of words with what they see.

"Dear God," Duke says, still stunned at the scene he's witnessing.

Both he and Martinez are in a state of shock, unsure of what to do next with what they've just observed.

CHAPTER 11

Enough

Reid, Slater, and the other Terror Squad members are sitting at their desks in their safe house going over some paperwork when Martinez and an angered Duke make their way into the building.

"So this is where you are your thugs hang out?" Martinez comments, looking around the space, noticing the griminess of the area. "Suits you. Dirty as fuck."

"Fuck you, Martinez," Slater says, rising from his desk, approaching both her and Duke. "What the fuck are you two doing here anyway?!"

"Relax, Slate, I told them to meet us here," Reid says as he quickly gets between the bunch. "They were summoned here, just like you were, so take a seat and chill out."

Slater grunts, but does as he's told, slowly making his way back over to his desk. Reid turns his attention to his guests and smiles.

"Can I get you two anything while we wait?" He asks.

"I don't want shit from you!" Duke fires back with anger in his eyes. "Not after the bullshit you pulled!"

"Look, I told you to hang back while we took care of this," Reid says, rolling his eyes. "What happened couldn't be helped. If you read the report, you'd see-"

"Fuck your report!" Duke exclaims as he gets into Reid's face. "He was a lead! He could have led us to the real killer, or even better, flipped, which could have ended this case!"

"The man opened fire on me and my men. We did what was necessary to get the job done. Now if you have a problem with my methods, maybe you need to file an official complaint," Reid replies, not backing down.

The two men are heated when in walks Billick and Irvin.

"That's enough, you two!" Billick yells, getting the attention of both men.

He looks around the area and notices a few members of Reid's crew who were not part of the official circle of trust in terms of the investigation.

"Explain yourself, Reid," Billick commands. "Why are all these men here?"

"The cats out of the bag, sir, with all due respect," Reid fires back. "Your guy broke his cover last night showing up at the scene last night. All my men are vetted, and I trust these men with my life."

"I don't give a damn if they're vetted or not, get them out of here!" Exclaims Billick.

Reid sighs before looking at his men and nodding them off. A disgruntled Slater also walks out leaving Duke, Martinez, and Reid alone with Billick and Irvin. The commissioner takes a look at the area and shakes his head before turning his attention towards Duke and Reid.

"What the fuck happened out there last night?" He asks. "Was that the guy who killed Officer Williams?"

"Sir, he was part of a group who killed Williams," Duke explains. "The main suspect is still at large at this time. The plan was to arrest the suspect known as Fatboy and work him for a location on the leader of the attack. Apparently, Sergeant Reid had other ideas."

Billick turns his attention towards Reid, waiting for an explanation.

"Well, Sergeant. I'm waiting," the commissioner says, looking for answers.

Reid sighs before backing away from Duke and begins to recall the incident.

"Me and the boys were out at a local burger shop, starting wind down for the day when we received a call from your undercover," he says, starting from the beginning.

*****

Reid, Slater, and a few other members of his squad are sitting at an In and Out Burger restaurant laughing and joking with each other while enjoying their meals. Reid is at the center of the group, entertaining his fellow officers when he receives the call from Duke on his dispatch radio.

"I got you, copy," he says as he distances himself slightly so he can better hear Duke. "Roger that, white Hyundai, plates lima, three, lima, lima, zero, whiskey in Nickerson Garden. Which direction are they heading?"

Reid snaps his fingers, grabbing the attention of Slater who makes his way over towards him while he continues to listen to Duke's message.

"Ten-four, we'll have eyes on the suspect momentarily. Meet me on channel twenty one, channel twenty-one," Reid responds before switching radio channels and turning his attention to Slater. "Get the boys ready, we may have our guy here."

Slater nods his head before running off to let the rest of the team know what's going on. Duke checks in once again as Reid goes to his radio once more.

"Is this who I think it is," Reid questions, seeking confirmation.

A cryptic smile enters his face after Duke tells him he's one of the suspects of the William's shooting.

"Alright, sit tight, we'll take care of it," Reid instructs as he heads over to his unmarked vehicle with Slater driving.

Reid becomes irritated as Duke pushes back towards him wanting the collar for himself.

"And I'm tellin' you to hang back! We'll take it from here. Six eight four zero out!" Reid exclaims before cutting off his radio.

"I'm gettin' sick of his shit," Slater warns as he starts the car.

"Don't worry about him. He gave us what we need. I'll get the boys to run back and ping where that last transmission came from later, but first thing's first," Reid says before going into the glove box and pulling out a separate radio that's used between him and his squad. "Alright, fellas, seems like we have a suspect who was involved in William's death. Let's honor one of ours and get this asshole!"

Reid gives out the license plate number, car description, and last known heading to his squad, who all speed off in three separate cars heading to intercept Fatboy's car.

Around fifteen minutes later, Reid notices the vehicle in his sights, double-checking the license plate number, just outside of the Hacienda Village area. He goes back to his secret radio to alert his team.

"That's them. Gonna flash them, you know what to do," he says as he turns on his police lights.

Fatboy quickly pulls over his car to the side of the road, as Slater pulls up behind him. Reid nods his head as Slater takes point, getting out of his car and approaching Fatboy and his crew. Fatboy lowers his window, shaking his head, feeling as though he's being harassed.

"Officer, I know I wasn't speeding or anything, so why are you doggin' me here?" he asks.

"I need you to step out of the vehicle, sir," Slater says with his hand on his holstered gun.

"Man, I ain't steppin' out of shit," a defiant Fatboy responds. "I ain't do shit, and I know my rights. So unless you got something official, I suggest you break out and leave me on my way."

"Really? Did you extend the same courtesy to Officer Williams?" Slater asks with the other two cars of the Terror Squad all pulling up and quickly jumping out of their vehicles with their guns aimed squarely at Fatboy and his crew.

Fatboy shows a little nervousness for the first time, looking back at his crew before turning his attention back towards Slater.

"I don't know what you're talking about," he says, causing Slater to smirk.

"No, I guess not," Slater says before moving outside of the line of fire, signaling his team. "He's all yours, boys!"

Before Fatboy has a chance to react, all the officers open fire at his car killing not only Fatboy but the other three members of the crew that were riding along with him. After a barrage of shots, Slater raises his hand, signaling a cease fire. He walks over and checks to make sure his victims were dead. Satisfied with the results, he looks over towards Wachowski, one of his team members.

"Yo, Wack, you're up," Slater responds.

Wachowski nods his head and quickly pops the trunk to his vehicle. He takes out a duffle bag filled with automatic weapons and makes his way over to Fatboy's car. He makes sure to plant the weapons on each of the members with the exception of Fatboy. He takes the last weapon and hands it to Slater, who quickly aims it at one of the vehicles the Terror Squad arrived in and fires several rounds into it. He then takes the weapon and plants it into Fatboy's hand to complete the setup. Reid chuckles as he exits the vehicle and looks over the crime scene.

"Nice boys, very nice," he says before looking at Fatboy in more detail. "Damn, this is a big fella, isn't he? Sure we got enough bullets in him?"

Slater laughs before taking out his pistol and firing one shot into the lifeless body of Fatboy. Duke and Martinez pull up just as Slater fired the shot and look on, stunned at what they're seeing. Reid taps Slater on the shoulder to make him aware they were being watched by both Martinez and Duke. The team leader turns on the charm as he makes his way over towards Martinez and Duke, trying to explain what happened.

*****

Duke laughs, stunned with disbelief after hearing Reid's version of what happened.

"What's so fuckin' funny?" An irritated Reid questions. "Those animals fired first! You think it's funny to put men in the line of fire like that?!"

"I'm laughing because your story is bullshit!" Duke fires back.

"You know god damn well they didn't fire at you. Hell, we pulled up and saw your psycho friend put a bullet in Fatboy's head ourselves!"

"The man was already dead when Slater fired that shot. He was a little frustrated after being shot at, and let one-off. It was inappropriate, yes, and I plan to personally reprimand him for his actions," Reid says, causing Duke to throw his hands in the air, frustrated.

"Sir, all due respect, but this isn't what I signed up for," Duke says to Billick. "I can't do my job if this man is running things. He and his crew's tactics are highly questionable. I wasn't a part of a hit squad back in Cincinnati, and I damn well won't be in one here!"

Billick sighs and he nods his head. He looks at the others in the room considering his next words carefully.

"Leave us," he says to the others.

Reid, Martinez, and Irvin all walk out of the room leaving Duke alone with the commissioner. Billick takes a seat at the edge of a nearby desk before addressing his subordinate.

"I know Reid's tactics maybe a little reckless at times, but he's the type of man you want on your side when the shit hits the fan," Billick explains.

"Sir, he killed the suspect along with the others in that car, who as far as we know weren't even involved with The Hand," retorts Duke. "Plus, killing the suspect throws me off my investigation of locating the main target. He and his crew are out of control."

"I hear ya, I hear ya," Billick says, trying to calm his officer. "I'll have a talk with him. Make sure he considers your investigation before going off half-cocked in the future. As far as him killing the suspect, per his report, everything seems on the up and up. The review board will look into it, I'm sure, but I don't see this going any further than that."

Duke shakes his head, amazed at what he's hearing.

"Sir, all due respect, he shot and killed those men!" Duke reaffirms once again. "I'm not buying it for one second that Fatboy shot first! I know the guy; he doesn't have it in him. He wouldn't do something like that unless he was ordered to."

"Were you there when the shooting went down?" The commissioner asks. "Cause if you weren't, then how do you know what went down?"

"I saw the shot into Fatboy's head when it was all over," Duke confirms. "Both me and Martinez saw that."

"And he explained what happened there. Like he said, Officer Slater will be reprimanded for his actions, so he's not going to get off scot-free," Billick responds.

Duke shakes his head in defiance, regretting taking on the job. He knew what he had seen, and he saw that both Reid and Slater took pleasure in taking the life of Fatboy and the others. Billick can tell that Duke isn't buying in with what he's saying and decides to take a different approach.

"Look, Officer Mitchell, remember why you're here," Billick quips, standing up. "We made you an offer to assist us with a problem. It took you longer to get in than we had thought, but you did manage to get in. So far, you haven't thrown us anything outside of this Fatboy suspect. I'm wasting man-hours protecting Officer Murphy based on your word and lost another two officers in Williams and his partner with no end game in sight. You want to impress me? Bring me that son of a bitch's head on a platter! Do your fucking job! If you can't do it, we still have an open file on you, and can go the other way with the charges if you want."

Billick's intimidation causes Duke to back down as he has no leverage to present. He sees what this investigation is all about, but at the moment, there's nothing he can do.

"Fine," Duke says begrudgingly. "You just make sure to keep your dog on the leash."

Billick chuckles, playfully punching Duke on the shoulder.

"Teamwork, that's the spirit," he says. "Now go on. Get out of here. I'm sure there's talk in The Hand about what's transpired. Let's see if Damu makes an emotional decision."

Duke nods his head and makes his way out of the room. When

he exits, he notices Reid is entertaining his men on the far end of the parking lot, laughing as if nothing happened. Martinez, who is leaning on her car and notices Duke walking out. She also sees the expression on his face and quickly makes her way over to distract him.

"Let it go, Duke. Let it go," she says, pulling at his arm.

Duke sighs as he's lead away from Reid and his bandits and back towards Martinez's car.

"How can you be okay with this shit?" He asks his partner. "I know what we saw, and they're going to get off with a fucking reprimand? Are they serious?"

"I know. It sucks, I get it. There's not a whole lot we can do, especially with the commissioner calling the shots," Martinez explains as they both watch Billick exit the building and joins Reid and the others. "I mean, you can file an official complaint, and it would have to go to the mayor since the commissioner is a part of the problem. You really think with your history that the mayor is gonna go for it?"

A frustrated Duke sighs when he notices Deputy Commissioner Irvin sitting in his car looking towards Reid and Billick. He looks as though he's not exactly thrilled with the situation as well. After making a mental note of Irvin's seemingly displeasure, he and Martinez get into her car and quickly making their way out of the parking lot and down the road.

Later that day, Duke is making his way down towards the Nickerson Garden Projects. He received a text from Terricka to meet her there, which is odd since they've normally only met at the hospital. He knows the meeting is probably about Fatboy's death, and after what happened between him and Reid earlier that day, he's conflicted about what he should do. He's thought about coming clean to Terricka and warn her about Reid and the others but realizes it's his feelings driving that way of thinking. Damu is still a criminal, and the sole organizer of multiple cop kills in the past. As much as he wants out from under Billick and Reid, right is right, and Damu and his followers needed to be stopped. As he approaches the address Terricka told him to come to, he's stopped at the front door by one of Damu's body-guards.

"Arms out, nigga. You know the drill," the bodyguard says.

Duke shakes his head but complies as he reaches out his hands to be searched. While he's being patted down, Terricka walks out of the building and frowns, quickly stopping the bodyguard.

"What the fuck are you doing?!" She exclaims.

"Damu's rules. He said no exceptions," the bodyguard responds.

"He's with me! He doesn't need to-"

"It's alright, Terricka. Let the man do his job," Duke replies, interrupting as he holds his arms out.

The bodyguard finishes patting him down before nodding him to move on. Terricka shoots the bodyguard a dirty look before leading Duke inside the building.

"Damn, what's that all about?" Duke questions as if he didn't know.

"Fatboy, Michael, Ed, and Q were all killed last night," a distraught Terricka replies. "All of them, gunned down in the middle of the fuckin' street!"

Duke acts as though he's stunned to hear the news as he and Terricka enter the back room, which is filled with about fifteen members of The Hand of God. Everyone is discussing the shooting incident amongst themselves, taking it as an act of war. Terricka leads Duke to the back corner of the room and looks at the unrest her people are showing. She shakes her head with sadness, knowing things are only going to get worse from here.

"It's starting," she says, scared to face the future. "A lot of people are going to die."

"Going to die? Who? Terricka, what aren't you telling me," inquires Duke.

Before Terricka can reply, Damu walks in with several Hand soldiers by his side, causing the room to go quiet as they wait for their commander's words. Damu looks around the room, fighting to contain his rage, before addressing his crew.

"As I'm sure you all have heard by now, last night we lost four of our members. The LAPD once again flexed their muscle and took out Cornell, or Fatboy as he's known to those that knew him, Michael, Ed, and Q. Now, the police said that these men were all armed and shot first, but we all knew these men. None of them were armed at the time of the shooting, and even if they were, none of them were dumb enough to shoot at a police squad car after being pulled over!" Damu exclaims as the room fills with chatter, all agreeing with their leader's points.

"This wasn't just a typical traffic stop! No, this was an act of war by the LAPD! This was a message sent to us to scare us, and flex on us hoping we'll back down! Let me tell you something, no matter what the LAPD throws at us, we are not going to back down! No, what we're gonna do is we're gonna push even harder! We have them running scared right now, which is why they felt the need for this cowardice attack! Blood must be answered in blood, and we're gonna make sure that Fatboy, Michael, Ed, and Q's deaths are avenged!"

The crowd's cheers and support fill the room as Damu shakes his head, knowing his followers are behind him.

"I'm fuckin' glad to hear that!" A voice says from the doorway, grabbing Damu and the other's attention.

Jules walks in the room, with his eyes filled with rage as well making his first appearance since he and Damu's falling out.

"Yeah, I'm real fuckin' glad to hear that," he says as he walks into the front of the room next to Damu. "The question is what's our next move? I'm tired of this sitting on the sideline shit! I want these bastards to bleed for this shit! So what are you gonna do about it, nigga?"

Damu smiles, thrilled to see his second in command back. He reaches into his pocket and hands Jules a sheet of paper.

"I have in my possession the safe house that Reid and his bandits are hiding at," Damu says, stunning Duke and all those in the room.

They have been looking for Reid and his Terror Squad members for months, and to finally have their whereabouts is a big win for The Hand. Terricka gasps, stunned that her father hadn't told her about this before the meeting. Jules looks at the address with a sinister grin, nodding his head. He's been dreaming about taking out Reid and the others for quite some time, and with that one sheet of paper in his possession, he's able to make his dreams come true.

"Fuck yeah," he says, looking towards Damu. "I'm ready to ride on these niggas, for real."

"And you shall, young brotha. You shall," Damu responds. "Get a surveillance team together. I want each side of that building checked out. Who comes in, who goes out, shift changes, I want to know it all."

Jules looks at his leader as if he's offended by the orders given.

"Surveillance? Man, get the fuck outta here with that bullshit!" He exclaims, surprising his leader. "These niggas took out my friends. I'm not tryin' to sit around and watch them. I'm looking for action!"

"Jules, I understand that you're upset, as are we all, but don't be foolish," Damu quips, chastising his second in command. "You run in there guns a blazing, you're gonna get yourself killed!"

"Nah, I don't see it like that. We outnumber them by quite a bit. If we storm the place, there's no way they could stop us in time," Jules retorts before looking towards the rest of the group. "How many of our people have fallen to these muthafuckas? Specifically, this crew? We've been waiting for far too long to take these fools out, and now that we finally have a lead on them, he wants us to wait?! Is that what you want to do?!"

There is a slight discussion between the group amongst themselves, some agree with Damu's caution, and some looking for action, just as Jules. Jules looks at his leader once more, hoping he will see things his way.

"Damu, I owe you my life for all the things that you've done for me. I love you, my brother, but you're wrong about this,"

Jules says to his boss, respectfully. "I'm sorry, but I can't follow your path any longer. I'm ready to act, and it's time to show these pigs that there's consequences for their actions. Please, brother, reconsider."

Damu shakes his head in refusal, disappointing Jules.

"I'm sorry, old friend. You're making a mistake if you're thinking on moving on Reid that way. You will not survive," Damu warns.

"Listen to Damu," Duke yells from the back of the room, infuriating Jules even more. "Reid and his crew may be dirty, but they've been trained! You can't go in there not expecting a huge casualty count! Too many unknowns behind those walls!"

"Man, fuck you!" Jules fires back angrily. "You just scared we gonna knock off more of your kind. I expect that shit coming from you!"

"What about me, Jules?" Terricka says, stepping up. "You know me. I have more hatred for Reid and his thugs than anyone else in this room! I would love nothing more than to see them get what they deserve, but not like this, Jules. We have to be smart about this."

"You never really was about this life," Jules points out. "All your court cases, suits filed, and meetings with the top brass and for what? Niggas are still gettin' killed daily. Now that we finally have what we've wanted, now that revenge is so close, you want me to back down? I guess you really are daddy's little girl."

"It doesn't have anything to do with me and my father's relationship!" Terricka snaps back. "This has to do with what's smart, and what's stupid! We will continue to fight in the courts and everywhere else, but what you're proposing is suicide! Plain and simple!"

Jules chuckles, disappointed with his old friend's response. All of the respect he once had for both her and Damu is gone.

"Remember in one of your speeches not too long ago, you said *'Better to die on your feet, than live on your knees'*? I'm done crawling," Jules replies before turning his attention to the rest of the group. "Y'all are gonna have to make a choice. Either we continue to live on our knees, or we take the fight to them! It's time to step the fuck up! So who's gonna ride with me to take out the pigs that killed our friends?"

After a brief discussion, around ten of the attending members decide to join Jules's side as they rise and take their place behind their new leader. A smirking Jules looks back at his former leader Damu as if he's taunting him.

"There you have it," Jules says. "The people have spoken. Action is what we need, brother. I hope you find peace from the sidelines."

Jules makes his way out of the room, with his supporters following close behind. Duke, knowing that Jules and his crew are about to make a mistake, is about to catch up with him when Terricka pulls his arm.

"What are you doing?" She asks.

"I've got to stop this," he says. "Stay with your father. I can't let him do this!"

Terricka tries to hold Duke back, but he jerks his arm away from her and runs out of the building, looking to chase down Jules. She also realizes that Duke knows her secret about Damu being her father, and can tell he's bothered by her holding that back from him.

Outside of the building, Jules and his supporters are scattering, as he assigns each team a car, prepping to go onto the hunt. Duke notices him and quickly approaches Jules hoping to convince him against the attack.

"Jules, you can't do this shit!" He exclaims to an unconcerned Jules. "These men are trained, and even if you get the drop on them, they will win!"

"Oh, and we're not trained?" Jules snaps back. "You forget there's a lot of military soldiers part of the team. I don't even know why I'm discussing this shit with your ass."

Jules turns to walk away when Duke pulls him back.

"Listen to me, man! You're leading these people to their deaths!" Duke exclaims. "I'm sorry you lost your friend, but how many more have to die before you see this is the wrong approach? A real leader thinks of his men before his vengeance."

Hate has filled Jules's heart, and he's not going to allow anyone to deter him from his self-anointed path of justice, especially a former police officer.

"There will be blood tonight one way or the other. Either you get the fuck out of my face, or be the first victim to add to the spilled blood," a threatening Jules responds, standing toe to toe with Duke.

The two men size each other up for a moment as Jules waits for Duke to make his move. Duke can tell there's nothing he can do to prevent the ex-Hand member from backing off his attack. He backs down, allowing Jules to go about his way, shaking his head with confusion. While he despises Reid and everything that he and his Terror Squad stand for, he isn't about to let them get into a gunfight that would end many of The Hand's members' lives. As Jules and his crew load into their vehicles, Duke makes his way down the block to a secluded area before pulling out his cell phone. He dials Reid's number and waits for an answer.

Back at the safe house, Reid and his team are working on paperwork from their desks when his cell phone suddenly rings. He checks the caller ID and rolls his eyes before answering.

"What the hell do you want?" Reid asks, knowing it's Duke calling him.

"Listen, your cover's been blown! I don't know how, but they know where you're at!" Duke warns.

"Who?" Reid questions.

"Hand of God members! They know where you're at, and there are about ten guys on the way to your location now! You need to get your men out of there before it's too late!"

Reid stands from his desk and looks around, deciding on their next move.

"Thanks for the warning," he says before hanging up the line.

He looks at his crew, who are all looking at him, confused about what's going on.

"Gear up, fellas. We're about to have company," Reid says.

A smirking Slater nods his head before jumping up from his desk to get prepared for the attack.

Back in Nickerson Garden, Damu and Terricka are sitting with each other after the rest of the crew has cleared out. Both are showing concern in their eyes, wondering if the cause is done.

"I can't believe after everything you've done for him that he would do that to you," Terricka says with a few tears in her eyes. "What are we gonna do?"

"We will continue to move forward," Damu says. "This doesn't change anything. We still have a job to do, and we're going to see it out till the end."

"With what people? Jules took some of our best men! And what will happen if they do pull this off? They will taint everything we've been fighting for," Terricka responds to her father. "I mean, we're lacking leaders now. You can't be everywhere at once."

Damu nods his head, understanding where his daughter is coming from. He knows Jules has hit The Hand of God with a devastating blow, which the group will struggle to recover from. Still, he has faith that he's doing the right thing, and it will correct itself in due time.

"People can be replaced. Even me one day," Damu says while considering the future. "What do you think about Duke?"

Terricka looks at him, confused about why he would ask her such a question.

"Duke? What about him?" She asks.

"I'm thinking about him taking Jules's place at my side," Damu responds, stunning his daughter.

"Are you serious?" She asks. "We don't know him like that! He's already shown he's not ready to do the dirty work. I mean, I like him and all, but not like that," Terricka responds.

"I think you like him a little more than you're letting on," Damu deduces. "It's true, he may not have the nerve for the dirty work, but he's a level head. Someone that can keep us honest. I've had him working with the youngsters, and they're following his lead. He knows how to be a leader, and besides, it's not like I'm going to be doing this forever."

"Don't speak like that, dad," an emotional Terricka responds. "I hate it when you do that."

"Always looking to the future, my dear," Damu responds with a smile. "We should never fear what the future holds, but we should always do our best to plan for it. Never in a million years did I think I'd be the leader of the social justice cause like I am today. With you, I've never been prouder how you've turned out, and I'm sure D-Rag would be proud of how Duke turned out as well."

Terricka sighs, nodding her head, thinking about Duke, and if he's the one to lead them into the next stage. Damu's smile slowly fades as he looks at his daughter, wanting to get something off his chest for quite some time.

"I never wanted this life for you, you know," he admits to his daughter. "I'm proud of you, and everything that you've accomplished, but Terricka, this is not the thing I want you to spend the rest of your life on."

A stunned Terricka looks on as if she's offended.

"Oh, so it's fine for Duke to live the life, but for me, it's not good enough?" She fires back.

"No father wishes such a hard life on his daughter," Damu replies. "When it comes to that, I'm like every other father. I wanted to see you with your own family, having my grandkids, and living a normal life. The reason I'm fighting is for you and your future kids to have a better life. I never imagined you joining the fight, but there you were just as militant as I was. I've told you before, I never want you to have to take a life or be a part of that side of the business. Be a social justice lawyer, fight for your people in the courtroom. This other stuff, however, I think it's time for you to put it all behind you."

Terricka is almost in tears once again, knowing that when her father says *'I think it's time'* he really means that she's done with The Hand. Damu knew that this is the beginning of the end with Jules leaving, but didn't want to admit it to his daughter.

"Dad... I'm... I...,"

"I'm sorry, Terricka. The heat Jules is going to draw is going to be catastrophic. I can't let you be a part of this anymore. After I take out this Officer Murphy, the one who is in charge of Jamie Powell's death, I'm going to go underground for a while. There will be no peace for me. No time soon anyway. I don't want you involved anymore," Damu says to a devastated Terricka.

He hugs his daughter, as the two embrace one last time before quickly making his way out of the room. A distraught Terricka bursts into tears knowing she may never see her father again. The cause that she loves so much is abruptly leaving her, and the pain of losing it is too much for her to handle. Several moments later, Duke makes his way back into the building and notices Terricka sobbing. He initially is there to go at her for not telling him about her father. Seeing her in the state she's in, however, he decides against it as she slowly looks up towards him, her face still drenched in tears. The two are silent as Duke makes his way over towards her, unsure of what to say. After a few moments, Terricka rushes into Duke's arms, crying profusely. Duke embraces her, not sure what's going on but willing to give the lawyer comfort in his arms.

CHAPTER 12

Smoke Them Out

A few days later, Deputy Irvin finds himself sitting at The Coffee Corner shop located next to the farmers market, enjoying a cup of coffee while he checks out the latest news on his tablet. The shop is a place where Irvin goes to unwind from the day to day operations of the precinct. It's just far enough away from his office that his anxiety can rest, and with the beautiful weather, it is a perfect day to sit at the outside table. His mood is ruined when he notices both Duke and Martinez approaching him. He sighs as the two partners stand, awaiting the Deputy Commissioner to acknowledge their presence.

"I come here on my lunch break to get away from the job," Irvin points out. "I suppose you two have a reason to be here."

"Yes, sir. Reid and his group must be taken down," Duke responds with a determined look in his eyes.

"Ah, this is about the night in question I take it," Irvin replies, closing his tablet, giving Duke and Martinez his undivided attention.

"It's about much more than that, sir," Martinez chimes in. "Reid and his crew are nothing more than a vigilante team at this point. They kill with impunity, and nobody's doing anything about it."

Irvin sighs, shaking his head having to deal with the situation from a few nights ago once again.

*****

On the night in question, Jules and his followers are just outside the Terror Squad's safe house. They all have black masks on covering their faces and are hand signaling each other instructions as half the men remain with Jules, and the other half head towards the back entrance. Jules waves one of his supports forward, who lowers his weapon and works at picking the lock. The others wait patiently with their weapons drawn, looking around the area to make sure they aren't noticed. After a few moments, the locksmith opens the door, much to Jules's delight. Jules takes the lead as he and the others quietly enter the building.

It's pitch black in the building as Jules, and the others tiptoe through the building, making sure a sound isn't heard while they slowly approach. They get deeper and deeper into the building and make it to the main area where Reid and the other's desk are located. Jules notices the other half of his team entering the area on the other side and signals them to hold their position as he tries to make sense of what's going on. There's only one slight strip of light giving the faintest light in the room from a street light outside the building. Jules and the others are confused, believing that they missed their chance.

"Looks like they're gone," one of the supporters says.

Before Jules can respond, the supporter's head bursts, as blood splatters everywhere, killing him. Jules and the others look around with their weapons drawn but don't see anything in the darkness. Two more Hand members fall to the ground after being fatally shot, as the rest of the group try to take cover as best they can. They are under attack as bullets whizzed by their heads. Jules takes cover under one of the desks in the area. He watches as one of his members fall in the aisle, his eyes looking towards Jules reaching out to him. Jules tries to make his way over to pull his follower from harm's way, but it's too late as the follower's body goes limp while the life slowly fades away from his eyes. A scared Jules doesn't know how to react as the gunshots get louder and louder. After a few moments, feeling he has nothing to lose, Jules decides to do his best and head for the exit. He breaks cover, firing multiple shots randomly in the area before trying to sprint out of the building. Before he can make it, he's gunned down with two bullets into his back sending him crashing towards the ground. He's struggling to hang on as Reid, and the others reveal themselves, wearing all black and night vision goggles. Reid looks around and notices Jules is the last of the crew still alive. He and the others remove their goggles as Reid motions to one of the Terror Squad members to cut the lights back on. With a smirk, both he and Slater approach the fallen Jules as Slater kicks the gun out of their would-be attacker's hands. He bends down and turns Jules over to make sure Reid can see Jules's eyes.

"Well, aren't you a piece of work," a smirking Reid says, bending down to get a better look. "I just want you to know that it was Duke who did this to you. He's working for us. Isn't that lovely?"

Jules's eyes are big angry that he's been betrayed. He knew they shouldn't have trusted him. Once a pig, always a pig, was what he told Damu, but his old leader would hear nothing of it. A struggling Jules begins coughing up blood, which disgusts Reid as he rises looking towards Slater.

"Take care of this cause that's just nasty," Reid said as Slater takes his gun and shoots Jules in the head, killing him.

"Oh, shit, that reminds me, Slate, I need to get with you on that reprimand," Reid jokingly responds, causing Slater to burst into laughter.

The rest of the squad begins to look over the area to see what could be salvaged from the attack while a lifeless body of Jules stares towards the ceiling as if he is looking at God himself.

*****

Martinez and Duke, who both have taken a seat across from Irvin, continues to try and convince the Deputy Commissioner that Reid and the Terror Squad were out of control.

"Deputy, sir, I made that call to warn Reid. I told him to get out of there," Duke says. "I gave him fair warning, and instead of evacuating, he and his squad killed those men!"

"Reid killing a bunch of gang members, or domestic terrorists that were coming to kill him is justified," Irvin responds. "Come on, even you can see that he was justified!"

"What about Fatboy?" Duke fires back. "You know good and damn well they weren't justified with that killing."

Irvin is silent, backing down slightly. He didn't agree with how the way things were handled with the Fatboy shooting, but Billick wouldn't listen to his thoughts about the situation.

"Why come to me? Why not bring it directly to the Commissioner. It's his operation," Irvin suggests.

Martinez and Duke look at each other, having already attempted to go to the commissioner.

*****

The day prior, Duke, Martinez, and Reid were in the commissioner's office going back and forth arguing about how things were handled in both the safe house shooting and the Fatboy shooting. Billick is sitting behind his desk, frustrated with all the arguing, and has finally had enough.

"Okay, quiet. Quiet I said!" He exclaims, silencing the room and turning his attention towards Martinez and Duke. "I understand that things got a little crazy, and Duke, you did a good thing giving Reid a heads up. What I'm trying to understand is one, how did they get the location to the safe house, and secondly, what did you expect him to do? They're coming after him and his men? Don't they have the duty to protect themselves?"

Reid nods his head with agreement as Duke sighs.

"Sir, all I'm saying is that it's a pattern," he says, trying to make the commissioner understand. "Everything he and his terror squad do is aggressive to the point where the bodies are starting to build. You already have protests all throughout the streets. You really think this is gonna help matters?"

"You saw the security footage," a defensive Reid fires back. "You

saw them coming into my safe house with their weapons out looking to kill me and my men! What we did was justified!"

"Oh, fuck you! You could have got out of there when I called you!" Duke fires back. "You could have left or at the very least call it in and bring others into the area. No, you wanted them to roll through. Your own personal shooting gallery!"

"Maybe, just maybe, if you'd give us a fix on your man Damu this thing would have been over by now," quips Reid. "By the way, when you made that call, where was he? I'm guessing in the area!"

"He does bring up a valid point," Billick interjects. "You've been deep cover for a while now, and yet Damu is still at large. Why is that?"

"Sir, per my report, you'll see that he moves around, and I don't know when-"

"I'm up to speed on your reports, Officer. I'm well aware," Billick interrupts. "I just find it odd that you're never able to give his where-abouts to your back up until it's too late."

"Sir, I can concur, he gets me the information, but once I check it out, everything's abandoned," Martinez points out.

After a few moments, Billick sighs, turning his attention back to-wards Duke.

"Officer Mitchell, can you please give us a moment," he asks.

Duke nods his head and heads out of the office leaving Reid and Martinez alone with Billick.

"So, where are we with Damu? Seriously," he asks.

"Sir, I've been in both Nickerson Gardens and Imperial. I don't see much involving The Hand, other than graffiti here or there. Duke's been straight up. I've been keeping an eye on him," Martinez replies, sort of covering for Duke.

Billick shakes his head and turns his attention towards Reid.

"Well?" He asks.

"I have a few things I'm looking into, but I'm not going to lie to you, sir, I don't exactly trust the guy," Reid replies.

"You don't trust the guy who literally called to give you a heads up on a group of killers coming your way, saving your men, and probably you?" A confused Martinez fires back. "I'm just saying, if he wanted *you dead, he probably wouldn't have said anything."*

"True, but how did they find us?" Reid fires back. "He probably fucked up, and then tried to fix it. Sir, I'm telling you this guy is no good."

"Maybe, but he's the only person who can get you in a room with Damu," Billick points out. "He'll come around, and when he does, I want one of you to take the shot."

"Excuse me?" Martinez responds, shocked to hear those words coming from the commissioner's mouth.

"You heard me!" Billick snaps back. "If we take that son of a bitch alive, he'll be a martyr. It'll spark all kinds of protests like we got going for that Jamie Powell idiot right now."

"I get that, sir, but you're talking about murder, and I don't think-"

"I'll get it done, sir," Reid interrupts, shooting a look at Martinez. "I'll make sure he's taken care of."

"Good, then it's settled. Keep me posted," Billick says, dismissing his subordinates.

Both Reid and Martinez exit the commissioner's office heading their separate ways. Martinez is still stunned Billick would ask her to do such a thing as she puts her cell phone into her pocket before heading to the elevator.

*****

Irvin finishes his coffee, still not convinced after hearing both Martinez and Duke out.

"He's the commissioner," Irvin points out. "If he's not willing to do anything about Reid and his squad, what makes you think I can?"

"He's literally sanctioning a hit on Damu," Martinez points out. "I mean, shouldn't that count for something?"

"I get it, I really do. This whole situation is out of wack, but without evidence, I ask again, what do you want from me? It's your word versus the Commissioner, Reid, and his unit. I promise you it won't make it to the review board." Irvin replies, causing Martinez to lose hope.

"I guess nothing. Sorry to have bothered you, sir," she says before making her way from the table.

Duke sighs as he stands as well. Before he leaves, he decides to give the deputy one more thing to think about.

"Good men who do nothing are just as bad or worse as the ones doing the dirt," he says. "Take it from me. I was one of those good men who did nothing. If I had to do it all over again, I'd like to think I'd change things, but this blind loyalty I have for this badge... I'm just sayin', sir, be the better man on this."

Duke hurries off to catch up with Martinez, as a conflicted Irvin leans back in his chair trying to process everything that was just told to him.

Sitting just outside the hospital area where The Hand of God members normally dwell is Slater and another Terror Squad member in an unmarked car that blends with the surroundings. They are looking around the area cautiously when Reid pulls up in another unmarked vehicle, parking right behind them. He quickly grabs a couple of fast food bags, and drinks before exiting the vehicle and hopping into the back seat of Slater's car.

"How goes it, boys?" He asks, handing Slater and the other member their food.

"Pretty slow so far," Slater responds. "You sure that boy gave us the right information?"

"Yeah, Wink is the best tech man the department has to offer. If he said Duke made a call right here, that's where it was made," Reid says, looking around the area.

"There's nothing around here though. Most of these buildings are abandoned. I guess they could meet around here or something, but please tell me you're not going to have us here all night looking for this guy," pleads Slater before taking a bite of his burger.

"It's the boss man's call on this one," Reid points out. "If we can't catch the son of a bitch, we're damn well gonna send his ass a message."

Reid is about to exit the vehicle when he notices a car pulling up several blocks down from the distance.

"Pass me the binoculars," he says to Slater.

Reid takes the binoculars and gets a good look at the car pulling up. A couple of members of The Hand exit their vehicle and head down the sidewalk making their way into the courtyard.

"Hey, start the car, move up a few blocks," he orders Slater, who is just getting into his meal.

"Come on, Reid, I got shit everywhere," he says.

"I see something, asshole. Move the car up before we lose them!" Reid exclaims.

Slater sighs as he starts the car and moves up a couple of blocks as ordered.

"That's it, right here," Reid says as Slater parks the car.

Reid peers out of the back window and watches the individuals he saw earlier ducking into a building just out of their sight range. He takes a look in the binoculars once more, trying to get a better view of things, and notice the bodyguard sitting at the entrance to the hidden hospital. A wicked grin enters his face as he lowers the binoculars.

"Pop quiz. What kind of building that's abandoned in the middle of the projects would need a doorman to allow people in?" He asks.

"What the fuck are you talking about?" Questions Slater.

"Take a look, building at the far right, just at the corner," Reid says while handing Slater the binoculars.

Slater quickly wipes his hands and peers through the binoculars himself trying to see what his unit leader sees. After a few moments, he notices the bodyguard as well. He also notices two people exiting the building, making it seem like it's a high traffic area.

"Oh shit," Slater says. "That might be the spot."

"You damn well best believe that's the spot," Reid says as he pulls out his cell phone, dialing Billick. "Let's see what boss man wants us to do."

After several rings, Billick answers the line.

"Yes, sir. Sorry to disturb you, but we may have a lead on our guy. Seems like they're using an abandoned building as a hideout… No, we don't have eyes inside the place. Not sure if he's in there or not, but they have security outside protecting the entrance… If you want, we can set up and-… Okay… yes, sir… no problem… I'll see to it that the message is sent," Reid says with a cryptic grin before hanging up the phone.

"Well, what did he say?" Slater asks.

"Damu has boss man really pissed," Reid says with a chuckle. "Shit, even I think this is too much, but an order is an order. We're going to smoke 'em out, boys. Whether he's in there or not, it doesn't matter. Time to let these thugs know that we still run these streets. Get on the radio and get the rest of the squad down here. Bossman wants a message sent, and we're going to give it to him."

Slater nods as the other Terror Squad member goes to the radio as instructed to hail the others in the team and make them aware of their dastardly plan.

Later that day, Terricka is at her apartment staring out at the magnificent view from her couch almost as if she's comatose. The city's glimmer doesn't distract her as she's still struggling not only with the recent loss of her friends, but also the loss of her position in The Hand of God. She wanted nothing more but to someday take her father's place at the head of the organization, but with the way everything has worked out in the past days, it seems like a distant dream, never to come true. Her gaze into the city's abyss is interrupted by a knock at her door. Unable to find her slippers, she tiptoes on the cold tile to answer the door, surprised to see Duke.

"Duke? What are you doing here?" She asks.

"Hey. Sorry to drop by unannounced, but I wanted to check on you and see how you were doing," he says. "Can I come in?"

Terricka nods her head and allows him to enter the apartment. He can tell she's struggling by her appearance and with the disorganization in her apartment, which is a stark contrast to what it was when he last was there. Terricka makes her way back over to her couch and stares out towards the city again with Duke taking a seat next to her, sharing the view.

"I know I haven't been around much since hearing about Jules, and I'm sorry," Duke says. "I did everything I could to prevent that from happening, but he wouldn't listen."

"You're fine, Duke. You don't have to apologize for what happened," Terricka replies. "Truth be told, what could you have done to stop him? Jules was arrogant and foolish. What happened to him isn't your fault or anyone's fault but his own."

While Terricka's words were genuine, Duke didn't agree. He's the one that called Reid that alerted him about the attack, which allowed him and his unit prep time. He put his faith in Reid to handle things differently, a faith he no longer had. While it was foolish for Jules to attack a police safe house head-on, it didn't exonerate Duke from his guilt for his hand in Jules's demise.

"I went to see his mother, you know," Terricka continues. "Jules's mother. Such a sweet lady. She's lost two sons now to police shootings. Duke, what's the point of it all? The more we push back and the more we fight, the more people are killed. I grew up with Fatboy, Jules, Q, and all the rest of them. These aren't just random people like Jamie Powell or the other thousands of people who are killed by police each year. These were people I knew. People I've sat with, been in their homes, played with their kids. These are people I loved, Duke. What have we've been doing all this time if not to save them?"

Duke sighs as he can tell the pain is taking its toll on his friend.

"Terricka, what you're going through is normal," he explains, trying to calm her down. "You've lost a lot of good people this past week, but you can't give up the battle. The streets need you. You're too important to back away now."

"The streets need me?! My own father doesn't need me!" Terricka exclaims as tears start to fall from her eyes. "I've been through it all with him, and just like that he cuts me out! And to make matters worse, he said he wants you to be his second in command!"

A stunned Duke is speechless after hearing Damu's request. Terricka notices his mood and chuckles to herself in disbelief.

"Oh, I see you haven't had that conversation with him yet," she says, rolling her eyes.

"No, I... Why me?" Questions Duke. "I'm nowhere close to the type of person Jules was. Hell, I just found out that he's your father a couple of days ago. If he didn't trust me with that, why would he trust me with anything else? I'm no cop killer."

"Exactly! He said he needed you for balance or some shit. Truth is that he's just doing anything he can to keep me out. I was good with Jules being the number two because he did come up in the cause. You though? You've been here a little over a month? What have you done to earn that spot?" A jealous Terricka quips. "You're not even down with the cause like that, and he chooses you? Give me a fuckin' break!"

Terricka turns away from Duke, who tries to comfort her wiping her tears away as best she can. Duke takes a deep breath as he gazes out of the window, wanting to tell Terricka the truth about everything.

"Look, Terricka, I didn't ask for any of it. You're right, I'm not down for the cause the way your father and Jules are. I like the things The Hand stands for when it comes to the hospital, giving back to the community, and helping out the youth. I can dig all of that. I will never be down with killing cops. Never. Two wrongs don't make a right, and I would never take leadership in something I don't fully agree with," Duke explains. "Your father is doing you a favor by not letting you get involved. He's protecting you."

"How the fuck is he protecting me?" Terricka snaps back.

"Have you ever killed anybody?" A curious Duke inquires. "Taking a life isn't as easy as the movies make it seem. Your father knows that, and I know that."

"He never gave me the chance!" Terricka exclaims. "I'm just as good as any one of you guys! Just cause I'm a woman or daddy's little girl, he doesn't think I can handle it."

Duke sighs, lowering his head, recalling the first person he killed in the line of duty back with his stint with the Cincinnati PD.

"My first kill happened on a drug raid," he says, opening up. "We hit this trap house after following a re-up to the address. The plan was to catch them dirty, and take them right there, but apparently, the dealers had other ideas."

Duke tenses up slightly, as Terricka notices his mood change.

"While clearing out the room, I kicked open a bedroom door or something. Here is this teenager with his gun aimed right at me, ready to open fire," Duke recalls as the memory starts to weigh on him. "He fired, just missing me, and I'm talking by about inches. Before he could get off a second shot, I took him out. I still remember the bullet hitting him square in the head, and watched as his body hit the ground. It was like it was in slow motion."

Terricka didn't have any idea of the baggage Duke has been carrying around. Even though the incident happened years ago, she could tell he isn't completely over it.

"That kid's death haunted me for months," Duke admits. "There were a few others I had to open fire on after that, but that one, that first kid... it... you never recover from that. So when I say I understand what your father is trying to do, I meant it. Once you've killed someone, there's no turning back. You're scarred for the rest of your life. My only fear was that it started to get easier after each victim. You tell yourself that it's either you or them and that it's justified, but in the end, you never forget your first. This is coming from me, and I was on plenty of drug raids back then."

A stunned Terricka reaches out and grabs Duke's hand to comfort him. While she has always prepared for the day that she may have to execute someone herself, she has never seen it from Duke's point of view. It brought her insight into a world she knew nothing about.

"I think you're fighting this thing the right way, using a system built against us, for us," Duke points out.

"It's all bullshit though," Terricka fires back. "What good am I doing out there?"

"What, are you kidding me? Think of all the folks you got off," Duke points out.

"Like who?"

"Well, me for starters," Duke says with a smirk. "And I'm sure the list goes on with many people who were falsely accused. I know, it's not what you wanted, but your role in this thing is bigger than you'll ever know. All this cop killin' shit though, it's going to bring you nothing but stress and pain, not to mention heat from the police and feds."

Terricka sighs, nodding her head with agreement when a question suddenly hits her.

"If you felt this strongly about the cop killings, why did you join up with us?" She inquires. "I mean, I know you weren't a part of it or anything, but knowing what we did, why be with us?"

Duke sighs, knowing the time has come to be truthful with his friend. With things falling apart as they were, it is time for him to come clean and tell the truth about his undercover work with the LAPD. Before he can confess, his cell phone suddenly starts ringing, saving him for the moment. He checks the caller ID and notices it's Martinez calling him.

"Let me take this real quick," he says, rising from the couch and making his way into the kitchen area for more privacy.

"Yeah, what's up?" He answers once he's away from Terricka.

His face drops as the news from Martinez startles him.

"Oh my god, are you serious?" He asks, looking back towards Terricka.

She notices his glance and curiously walks over as Martinez continues to fill him in on the latest news.

"Alright… yeah… I'm on the way," he responds, hanging up the phone.

"What is it? Is everything okay?" Terricka asks.

Duke is silent as the information he just heard has him shook.

Terricka becomes concerned as she awaits a response. After gathering himself, Duke explains what Martinez just informed him. The news shatters her as she backs away with sadness entering her face. After gathering themselves, the two make their way out of the apartment and down to Terricka's car.

CHAPTER 13

The End is Near

The sun has just set with darkness settling everywhere but the Nickerson Garden Projects. A fire to the hidden hospital lights up the night, along with firefighters and police in the area. Onlookers try to get a peep of the blaze but are taped off as even with the fire being a good distance away from the curb, it's burning so hot that its effects can be felt from afar. Firefighters continue to battle the blaze as Duke and Terricka pull up on the curb in Terricka's car, speechless with all that's going on. They quickly exit the vehicle and run towards the taped off area, but are stopped by police who won't let them by.

"You gotta let me in! I know that building! I have friends that might be in there!" Terricka yells.

"Ma'am, I'm going to need you to calm down," the officer says. "It's too dangerous to let anyone in."

"You don't understand! I need to get by! Please!" A distraught Terricka pleas with the officer.

He continues to give Terricka a hard time until Martinez notices the commotion.

"Hey, it's cool. Let them in," she says to the officer.

Terricka's surprised to see Martinez as both her and Duke make their way behind the line towards her.

"What have you got so far?" Duke asks.

"Well, they were able to evacuate all the people out that they located, but Duke, I'm gonna be real here, there is no way to know how many people were in that building," Martinez reports as a confused Terricka looks on.

"Any idea what happened?" Duke questions.

"It was Reid and his bandits. They did this shit," Martinez says as she hands Duke a Back the Blue flyer that was found by the building. "There's like hundreds of these all around the building. They wanted us to find this."

"It's an invitation," Duke replies, crumpling up the paper. "They wanted these flyers to be found to provoke a confrontation. Son of a bitch!"

After a few moments, it hits Terricka, where she's seen Martinez before.

"Hey, wait a minute. Aren't you Angela? Duke's old girl," Terricka says, trying to understand what's going on. "I remember, at the rally. You were wearing a skimpy outfit and everything. What are you doing here?"

Martinez looks towards Duke, who gives her the okay to come clean.

"I'm Detective Valentina Martinez with the LAPD. Angela was my cover story. I'm working the investigation on The Hand of God," Martinez says, shocking Terricka.

She quickly puts two and two together, looking at Duke, who tries to explain his side of the story.

"Terricka, calm down. Look, I was about to tell you before all this went down," Duke explains.

"Oh my god, you're a cop?! Are you fuckin' kidding me right now?!" Terricka exclaims, feeling like a sucker.

"It's not what you think. Look if we can-"

"Don't touch me!" Terricka fires back when Duke tries to pull her off to the side. "I see it now. You were workin' me this whole time! And my dumb ass fell for it hook, line, and sinker!"

"Terricka, if you will let me explain, I'm sure we can-"

Terricka silences Duke with a vicious slap to the face, hurt by his betrayal. She starts swinging on Duke several more times as he covers himself up, resisting her blows. Martinez is about to jump in when Duke waves her off and grabs Terricka pinning her on a nearby squad car, trying to calm her down.

"Terricka, damn it, will you listen to me!" Duke exclaims as Terricka struggles to get away from his grasp.

"Get off of me!" She yells, causing Duke to finally release her and back away cautiously.

Terricka is out of breath, panting as she wipes tears from her face looking towards Duke with a scowl.

"I know this is upsetting, and you have every right to be pissed, but right now, I need you to tell me was your father in the hospital?" Duke asks a defiant Terricka, who goes silent. "Terricka, please, they are gonna kill him. If you know where your father is, you have to let me know."

Terricka continues the silent treatment, not knowing if she should trust Duke after what he's done. Feeling he's not getting anywhere with Terricka, Duke is about to walk off when Terricka finally breaks his silence.

"He wasn't in there," she says, catching Duke and Martinez's attention. "There were a lot of sick people there. They didn't deserve this."

"No, they didn't," Duke says, cautiously approaching the lawyer. "It's Reid and his Terror Squad that is responsible for this. I know you don't trust me right now, and I don't blame you, but if we don't find your father, they will kill him. There won't be any arrest or bail. They have been given the green light to kill him. If we have any chance to save him, you need to tell us where he is. I give you my word I will protect him. Terricka, please."

An emotional Terricka struggles to keep it together not knowing what to do. She didn't want to betray her father, but if what Duke is telling her is correct, she needed to do the right thing to keep him alive. After going back and forth with her choices in her mind for a couple of moments, she finally makes a decision.

"I spoke to him maybe about an hour or so before you came by. All he said is tonight is the night," she responds.

"What does that mean?" Martinez asks.

Terricka hesitates for a moment before responding.

"He's going after Jamie's killer," she answers. "He's going to balance the scales of justice tonight."

Duke's eyes are wide, realizing that Damu is walking into a trap.

"Shit! We need to go! Now!" He yells.

"Alright, I'll get the address and call you along the way. I'll meet you over there after I wrap up things here," Martinez says before running off to her squad car.

"You better let me drive," Duke says, waiting for a response from Terricka.

She still doesn't fully trust him but hands her the keys as he quickly leads her back to her car. They quickly make a U-turn and quickly screeches down the road hoping to stop Damu before it's too late.

As they drive down the street, Terricka quietly looks over at Duke, her head filled with questions after his big revelation. Duke can feel her glance and tries to avoid eye contact to focus on the road. After a few more moments of silence, Terricka can no longer help herself.

"Was it your plan to sleep with me that night?" She inquires. "Was that part of your duty or something? All the flirting, the looks... It was all to work me to lead you to my father, wasn't it?"

"Terricka, I know you're upset, but this isn't the time to-" Duke says before looking over at her and noticing the sadness in her eyes.

After a few moments, he sighs and responds.

"No, me sleeping with you wasn't a part of any duty or anything," he admits. "I didn't even know Damu was your father until that night with Jules. Well, I suspected as much, but I didn't really know until then. At the beginning of all this, when I met you at the corner store, I had no idea you were a part of The Hand. When I found out... I... I don't know. I didn't mention you in any of my reports. Martinez suspected something, which is why she set up that whole Angela thing, but even she didn't

192

know about it until probably a few minutes ago."

Terricka continues to gaze at Duke, trying to read him. What he says seems genuine. After years of being a lawyer, she's keen on using her intuition to see if someone is lying and is not getting that vibe from Duke, who glances over at her.

"That night of sex wasn't me doing my job. It was real. My feelings for you always was real. I'm sorry about all this. This is not the way I wanted to have this conversation. I guess I knew I would eventually, but not like this," Duke continues, hoping to calm his friend a little bit.

Terricka sighs, shaking her head as she sits silently for the rest of the ride. Duke returns his attention towards the road, hoping that they aren't too late.

Just outside of Murphy's home, Damu, and several of his followers are sitting in a car down the block surveying the area, waiting to make their move. Damu seems to be in a daze staring into space, realizing what he's about to do. Never has The Hand attempted a cop kill at a cop's home. It's out of character, but Damu knows the end is near. After hearing about the hospital being burned down by Reid and his crew, rage and anger flow through Damu's blood, which clouds his judgment. He wants to strike back at the LAPD, and the only way he's able to have his revenge is to take another perceived dirty cop in Murphy. After a few more moments of silence, Damu snaps out of his daze and checks out the home once more.

"Remember, no civilian casualties," he reminds his men. "He has a wife and kids. I don't want any harm to come to them. Just Officer Murphy."

His followers all nod their head with agreement as Damu opens his car door.

"Let's go," he says, exiting the vehicle.

Unknowingly to Damu and his men, there is a hidden camera set up looking over the block being monitored by several officers, including Reid and his Terror Squad, who is in a house the department rented out across the street from Murphy's home.

Reid is sipping his coffee checking out the monitor when he notices Damu and his men cautiously making their way towards Murphy's home. A cryptic grin fills his face as he grabs Slater's attention.

"What I told you?" He says, pointing towards the monitor. "Them boys are too predictable. Let's go get this cock sucker. No need to bring him. This ends tonight."

The Terror Squad unit all offer their support and agreement as they all quickly prepare to move.

At Murphy's doorway, one of The Hand's members is working on picking the lock to the building, while another one has disabled the alarm system but cutting a connecting wire to the house. The locksmith finally hears a click signifying he's unlocked the door. He turns and motions to Damu that he's ready to move. Damu acknowledges him and motions to the rest of the team to prepare to move. Before they can enter the home, a single shot fires from across the street, hitting the locksmith in the shoulder as Damu and the other quickly take cover and turn their attention across the street to see if they can locate where the shot came from.

Inside the home, Murphy is awakened by the shot and quickly jumps out of bed, going into his nightstand and pulling out his gun. Shannon wakes up as well as she watches her husband walk over and peek out of the window curtain.

"Dave, what's going on?" She frantically asks.

Murphy waves her down to quiet her as he can tell someone is on their porch, but can't view them from his upstairs bedroom.

"Get the kids and go into the bathroom," he whispers to his wife. "Go quietly."

Shannon nods her head as she quickly jumps out of bed and heads out of their room towards her kid's rooms. Murphy follows making sure that his family is safe in the bathroom as he tries to peer down to the main floor to see if he can see anything.

On the porch, Damu and the others do their best to slow the bleeding of their fallen member. Several more shots ring out from across the street as Damu, and the others continue to take cover.

"Anyone see anything?" Damu asks while peering across the street as best he can while remaining covered.

"I don't see... wait a minute... Oh my god!" One of the members responds in fear when he notices Reid and his Terror Squad officers all approaching them from across the street.

"Light 'em up, boys!" Reid orders as they open fire with a barrage of bullets towards the porch.

One of The Hand's members is struck multiple times and is killed instantly. Damu and the other two members left duck as low as they can, hoping to avoid being struck.

Down the street, Duke pulls up by the intersection and is horrified with what he's seeing with Reid and the others firing at Murphy's home. Terricka is speechless when Duke suddenly passes up the block.

"What are you doing?!" Terricka ask.

"Gonna try the back way," Duke explains as he quickly turns down the next road.

He arrives on the opposite side of Murphy's house after a quick call to Martinez to let her know what's going on. He readies his gun before looking towards Terricka.

"Look, stay here and keep your head down," Duke says.

"Fuck that! I'm going with you!" Terricka fires back as she readies herself to leave the car.

"Terricka, it's not a good-"

"Duke! We're wasting fuckin' time right now! My father might be dying! Either you're gonna go in there with me and be my protector, or I'll go at it alone and take my chances. Your call," Terricka interrupts, waiting for a response.

After hearing increased shooting coming from the front of the home, Duke sighs, knowing Terricka is leaving him no other choice but to take her, and nods his head with approval.

"Stay behind me, and keep your hand on my shoulder at all times," he commands.

Terricka nods her head as the two exits the vehicle and

makes their way into Murphy's backyard. Terricka places her arm on Duke's shoulder as instructed as he cautiously leads her towards the back door.

In the front of the home, Reid and his Terror Squad have Damu and his followers pinned down on the porch. They are slowly advancing towards the porch firing at a fast pace when an idea hits Damu.

"When they reload, into the house!" Damu says.

"What about James?!" One of the members exclaims.

'Brother James is already gone," Damu says, looking down at the locksmith who has bled out. "On my mark!"

The other two remaining members nod their heads waiting for the order to move. The rate of fire decreases as Damu can hear Reid and his crew starting to reload.

"Now!" He yells before leading his men crashing into the front door.

Before Damu and his followers can gather themselves, two shots are fired at his followers from above, sending them falling to the ground. Damu, acting on instinct, turns and fires his gun that hits the shooter, Murphy, in the shoulder on top of the staircase that sends him tumbling down the stairs. Damu smiles as he walks over to the fallen Murphy and kicks his gun out of reach.

"Officer Murphy, I assume," he says, causing Murphy to look up towards him.

"Who the fuck are you?" Murphy asks, still trying to gather himself.

"I'm the last thing you're ever going to see," Damu answers as he aims his gun towards Murphy. "I'm in a bit of a hurry, so please forgive me."

Damu is seconds away from pulling the trigger when Duke and Terricka burst into the home from the back entrance and make their way to the living room. Duke has his gun pointed towards Damu when he notices The Hand leader has Murphy in his sights.

"Drop your weapon, Damu!" Duke screams, surprising Murphy, who is thriving in pain.

The unfazed Damu chuckles as he turns and notices Duke and Terricka.

"I been waiting for this moment, Duke," Damu says, still with his gun pointed firmly at Murphy's head. "I didn't think it would be now, but I knew eventually you'd come for me. That is what you're here to do, correct? The commissioner brought you in just to deal with me, right?"

Both Terricka and Duke are stunned as Damu reveals he knew all along that Duke is an undercover officer. Terricka is especially surprised as she attempts to walk towards her father, only to be blocked off by Duke.

"Stay back, Terricka," he says, keeping her out of harm's way.

"You... you knew he was a cop?" A confused Terricka asks her father. "Why didn't you tell me?"

"Yes. I knew it from the day you brought him to me what he was," Damu admits. "I didn't tell you because I wanted to protect you. You are what's good about the cause, Terricka. You never believed in your importance, but what you do is more important than anything that I or any other members have done. You are the true face of The Hand of God, and I wanted you to show him the truth, something you wouldn't have been able to do had you known his intentions."

Terricka is beside herself with emotions, feeling betrayed by not only Duke but also her father.

"How could you have possibly known?" She asks.

"That doesn't matter right now. What matters is I need you to put your gun down, Damu," Duke interjects.

"I'm sorry, Duke, I can't do that," Damu says cocking the hammer back on his gun, making Murphy and Duke nervous. "This man needs to pay for his sins. He needs to pay for Jamie Powell's spilled blood."

"Do it," Murphy says, grabbing everyone's attention. "Do it. I deserve it. I wish I could go back and undo what I did, but all I see at night when I'm sleeping is that kid's face. He didn't deserve to die like that. Please, you'll be doing me a favor putting me out of my misery. I… I can't deal with the guilt anymore."

Damu hesitates to pull the trigger as he didn't anticipate such a response from Murphy.

"Leave my dad alone!" David yells, grabbing everyone's attention after making his way out of the bathroom overhearing the commotion from upstairs. Shannon tries to pull him back, but he jerks his arm away from her and stands just above the stairwell.

"David! Get back in the bathroom!" Murphy yells to his son.

"I'm not gonna let them kill you!" A tearful David replies.

"David, listen to me. You're the man of the house now. It's up to you to take care of your mother and sister. Please, son, do as I say," Murphy says as he grimaces in pain.

A tear-filled Shannon makes her way over to her son and grabs him as they both take one last look at Murphy. David wants to be defiant and fight the intruders, but he looks at his father, and after a few moments, he slowly nods his head, accepting his role with the family before retreating into the bathroom with Shannon. The room is tense as Damu turns his attention back towards the fallen Murphy. Duke still has his gun pointed in Damu's direction, praying that Damu doesn't follow through with his plan. Before The Hand of God leader can make a decision, a shot fires from the front doorway striking Damu from behind, who grimaces in pain before falling to his knees. Duke quickly turns his attention to the doorway to see both Reid and Slater walking through the front door with their weapons drawn. A smirking Reid, who is the one who fired the shot that has Damu on the ground, walks in and quickly kicks the gun away from Damu. Terricka is filled with rage as she looks to approach her father, but once again is held back by Duke.

"What the fuck is the matter with you?!" Duke exclaims. "You didn't have to do that!"

"The fuck you say? I'm under orders from the commissioner, as you know," Reid says before Slater shoots the other downed members of The Hand, making sure they're dead.

"Are you outta your fuckin' minds?!" Duke reacts after witnessing Slater's heinous act.

"Now look here, Officer, you and your girlfriend are free to go whenever you're ready," Reid says before checking out Terricka once more. "Hey, aren't you that loudmouth lawyer that hates cops?"

A distraught Terricka remains silent as Reid chuckles, turning to Slater.

"Check this out, Slate. Our man here is banging Ms. Civil Rights," He says, mocking both Duke and Terricka. "Jesus Christ, this has been a day, I swear. What's baby girl doing here, Duke? Commissioner is going to have your ass for bringing her along."

Duke frowns as Reid's attention goes to Damu, who is still on his knees, holding his bleeding stomach, where the exit wound is. He crouches down to get a better look at the man he and his Terror Squad has been chasing all those months.

"So you're the man," Reid replies, nodding his head as if he's impressed. "I gotta give it to you, boy. You've been a pain in our ass for a while. I'm so happy it was me that caught up with you."

"Let me do him," Slater responds, filling Terricka with fear.

"No!" She yells, finally breaking away from Duke and rushing over to her father to cradle him, blocking Reid. "Leave him alone! He's down for God's sake!"

"Pretty lady, you are one for your people, I'll give you that," Reid says as he aims his gun towards both Terricka and Damu. "But, orders are orders, and I have no problem taking you out with him."

Duke has head enough as he aims his weapon towards Reid, causing Slater to aim his gun back at him.

"That's enough, Reid! I'm taking him in the right way," Duke bellows.

"Um, no you're not," Reid fires back, clutching his weapon rightly. "We are under orders to kill this man. Unlike you, I follow orders."

"Orders or not, you know this shit is wrong! Back off!" Duke responds, causing tension between everyone.

There's a standoff with Duke aiming towards Reid, Slater

aiming towards Duke, and Terricka covering her father with Reid towering over her with his weapon firmly on his side. Realizing Duke isn't going to let up, Reid sighs shaking his head in disappointment.

"Take him," Reid utters, causing Slater to fire his gun towards Duke.

Duke is able to react quickly but takes a bullet to his shoulder. He's able to retaliate, shooting Slater in the head, killing him before he himself falls to the ground, throbbing in pain. A distressed Reid slowly leans down towards his fallen ally as rage fills him realizing Slater is dead. Before he can respond, Terricka gently lays her father down on the ground and grabs Duke's gun, which he had dropped, and aims it towards Reid, who rises and slowly turns around to face her.

"What the fuck are you gonna do with that?" Reid says, slowly approaching her. "You ever killed anybody before, missy? Cause the way you're shaking with that gun, I'm guessing you're not an expert."

With tears streaming down her face, Terricka continues to aim the gun towards Reid, backing up slightly as he approaches her.

"Go ahead, bitch! Shoot me! You don't have it in you! Do it!" Reid yells, startling Terricka. "If you don't, I will, and I promise you there's no pussy on this boy. I'm gonna kill your boyfriend there, the cop killer, and you. So if you're gonna do it, then do it!"

Terricka struggles to hold the gun and has backed herself into a wall, cornering herself from the slowly advancing Terror Squad leader. The gun is digging itself into the chest of Reid, who is face to face with her. The two have a stare off, with Reid daring her to take the shot. As much anger and hatred that filled her heart towards Reid, she couldn't pull the trigger even knowing that he would kill her if she didn't. Realizing that his intimidation tactic is working, Reid snatches the gun from Terricka's hands, shaking his head as if he's disappointed.

"That's the problem with you and your kind. You don't have

the balls to do what's needed to survive. All talk at them rallies, but when the real comes calling, you shrivel up like a scared little cock," Reid says before punching Terricka in the stomach, sending her to the ground next to Duke gasping for air. "I hope the pussy was worth it, Duke!"

Reid raises his gun towards Duke, causing the former Cincinnati Officer to brace for the end. Before Reid could act on his threat, he is shot from behind by Martinez, who had made her way through the back entrance, undetected. He slowly turns around and notices a fierce Martinez, one he's neglected her entire time on his squad, staring him down. Before Reid can make a move to retaliate, Martinez fires several more shots into his body, causing him to collapse onto the floor. She cautiously walks up towards his fallen body and confirms he's dead before holstering her weapon. After breathing a sigh of relief, she quickly walks over towards Duke to check on him.

"I'm fine, I'm fine. Check on those two," he instructs.

Martinez nods her head and walks over and checks the status of both Murphy and Damu before calling in on her radio for an ambulance. Terricka crawls towards Duke and checks him out, noticing blood everywhere feeling that she failed him.

"I... I couldn't do it. You were right, it's not in me," Terricka whimpers, ashamed of her actions.

"That's a good thing," Duke grunts, struggling with his wound. "It doesn't need to be in you. That's what makes you a better person."

Terricka slowly nods her head, when her attention is grabbed by her father, who grunts in pain. She quickly makes her way over to him and cradles him once more, noticing he's lost a lot of blood.

"Dad, stay with me, dad!" She exclaims, watching Damu fading with every moment that goes by.

"I... I told you this was the end, my child," Damu struggles to say. "The old way, my way doesn't work anymore. I always knew it wouldn't last. I'm... I'm sorry I won't be able to... see it through. I... I want you to... promise me that you'll work to keep the cause going... but... but you and Duke need to find... find another way... a better way. Don't make... the same... mistakes I did. Promise me, Terricka. Promise me."

The tears begin to flow down Terricka's face as she nods her head with agreement before hugging her father.

"I promise, dad, I promise I will keep things moving," she says as Duke makes his way over.

Damu looks towards him and reaches for his hand. Duke kneels alongside the fallen Hand leader and holds his hand, hoping to comfort him. Damu then joins Duke's hand and Terricka's hand together, signifying a union between the two new Hand of God leaders.

"Take care of each other... and... take care of our people," Damu struggles to say.

After a few coughs, Damu's hand goes limp, sliding away from Terricka and Duke's grasp. A grief-stricken Terricka begins sobbing when noticing her father is gone. She clutches him tightly crying as Duke hugs her to show his support for her father.

Thirty minutes have gone by as the street in front of Murphy's home is now lit with emergency lights from ambulances, and police vehicles as the tapped off area are filled with personnel trying to decipher what happened that night. Duke is sitting on the back of an ambulance getting his arm tapped up when he notices Murphy being removed from his house on a stretcher hooked with an IV. Shannon and the kids follow the paramedics out of the home when Shannon makes eye contact with Duke. She mouths the words 'Thank you' before making her way over to the ambulance her husband is being loaded in. As the paramedic finishes his wrap on work on Duke's arm, Martinez walks over to check on her partner.

"Did they take care of you?" She asks before sitting next to him.

"As much as they can, I guess," Duke says, looking around the area. "How's the investigation going?"

"Well, they are about to bring in the remaining Terror Squad folks shit pending an investigation. My guess is that we'll see several arrests once all that's said and done," Martinez reports, smiling. "I mean, they can claim they were following orders, but shooting into a house, lighting a fire to an occupied building, and murder are all still felonies last I checked. Officer Murphy may have some spinal damage but seems like he's gonna pull through. You and your boo are in the clear too, although you may need to coach her on a couple of things."

Both Duke and Martinez look over towards Terricka, who is being attended to by a couple of investigating officers. She looks comfortable with her interaction causing Martinez to giggle.

"Okay, maybe not," she replies. "Forgot she's used to dealing with us. I guess everything's a win. You did good work tonight. I'll admit, I had my doubts when we first started, but you proved me wrong."

"I realized some things too," Duke responds as he straightens himself out. "Tonight Damu told me he knew about me the second he saw me. I started thinking, how could he have possibly known the second he saw me? There's only four people who knew about me being undercover back then. Billick, Irvin, Reid, and you. Out of the four, who is most likely to leak my undercover investigation?"

Martinez giggles once more, shaking her head.

"So you have it all figured out, do you?" She replies.

"Well, I am a detective," Duke quips.

"Not a very good one," Martinez playfully fires back.

"How did you get involved with all this?" Duke inquires. "Did you know they were out here killing cops?"

Martinez sighs, knowing she had a lot to answer for.

"I came across Jules about a year or so ago," she says, going into her story. "We use to date when we were younger. I used to like them militant troublemakers when I was young, but as I got older, I wanted something different in life. I went on to become a cop, and it irked him to no end with everything that he had been through. With his beliefs and mine, it was obvious the relationship wasn't gonna work out, so we went our separate ways.

That is until I came across him like a year ago. I thought he was there tryin' that whole 'I miss you' hustle, but he wasn't. He had heard about me bumpin' heads with the corrupt folks in my department, and long story short, he introduced me to Damu."

Duke is hanging off Martinez's every word as she continues her story.

"When I first met him, I wasn't impressed. Just figured he's someone looking to add bloodshed into the world. When he broke it down with me though, and showed me the statistics of the police brutality cases and the repeat offenders, I gotta say I was tripped out over it," she says as a sly grin enters her face. "I saw myself how officers who killed minorities were let off with slaps on the wrists, if anything. No matter the amount of evidence, they were getting off. Plus, for every viral case, they're about a hundred cases that go unnoticed. I knew we had our issues as a department, but I would have never imagined it was that bad."

"What about the killing of officers?" Duke whispers. "Doesn't that bother you?"

Martinez thinks before responding, trying to remember her state of mind at the beginning of her Damu agreement.

"There was this Officer, Antione Winfield. Real cocky asshole, black guy who loved to flex on people," Martinez recalls. "Anyway, he got off on an assault charge that ended up killing this eighteen-year-old. No weapon, no anything. Kid spit in his face during his arrest, and he beat this kid within an inch of his life. The kid died several days later due to complications. The department made up some bullshit ass story about how the kid charged him with a knife or something. At least that's what I heard. He was assigned six months of desk duty. Duke, when I tell you I stared at the photos of that dead kid for hours-"

Martinez catches herself struggling to maintain her emotions.

"Anyway, this is a man who didn't deserve to live. The brass weren't going to do anything about it, so I turned to the one man who would," Martinez admits. "At first, I wasn't happy with it, but I kept reminding myself of that picture to justify it. That asshole deserved every bit of what he got. After that, it got easier I guess. You can tell me it's wrong, but you don't know the things I have seen. I was gonna clean up the department one way or another."

Duke sighs when a thought hit him.

"You're the reason Jules disappeared," Duke deduces. "You knew we wouldn't find him that night. You knew about the hospital in the area and why we were there, but you knew he wouldn't be there. Why even give him to me if you were trying to protect him?"

Martinez giggles, refusing to acknowledge her tampering into the case. Duke can her giggles were a deflection and that she's still hurting inside over her old lover's death. After a few moments of silence, Duke decides to move the conversation along.

"So what happened with Fatboy? You didn't warn him?" Duke inquiries.

"Fatboy was unfortunate," she responds as the smile falls from her face. "I didn't know him personally. I figured Jules would get word to him, but for whatever reason, he didn't. I guess we'll never know now."

Duke nods his head as Martinez looks on, wondering how he's taking the reveal of her involvement.

"Well?" She asks. "What do you have to say about it?"

"I mean, what do you want me to say? I guess I hope Murphy is off your hit radar now," he replies.

"Murphy was a Damu thing. I kept him up to date with the investigation and such, but after I saw the body cam, I changed my mind," Martinez explains. "Duke, that shooting could have happened to any of us. It was too dark to see for sure. After pulling his record, and seeing there wasn't a history of violence like talking about it, I was done with it. I told Damu that, but he didn't want to hear it. He took the initiative on his own."

Duke nods his head with understanding causing Martinez to look at him suspiciously.

"That's it?" She asks. "I just admitted to you that I'm guilty of being an accessory to murder, and that's all you have to say to me? By department regulations, you should be placing me under arrest for my involvement, or you could face charges yourself."

Duke looks towards Martinez for a few moments before shaking his head.

"My arm hurts right now. I don't hear too well when I'm in pain," he responds, smirking.

Martinez chuckles as well as they notice the coroner removing Reid's body out of the home.

"You know what I am pissed at? The fact Billick's ass is gonna get away with his part in this shit," Duke points out. "I mean, he ran a hit squad unit and allowed them to get away with all this shit."

"Don't worry about that. I'll take care of it," a confident Martinez responds.

"Please tell me you're not gonna kill the man," Duke replies cautiously, causing Martinez to laugh.

"Ye of little faith," she responds. "No, I'm done with that business. Officer Winfield aside, I did start to feel some kind of way with all this. Sometimes you get so lost in what you believe what's right, that you don't ask if it is right, ya know."

Duke nods his head as both he and Martinez notice Terricka heading their way. Once she arrives, she looks at Duke's arm, checking the work.

"How are you? Did they fix you up right this time?" She asks, referring to when he was in police custody bruised and battered.

"Yeah, I'm good. How are you?" Duke asks.

Terricka sighs as Martinez can tell the two needed to talk.

"Alright, I'm gonna get out of y'all's way here. Terricka, I really am sorry for your loss," she says before tapping Duke on his good shoulder and walking off.

Terricka takes a seat next to Duke, struggling to come to terms with everything that has gone on and with her heart still weighing heavy from the loss of her father.

"So, where do we go from here?" She quietly asks.

Duke is thinking for a moment, before looking towards her.

"We honor your father's wishes, and keep the cause alive," he replies. "We see who's left out there and give them the new mandate. Those who want to join us, we'll gladly accept them, with past transgressions forgiven. Those that still want to follow the old ways will be expelled. We need to make sure The Hand of God stands for the people. All this cop killing stuff is a thing of the past. I know it's harder to make changes the right way, but nothing worth doing is ever easy, you know."

Terricka sigh, but nods her head with agreement before laying her head on Duke's good shoulder.

"I'm scared," she says, looking at a future she's not comfortable with.

"Yeah, me too," Duke admits. "We'll make it though. We got to."

The two friends sit silently on the back of the ambulance while observing all the ruckus filling the area. They are at peace in the middle of the noise, still unsure of things to come, but at peace nevertheless.

EPILOGUE

In a swanky Hollywood Hotel, city officials gather for a yearly charity ball, black-tie event with live music and catering. The ballroom is filled with officials as high up as the Mayor's office who are all looking dapper in their tuxedos or ballroom gowns mingling with each other while enjoying drinks. In the mix of the crowd is Billick, who is sharp in his white tuxedo and red bow tie. He's in mid-conversation with one of the Mayor's advisors, when he notices Duke walking in, his arm still taped up, looking around the extravaganza. He stands out like a sore thumb in his off the rack suit and tie, which other guests immediately notice. A curious Billick excuses himself and makes his way over towards Duke with a big smile on his face.

"Officer Mitchell, I didn't know you were attending tonight," he says before shaking Duke's hand. "How's the arm?"

"Oh, it's good. It's all good," Duke says, smirking. "Yeah, the mayor offered me an invite to this thing. Honestly, I was gonna turn it down, but he insisted I show up. I won't be staying long though."

Duke looks around at the other guests and sighs.

"I guess I'm a little underdressed for this thing," Duke jokes, with Billick agreeing.

"Yeah, just a tad," the commissioner responds before leading Duke towards the refreshments table. "Look, I know we didn't have much of a chance to speak after that whole Damu thing went down, but I do want to take care of you for the work you did for us."

"Is that a fact?" Duke responds with a cryptic smile. "That's good to hear cause I thought you were trying to avoid me all this time."

"I would never do such a thing," Billick says as he picks up two glasses of champagne from the refreshment table, handing one to Duke. "It's time for a new regime, and I have a lot of ideas where I want to go from here. First off, the Terror Squad is a thing of the past. They were a little too aggressive at times like you mentioned before. I'm looking to change that. How would you like to head up and new special investigative unit? One where you'd have complete control over the cases you work and allows you to continue your work on maintaining police and citizen relations."

Duke nods his head as if he's impressed with Billick's offer.

"Wow, that sounds nice," he replies.

"Of course, it'll come with a substantial pay increase. I'm sure you could use the money to help out your grandmother," Billick suggests, causing Duke to laugh.

"Well, you are right about that. She could use a little more green coming her way," Duke replies. "Hey, I appreciate it, but I'm going to have to decline. You see, I got a better offer. One far more lucrative than you could offer me."

Billick looks at Duke with curiosity when right on cue, Deputy Commissioner Irvin joins both Duke and the commissioner by the refreshment table, along with two uniformed officers.

"Irv? What are you doing here? I thought you had something you had to do tonight?" Billick asks as Irvin looks towards Duke.

"Would you like to do the honors?" Irvin asks Duke.

"Gladly," Duke responds before turning his attention towards Billick. "Commissioner Billick, you are under arrest."

Billick laughs believing he's being set up in a ruse.

"Irvin, what is this, seriously? Did the Mayor put you up to this?" He asks.

"Sorry, Commissioner, but the mayor has nothing to do with

this, and the charges are real," Irvin responds before nodding to the accompanying uniformed officers who make their way behind Billick, who becomes defiant.

"Arrest me? What's the charge?" A now serious Billick asks.

"Well, accessory to murder for one," Duke points out. "And plenty of other departmental violations, but you know what, that's for later. The accessory to murder charge is the only one I care about."

"Bullshit!" Billick responds, starting to cause a scene that the other guests begin to notice. "I'm no accessory to any murder! Who did I allegedly help to murder?"

"You ordered Reid to kill Damu," Duke replies. "You've been running that little hit squad of yours for a minute. You had to know it was gonna come back and bite you in the ass."

"I don't know what you're talking about," a defiant Billick replies before looking at his deputy commissioner. "Irv, I can't believe you're buying this shit!"

Irvin looks towards Duke and nods his head, causing a more than happy Duke to go into his pocket, taking out his cell phone. He starts a recording where Reid and Martinez are in his office discussing Damu after Duke had left out of the room. Billick's mood changes as the audio has him ordering Reid to kill Damu. Duke smiles as he stops the recording and places his phone back into his pocket.

"You just can't trust anyone these days, can you?" He jokes as he downs his champagne. "Damn, this is some champagne. You may wanna finish yours, Commissioner. Oh, I mean ex-commissioner because no matter what happens after this, you'll never wear that badge again."

Billick thinks for a moment before downing his drink as well. A scowl enters his face as Irvin nods to the uniformed officers to take Billick into custody. They read him his rights before leading him towards the exit. He lowers his head in shame as they make their way towards the exit with the guests all chattering amongst themselves. He's now a castaway from their social society and knows they will always look down upon him no matter what happens. Duke grabs another glass of champagne and offers one to Irvin, who declines.

"This is some good shit," Duke says, downing another glass.

"How did it feel?" Inquires Irvin.

Duke thinks for a moment as he watches Billick being led outside of the ballroom.

"Oh, I think it's gonna feel a lot better here in a moment," he says with a smile as he quickly makes his way out of the ballroom himself.

As soon as Billick is led outside of the hotel, there is a group of protesters and media there waiting for him, including Terricka, who is leading the protester's chants. The commissioner is hit with a barrage of questions from the media while trying to hide his face from them. Duke makes his way outside and smiles while watching the commissioner making the perp walk down to a nearby squad car. Irvin joins him as well and is astonished at how many people are in the area. He looks at Duke curiously, wondering how he was able to set all this up. Duke shrugs, pointing towards Terricka.

"Don't look at me. It was all her idea," Duke says. "She had folks waiting for your arrival, and as soon as you entered, boom. What can I say? The girl is good with crowds."

Irvin shakes his head, thinking this is too much, but did find the humor in it. At the squad car, Billick takes one last look towards Irvin and Duke before finally being placed in the vehicle. After the vehicle, the protestors continue their chants as the media members film their story about the arrest. Irvin, seeing that his job is done, turns and shakes Duke's hand.

"Detective," he says before making his way down the stairs of the hotel.

Duke smiles as Terricka walks over and joins him at the top of the steps.

"That couldn't have gone better," she says with a smirk. "How'd he take it?"

"As good as anyone could in that situation," Duke replies. "I mean, at least he was dressed to impressed. Most perps get arrested in their drawers."

Terricka giggles as the two make their way down the stairs through the crowd, and unto the sidewalk where they begin to distance themselves from everyone.

"Tell Valentina thanks," Terricka says, referring to Martinez. "Without her, that bastard would have still been in office."

"Yeah, well with Reid and the others gone she was finally able to use what she had against him," Duke points out. "For now, we have to worry about the next guy who takes the throne. Is he gonna be a psychopath like Billick, or something else?"

"I thought Deputy Commissioner Irvin was gonna be the next man in line," Terricka replies.

"Well, since he's the one that broke this case, he very well might be," Duke says as the two continue to make their way down the block. "The mayor might have other ideas though. That is, unless a local lawyer with strong community ties can influence him one way or another. You know someone like that?"

"Get out of here with all that," Terricka quips while giggling. "You know the mayor is not gonna speak with me after what my father did. Probably pissed I'm still on the streets."

Duke stops and turns to Terricka to give her some news on his thoughts.

"I'm a hero right now. The person who saved one cop and took one in the line, all while breaking open a police corruption ring. Trust me, the mayor will meet with you on my behest," he says, acting as if he's cocky.

"I think your head is getting a little too big right now," Terricka quips.

"Perhaps. Why don't you ask the mayor when you meet with him on Friday? I got you a one o'clock meeting. He's very interested to hear your thoughts on police relations," Duke announces, surprising Terricka.

"Are… are you serious?" She asks, excitedly.

"Like I said, I'm the man right now in the city's eyes. Might as well use some of this fame before it fades," Duke replies. "If you want your voice heard, if you want the people's voice heard, here's your chance. It's a step in the right direction if you want it."

Terricka nods her head with agreement before catching Duke off guard, hugging him. Duke chuckles as embraces her as well. After a moment, the two continue down the sidewalk discussing ideas on how they can make a change in their community.

A year later, in front of the city's brand new Police Relations Public Center sits Terricka, Duke, and several other council members on stage in front of various guests and media members who are all enjoying the mayor's speech on a nice sunny day. Duke looks into the guests who are all in attendance and smiles as he sees his grandmother as part of the crowd.

"And without further ado, I'd like to bring up the woman who is responsible for the relations center, and the woman who also heads up the city's independent investigative panel, I give you, lawyer and social activist, Ms. Terricka Jackson!" The mayor announces, causing the crowd to applaud.

As Terricka makes her way towards the microphone, she pauses, taking everything in as she thinks how far she's come in such a short time. She quickly snaps out of it as she waves her hands trying to calm the crowd.

"Wow," she says with a smile looking out at all the guests. "I'll be honest, I never thought I'd see something like this in my lifetime. If you would have asked me if I would be here on this stage talking police relations with you a couple of years ago, I would have thought you were crazy, for real."

There are several chuckles throughout the crowd as Terricka continues.

"I'd like to thank the mayor for having me here today. Seeing all the hard work he's put in to make not only this happen, but also putting the investigation panel together shows true leadership and willingness to listen to the community, and we can't go further without acknowledging that," Terricka says as she and others in the crowd applaud the mayor.

The mayor smiles and waves at the crowd and Terricka as she gathers her thoughts.

"It's funny, I went from being the biggest advocate of defunding the police to one who supports police interactions. I was always on the side of the community, and still am, don't get me wrong. Throughout all my time opposing the police, and fighting against them, I never took the time to see things from their side. The independent panel was created to make sure dirty and corrupt cops are held accountable for their actions, and when we first started about eight months ago, all I could think about was putting cops behind bars," Terricka says before pausing. "We've done a lot of work, and because of the independent panel, we're able to either put away or have terminated seventeen officers for crimes against minorities."

Terricka's supporters all applaud, happy that the cops are finally getting what they deserved.

"One thing I didn't think we'd be doing is saving the jobs of cops," Terricka continues as the crowd dies down. "Over one hundred cops' jobs have been saved in the greater Los Angeles area by our panel. People, and I know some of you are not convinced, but being a police officer is a hard thing. It may be the single hardest profession in the world. Their job is to serve and protect, but with an escalation of violence in the world, plus a community that battles with them day in and day out, it's hard to see why anyone would want to do this for a living. A year ago, I would have never even thought about the struggle that good cops go through on a daily basis, and I say good cops because not all cops are corrupt, just like not all citizens are innocent."

Police supporters in the audience claps as a few of Terricka's supporters roll their eyes. Terricka notices the division in the crowd and shakes her head.

"I'm no fool. I know this isn't going to be an overnight thing, but in order for us to understand, we have to listen to what the other side has to say," she points out. "If we want to be heard, we also have to be willing to listen. I know some of you are indifferent with your opinions, and that's okay. The fact that you're here today speaks volumes as you're willing to see what the other side has to offer in order to start healing together. The Relations Center is just about that, relations. Detective Duke Mitchell heads the program, which includes everything from police training and tactics to community outreach. With him and the other officers who are part of the program, we're looking to heal together and repair a relationship that has been broken for far too long."

The crowd unifies their applaud this time, causing Terricka to smile.

"Like I said, it's not going to happen overnight, and trust me when I say that if there is a brutality case or shooting that's not warranted, I'm still going to be there to protect my people. My working relationship with Police Commissioner Irvin has gotten better over the past twelve months, although I think he still cringes when I show up at his office at times," Terricka says causing the crowd to laugh. "He made a sacrifice of having to deal with me, and I made the sacrifice to try and see things from his point of view. All I'm asking is that you, both police and social justice supporters to take the time and listen. That's what this center is all about, and I encourage everyone here to take some time and walk in the other side's shoes for once. There's been a lot of death on both sides of the line. I'm just trying to change that the best way I can. Anyway, thank you for coming. Come on down!"

The crowd applauds Terricka once more before the doors of the new center are opened for all to enter. Duke and Terricka meet just off the stage as they share a hug and a kiss. During the year's events, the two started dating as Terricka followed her father's advice trying to look for things outside of the cause. Having a support system is crucial with the death of her father, and she appreciates everything Duke has done for her in the past. As the two are walking towards the entrance of the center, they are blocked off by Martinez. She shoots a look of disappointment at Duke before smiling and hugging Terricka.

"Congratulations, girl. I'm so proud of you getting this all together," she says to Terricka.

"Thank you. And thank you for letting Duke be a part of it. I couldn't have done all this without him," Terricka responds, grabbing her lover in close.

"Yeah, about that, Duke, I didn't get your vacation request form to attend this event," Martinez says, turning her attention towards Duke.

"What the hell?! I sent you an email like a week ago saying I was coming here," a confused Duke responds.

"An email is not a request form. Come on, Duke, it's like five seconds of work!" Martinez fires back. "While we're on the subject of time, you've been three minutes late to your shift several days in the last couple of weeks. Am I gonna have to reprimand you?"

A look of disgust enters Duke's face as he can't believe he's having this conversation.

"It was only once! See, I never should have agreed to be in your unit," he fires back before turning to Terricka. "You see what I gotta deal with every day?"

"It was more than once, detective, including this morning," Martinez points out, as Terricka steps in.

"Well, I can attest to this morning. That was my fault. I kept him up all night doing some, well, work for me," Terricka mentions with a sly grin.

"Sorry, Terricka, y'all's sexual relations are not my concern," Martinez replies before turning towards Duke. "Seven A.M. sharp, buddy. Got me?"

Duke sighs as he grabs his head with frustration.

"Why was Slater such a bad shot? He could have saved me from all this," Duke replies, causing Martinez and Terricka to burst into laughter.

Both women grab one of Duke's arms as they lead him into the Relation Center hoping that their efforts will not only be a beacon of hope for the city of Los Angeles but also for the rest of the world.

Check out more great E.Nigma readings at:
www.enigmakidd.com

Contact/Social Media Info

Facebook www.enigmakidd.com
IG - enigmakidd
Snapchat - ericnigma
Twitter - @NigmaEric
Email - enigmakidd@gmail.com

To submit a manuscript to be considered,
email us at
submissions@majorkeypublishing.com

Be sure to LIKE our Major Key Publishing
page on Facebook!

Made in the USA
Middletown, DE
06 March 2021